Other *Mystery Scene* books available from
Carroll & Graf:

The Lighthouse

MARCIA MULLER and BILL PRONZINI

Carroll & Graf Publishers, Inc.
New York

Published by arrangement with the authors.

First published by St. Martin's Press.

First Carroll & Graf edition 1992

Carroll & Graf Publishers, Inc.
260 Fifth Avenue
New York, NY 10001

ISBN: 0-88184-885-9

Manufactured in the United States of America

For our good friend
Margaret D. Haley

Prologue

Mid-October

She ran through the night in a haze of terror.

Staggering, stumbling, losing her balance and falling some-times because the terrain was rough and there was no light of any kind except for the bloody glow of the flames that stained the fog-streaked sky far behind her. The muscles in her legs were knotted so tightly that each new step brought a slash of pain. Her breath came in ragged, explosive pants; the thunder of blood in her ears obliterated the moaning cry of the wind. She could no longer feel the cold through the bulky sweater she wore, was no longer aware of the numbness in her face and hands. She felt only the terror, was aware only of the need to run and keep on running.

He was still behind her. Somewhere close behind her.

On foot now, just as she was; he had left the car some time ago, back when she had started across the long sloping meadow. There had been nowhere else for her to go then, no place to conceal herself: the meadow was barren, treeless. She'd looked back, seen the car skid to a stop, and he'd gotten out and raced toward her. He had almost caught her then. Al-most caught her another time, too, when she'd had to climb one of the fences and a leg of her Levi's had got hung up on a rail splinter.

If he caught her, she was sure he would kill her.

She had no idea how long she had been running. Or how far she'd come. Or how far she still had left to go. She had lost all sense of time and place. Everything was unreal, nightmarish, distorted shapes looming around her, ahead of her—all of the night twisted and grotesque and charged with menace.

3

She looked over her shoulder again as she ran. She couldn't see him now; there were trees behind her, tall bushes. Above the trees, the flames licked higher, shone brighter against the dark fabric of the night.

Trees ahead of her, too, a wide grove of them. She tried to make herself run faster, to get into their thick clotted shadow; something caught at her foot, pitched her forward onto her hands and knees. She barely felt the impact, felt instead a wrenching fear that she might have turned her ankle, hurt herself so that she couldn't run anymore. Then she was up and moving again, as if nothing had happened to interrupt her flight—and then there was a longer period of blankness, of lost time, and the next thing she knew she was in among the trees, dodging around their trunks and through a ground cover of ferns and high grass. Branches seemed to reach for her, to pluck at her clothing and her bare skin like dry, bony hands. She almost blundered into a half-hidden deadfall, veered away in time, and stumbled on.

Her foot came down on a brittle fallen limb, and it made a cracking sound as loud as a pistol shot. A thought swam out of the numbness in her mind: Hide! He'll catch you once you're out in the open again. Hide!

But there was no place safe enough, nowhere that he couldn't find her. The trees grew wide apart here, and the ground cover was not dense enough for her to burrow under or behind any of it. He would hear her. She could hear him, back there somewhere—or believed she could, even above the voice of the wind and the rasp of her breathing and the stuttering beat of her heart.

Something snagged her foot again. She almost fell, caught her balance against the bole of a tree. Sweat streamed down into her eyes; she wiped it away, trying to peer ahead. And there was more lost time, and all at once she was clear of the woods and ahead of her lay another meadow, barren, with the cliffs far off on one side and the road winding emptily on the other. Everything out there lay open, naked—no cover of any kind in any direction.

She had no choice. She plunged ahead without even slowing.

It was a long time, or what she perceived as a long time, before she looked back. And he was there, just as she had known he would be, relentless and implacable, coming after her like one of the evil creatures in a Grimm's fairy tale.

She felt herself staggering erratically, slowing down. Her wind and her strength seemed to be giving out at the same time. I can't run much farther, she thought, and tasted the terror, and kept running.

Out of the fear and a sudden overwhelming surge of hope-lessness, another thought came to her: How can this be happening? How did it all come to this?

Dear God, Jan, how did it all come to this? . . .

Part One

Late September

The rocky ledge runs far into the sea,
And on its outer point, some miles away,
The Lighthouse lifts its massive masonry,
A pillar of fire by night, of cloud by day.

—Longfellow

Watchman, what of the night?

—Old Testament

Alix

Her first look at the lighthouse was from a distance of almost a mile.

They jounced through a copse of pine and Douglas fir, and immediately the rutted blacktop road sloped upward to a rise. Off to the right, the land bellied out to a distant headland; beyond that she could see the ocean again, the treacherous black rocks that jutted above its surface. Back the way they'd come, the shoreline curved and gentled and formed the southern boundary of Hilliard Bay.

She didn't see the lighthouse when they first topped the rise; she had scrunched around a little and was looking back to the north, to where buildings and fishing boats were outlined along the shore of the bay. The distance and the steely afternoon light gave them an odd, unreal look, like miniatures set out on a giant bas-relief map. But then Jan said, "Look!" and swung the station wagon off onto the verge. She twisted around again to face forward. And there it was, at a long angle to the left, perched atop a second, much narrower headland.

Jan set the parking brake and got out. "Alix, come on." He went ahead past the front of the car and stood shading his eyes from the cloudy sun-glare.

She stepped out, stretching cramped muscles; this was the first time they'd stopped since leaving the motel in Crescent City where they had spent the night. The wind was sharp here, and cold; it made the only sound except for the faint susurration of breakers. She zipped up her jacket and went to stand next to Jan, to peer with him at the lighthouse and its outbuildings. Her first thought was: God, it looks lonely. But it was just a thought; there was nothing negative in it. If anything, she was pleased. Cape Despair. The Cape Despair Light. With names like that, she had been prepared for a desolate crag topped by an Oregon lighthouse version of Wuthering Heights. No, this didn't seem so bad at all.

She began to view it in a different perspective, through her artist's eye. A round whitewashed tower—vaguely phallic with its rounded red dome—poking upward out of a white, red-roofed frame building. One large outbuilding and two smaller ones that were not much more than sheds. Clouds piled up behind the tower, dirty-looking, like soiled laundry. Cliffs falling away on both sides, on the south to a narrow beach so far away it seemed hazy and indistinct. A few wind-bent trees. Cypress? Probably. Patches of green grass, dun-colored rocks, gray-bright sky. There was a melancholy aspect to the whole, a kind of primitive beauty. Nice composition, too, seen from this vantage point and with those clouds bunched up behind it. On another day like this, she thought, it would be a challenge to try capturing that melancholy aspect on canvas. The idea both pleased and surprised her; she hadn't painted anything noncommercial in years.

"Alix? You're not disappointed?"

"Of course not," she said. "Do I look disappointed?"

"Well, you were so quiet. What were you thinking?"

"That I might like to paint this someday, if I have time. This view of the lighthouse."

Jan raised an eyebrow: the Alix Kingsley-Ryerson who had painted seriously was someone out of the past, someone he'd never known. But he said, "Good. That's good," and smiled at her, and she knew he was relieved that her first impression had been favorable. Behind his horn-rimmed glasses, his eyes were bright—that electric-blue color that seemed so vivid when he was excited. They had been that way for almost a week now, ever since the packing and last-minute preparations for the move had begun. The boyish eagerness eased her mind. For much of the year he had been mired in one of his periods of depression, and more prone than ever to severe headaches—working too hard at the university for some reason known only to him. Unlike hers, his way was to bottle up things inside, so tightly sometimes—this last time—that she found it impossible to draw him out of himself. It hadn't been until his application to the Oregon State Parks and Recreation Division had been approved that his depression started to lift. Now he seemed his old self again. The next year meant a great deal to him, more than she had imagined when he first broached the idea of an early sabbatical.

Jan was looking out toward the lighthouse again, bent forward slightly, his flaxen hair streaming out behind him. The wind was in his lighter blond beard too, ruffling it and pooching it out on the sides. Not for the first time, she thought he must have Viking blood. He was headstrong, forceful, independent, tenacious—all Viking characteristics. And he *looked* like a Viking; it required very little imagination to picture him at the helm of a Norse ship out of Novgorod, leaning into the wind with his hair streaming behind him that way. Jan the Bold. Of course, he *was* getting a little thick around the middle—the result of his fondness for beer. Jan the Paunchy.

She laughed in spite of herself, and he said, "What's funny?" with his gaze still on the Cape Despair Light.

"Nothing, really. I'll tell you later." She felt a surge of affection for him and thought: It's going to be all right. She squeezed his arm. "I'm freezing. Let's get back in the car."

"Right."

He got them moving again. The road dipped down through a hollow where clumps of tule grass stretched away on both sides.

Odd-looking grass: hundreds of big round tufts of it, like an army of porcupines with their backs arched, their quills drooping, their heads tucked down out of sight. As if waiting for something. Night? The right time to mass an attack on the few sheep that grazed among them? Fanciful thought, Ryerson—too many children's-book illustrations.

Once they came out of the hollow, climbing gradually again, the blacktop ended and the road degenerated into a gravel surface pocked with potholes. Jan had to slow the station wagon to a crawl. Still, there was no way to avoid all of the holes. The rough ride dislodged something in the mass of suitcases and clothing bags and cardboard boxes that jammed the back half of the station wagon; it made a clanging noise every time they rolled through one of the chucks.

The terrain had changed too, grown more barren. There were few trees this far out on the cape—just a scattering of cypress and hardy evergreens. No meadowland, as there had been for most of the previous two miles from the county road, and consequently no more sheep. There were large sections of bare ground, rocky and dun-colored; the patchy grass was thicker, and weedier; the Oregon grape and prickly broom that covered the rest of the cape grew only in isolated clumps out here. Most of the leaden sea and part of the shoreline were visible to the south, less of the sea and little of the shoreline to the north. When Alix twisted around again she could no longer see either Hilliard Bay or the tiny hamlet along its inner shore.

The lighthouse remained visible ahead of them, even though the road serpentined along the narrowing headland. She watched it grow, take on definition. Cape Despair Light. Built in 1860, when the cape bore its original name—Cap Des Peres, the Cape of the Fathers, after a pair of Basque sheepherders who had established the first homesteads on this lonely part of the Oregon coast and who each happened to have fathered eleven children. But Cape Despair was a much more appropriate name. Even after construction of the lighthouse, half a dozen ships had foundered and sunk in the savage storms that battered the cape and the rough, rock-strewn waters that lay off of it; close to a hundred men had died in those shipwrecks, forty-seven of them in 1894 when a coastal steamer ran afoul of the rocks in a dense fog. It was after that tragedy that mariners had dubbed it Cape Despair, and it was still commonly called that despite the Cap Des Peres designation on maps and in guidebooks.

They were only a few hundred yards, now, from the flattish tip of the headland on which the buildings sat. Alix leaned forward, pointing. "What's that big outbuilding on the left?"

"Used to be housing for the maintenance crew," Jan said. He had been here twice in the past three months for short visits. But he had known every detail of its history before that, of course; there was little about any North American lighthouse that he *didn't* know. "Coast Guard built it in 1940. Garage, workshop, and storage now."

"The other two?"

"The small one near the light is where the generator is housed. Cordwood, too. The one lower down, on the far side, is the pumphouse for the well."

"All the comforts of home," she said.

"It's not so bad. The well pump is electric; runs off the generator. And there's a phone line that got put in before the funding ran out. I told you that, didn't I?"

"Yes. And thank God for it. We won't feel so cut off up here if we can talk with our friends and my family once in a while."

"Just so you don't run up huge bills." But his smile told her he was only teasing.

The road petered out in a gravelly, rutted clearing that was supposed to have been widened and graded into a parking area for visitors. At the far end was a gate and a whitewashed board fence that extended in a somewhat erratic line past the buildings on both sides, almost to where the cliffs began their descent to the sea. The elevation here was a hundred and twenty feet. The tower rose another sixty feet; the light, when it had been operational, could be seen from a distance of twenty miles.

Jan stopped before the closed gate. The force of the wind was considerable on the exposed headland—enough to shimmy the Ford, as heavy and laden as it was. Alix felt the chill of it when he got out to open the gate; it made her shiver. She hadn't expected it to be this windy or this cold, not on a reasonably clear and otherwise warm late-September day. If it was like this on a *good* day, what would it be like during a winter storm? The thought was a little unsettling; she put it out of her mind.

Jan drove them over more rutted gravel to where an old rust-red pickup was parked near the largest of the outbuildings. The bed of the pickup was loaded with boxes, a chest of drawers, an old wheelbarrow. When he shut off the engine Alix could hear the wind skirling outside, the hissing pulse of surf against the rocks far below.

"That's Bonner's pickup," Jan said. He sounded the horn a couple of times; no one appeared. "Well, where is he? Inside somewhere sulking, I suppose."

"You can't blame him if he is, can you? We're taking his job away from him."

"I don't have much sympathy for him."

"No?"

"No. He's unpleasant and lazy. Look at all this. He hasn't kept it up."

"He's only a caretaker, not a maintenance man. . . ."

"Doesn't make any difference. He's lived out here for three years; he ought to have taken *some* pride in his surroundings, whether he was paid for it or not."

"Not everybody feels about lighthouses as you do, Jan."

"That's no excuse either. This is an important piece of history; he should have kept it up."

There was no arguing with him on the subject, so she let it go. But he was overreacting: the buildings didn't look all that bad, really, at least not from the outside. They could have used a fresh coat of whitewash—and the fence needed repair—but for a coastal light that had been out of service for more than twenty years, everything was in fairly decent shape. Especially the lighthouse itself. Alix studied it through the windshield. It was a variation on the Cape Cod style of lighthouse architecture: a compact two-story rectangular frame building—the watch house—with its three-story tower rising through the center. The tower had been fashioned of bricks made from nearby clay deposits, Jan had told her, the surrounding structure from the timber that had once covered this headland. High above, a catwalk circled the outside of the glassed-in lantern room. She could just make out part of the massive Fresnel lens mounted inside, a marvelous piece of nineteenth-century engineering rendered obsolete by modern technology.

She asked Jan, "Does the light still work after all these years?"

"I'll answer that after I've spent some time with it."

"You're not going to try operating it?"

"No," he said, "of course not. Come on, there's no sense in sitting here. We'll track down Bonner ourselves."

They found him inside the garage, in a workshop area toward the rear, packing tools into a wooden crate. "All of this stuff is *mine*," he said, as if challenging Jan to call him a liar. He also said he hadn't heard the horn, which likewise may or may not have been the truth. He was a dried-up little man somewhere in his fifties, with a bulbous head and dry brown hair combed sideways across the top. His eyes were dull and unfriendly, and so

15

was his manner. Alix decided Jan was justified in calling him unpleasant.

"Need another hour to clear out the rest of my belongings," Bonner said in sullen tones. "That is, if you don't mind."

"Why should we mind?"

"Keys on a peg inside the lighthouse door. I didn't leave you no provisions. Didn't see why I should."

"We didn't expect you to."

"Kitchen stove's almost out of propane. Enough for one more meal, maybe."

"I'm not surprised," Jan said. "Where are the empty cylinders?"

"Pantry."

"Where do we get refills?"

"A-One Marine."

"In Hilliard?"

"Closest place, ain't it?" Bonner looked at Alix for the first time. "You going to live out here too, missus?"

"That's right."

"Well, you won't like it."

"No? Why not?"

"Just won't. No place for a woman."

"They had women lighthouse keepers at Cape Blanco a hundred years ago," she said, quoting Jan. "Or didn't you know that?"

Bonner grunted. "I'll finish my packing now," he said to Jan. "You can find your own way around; you been here before."

It was cold in the garage; Alix felt chilled inside her light jacket. But the wind outside set her teeth to chattering. "I'm going to get something heavier," she said. She went to the station wagon, rummaged around among the clothing bags until she found her heavy pea jacket. Jan helped her put it on.

"It'll be warmer in the house," he said, "even if Bonner didn't bother to set a fire."

"God, I hope so. It's not always going to be this cold, is it?"

"Most of the time until March, probably. You'll get used to it, California girl. You lived in New York and Boston, remember?"

"How could I forget?"

"Suppose we take the grand tour? When Bonner leaves we'll unload the car; then I'll make us hot toddies."

"I could use the hot toddy right now."

"Hey, where's your pioneer spirit?"

"It froze to death about five minutes ago."

He laughed, a sound that was lost in the shriek and bluster of the wind, and started away across an expanse of thick weedy grass. Shivering, hunched inside her pea jacket, Alix followed his broad back toward their home for the next twelve months.

Alix

The kitchen depressed her.

It was a combination of things. For one, the walls were painted a battleship gray and the plaster ceiling was so smoke-stained that it approached the same color. All that gray made it gloomy, even when the sun shone obliquely through the window over the sink. The propane stove was another problem: it was old and crochety and you couldn't get it lighted without an effort. It was better than the one in the living room, though, the old wood-burner; *that* one smoked like crazy when the wind shifted and began baffling around the lighthouse tower and down into the kitchen chimney. They had had to open the first-floor doors and windows to air the place out, which of course robbed the first-floor rooms of most of their heat.

But the kitchen . . . it was still the worst room. The well water that came out of the taps had a brackish, mineral taste; they'd have to buy bottled water in Hilliard tomorrow. The refrigerator made funny humming, rattling noises, as if it were about to break down—or explode—at any second. As for the pantry, it wasn't even attached to the kitchen; you had to go down three steps and through a small cloakroom to get to it, which made it inconvenient and not much good for anything except as a storeroom for bulk supplies. But at least it had an outside door, so you didn't have to trundle the supplies through the kitchen and cloakroom.

And then there was the *other* well, the abandoned one under the trapdoor in the pantry floor. One of the early keepers, a man named Guthrie, had sunk the well in 1896 on open ground a short distance away from the original building; it was slightly less than twenty feet deep. When the next keeper took over in 1911 he had built the pantry as an addition and cut the trapdoor to give access to his water supply. (Jan knew all about this but had neglected to tell her beforehand.) The well had long since dried up, and once that happened it had been used as a refuse dump for a while. Jan had shone a flashlight down inside it to reveal rocks and scrap metal and God knew what else. Rats, for all she knew. She had a horror of rats.

Well, there wasn't much she could do about the pantry—except to put up more shelves, maybe, and make sure the trapdoor stayed shut—but the kitchen itself would have to be dealt with. There was no way she was going to live here a full year surrounded by all that dingy gray. Repaint the walls, and either paint or replaster the ceiling, depending on whether or not she could get the smoke grime off. Put some color in, some of the Metropolitan Museum posters she'd brought. . . .

She smiled wryly, aware of the fussy domesticity of her plans. Here they were at the beginning of their big adventure, and all she could think about was painting the kitchen.

But *was* it going to be an adventure? she thought wistfully. At the moment it seemed no more exciting than a child's vacation at the seashore. Well, perhaps that was appropriate. Often when she thought about herself, she felt as if she were a mere child; felt that nothing real had ever happened to her, nothing that constituted a test of her mettle. Everything in her adult life—after a bit of initial career and romantic disappointment— had been too easy. And she herself had remained untouched by life, growing from a pleasant, smiling child into a pleasant, smiling woman with few problems.

True, Jan had remained in love with her, hadn't tired of her or outgrown her. But sometimes she wondered just how much good she really was to him. There was a dark, brooding side to his nature that she didn't really understand and in which she couldn't share; there were problems he encountered with which she couldn't help. If she had experienced more, lived more, *felt* more, wouldn't she have grown in step with him? Or was she one of those people who were condemned to forever exist in the shadowland between childhood and adulthood?

Weighty questions, Ryerson, she told herself. Too weighty to be thinking about tonight. Fussy domesticity suddenly seemed a better subject, and she began to contemplate the rest of their living quarters.

They were habitable enough. No, she might as well be fair: they were more or less comfortable. Along with the kitchen, cloakroom, and pantry, the ground floor was comprised of the living room and one large bedroom. The bedroom had two good-sized windows facing seaward, and since it offered the most natural light, they had agreed she should use it as her studio. The second floor consisted of a bathroom and two bedrooms—the largest of which they would sleep in, the other use for Jan's study. Above that, built into a bubble-like niche in the tower, was the lightroom, where the keepers had stored cleaners, polishes, and supplies for servicing the light. There was even a barrel of sand in there, for use in the event of fire.

One drawback was the small hot water heater—only thirty gallons, barely enough for one of Jan's protracted showers—but that wouldn't be a problem. She'd taken cold showers for years, had gotten to like them when they'd been living on the back of Beacon Hill in Boston, in a building that lacked heat of any kind, including hot water. But the main drawbacks to the rooms and their arrangement were the drab white walls, their chilliness—small propane heaters were the only source of warmth in the bedrooms—and the enclosed inner stairway that took up part of the living room and led upward to the second floor and then through the tower into the lantern room. But she felt she could live with all of these too. If the dingy white color in the bedrooms and living room became too oppressive, she could always talk Jan into helping her paint them, along with the kitchen.

She finished drying the supper dishes—she and Jan had always taken turns with the domestic chores—and glanced up at the ceiling and thought again that she would have to get out the Ajax and 409 and see how much of that accumulation of grime would come off. But not tonight. She was so tired her legs felt achey. Some preliminary cleaning; Bonner was not much of a housekeeper. Unpacking. Finding places for things, rearranging other things. Making up the four-poster bed; setting out towels. And she had only just scratched the surface. A move like this was no summer vacation lark; it was a transplanting of an entire household, the same sort of upheaval you went through when you made a permanent move.

She thought of their big mock-Tudor house in Palo Alto and

wondered when she would see it again. Not until Christmas, at the earliest—*if* they decided to go home for the holidays. But the house was in good hands: her cousin June was dependable and conscientious—you couldn't ask for a better house-sitter.

Alix went into the empty living room. Jan had gone upstairs after supper; she wondered what he was doing. Whatever it was, he was being quiet about it. Curiosity took her up to the second floor. In the hallway that skirted the curve of the tower wall, she called his name. But he wasn't in their bedroom or in his new study; his answer came echoing down from above.

"Up here. In the lantern."

She went back to the stairs. The hollow of the tower was like a speaking tube: from the lower floors you could hear clearly when someone spoke from the lantern room in a voice not much louder than normal, and the same was true vice versa. Not even the constant muttering of the wind affected the acoustics inside.

The two flights of stairs leading up to the lantern were steep, creaky, and worn to a shine in the center of each riser. Just above the second-floor landing you had to pass through a metal trapdoor, hinged open and fastened that way with a hook; the reason for the trap, Jan had said, was so that men working in the lightroom and the lantern above wouldn't disturb their family members below. A pair of low-wattage electric bulbs, one on the wall halfway up each flight, did little to dispel the damp gloom. Climbing, she thought it was a good thing neither of them would have to do this every day—Jan especially, with the extra weight he was carrying. She wondered again if she could get him to diet while they were living here. Probably not. Well, maybe she could at least talk him into doing aerobics with her. She had started working out a couple of years ago, after her second miscarriage, and had kept it up because she knew it was good for her, kept her own weight down. And it was better than tennis or racquetball, the big "in" sports back home, neither of which she had ever been any good at. Too uncoordinated: all arms and legs, with an uncanny knack for stumbling over her own feet. Anyhow, lifting a book was the second most strenuous exercise Jan ever indulged in. "I'd prefer to have my heart attack screwing or reading quietly in a chair," he'd said more than once. A sedentary Viking. . . .

There was a three-foot-square opening in the floor of the lantern room, but no trapdoor there. Dusky light showed above it; it must be about eight, close to dark outside. She climbed through the opening. Yes, almost nightfall. Through the lantern windows she could see that the sun had set and there were hints of violent reds and purples among the clouds massed on the horizon.

Jan was on his hands and knees to one side of the massive light, using a flashlight to do something she couldn't see. He said, "Be with you in a minute," in a distracted voice.

She moved closer to the light. It fascinated her—its size, its intricate construction. A First Order Fresnel, Jan had told her, built in Paris in 1872 by the firm founded by Augustin Fresnel some fifty years earlier. A beehive of glass prisms set in brass— more than a dozen bull's-eyes, around which other triangular prisms were placed—it measured fourteen feet in height and six feet in diameter, and weighed better than three thousand pounds. The hand-polished prisms were capable of taking all the light that struck the inside surfaces of the glass and redirecting the rays into one flat beam that could be seen more than twenty miles at sea. The lenses were rotated by hand-wound clockworks powered by means of a descending weight. It was the clockworks, she saw, that Jan was examining with his flashlight.

The huge lens took up most of the space in the lantern room. The enclosure was decagonally shaped, each of its sides constructed of heavy iron-plate for the bottom two and a half feet, then of window glass some thirty inches by thirty-six inches set in narrow metal sashes topped by six inches of metal. The metal parts and the floor were painted a dark red color, faded and peeling now in places; the window sashes were a dull white, as was the domed ceiling. On the north side, set into the metal a few inches above the floor, was a door that reminded Alix of an oversized pet-door. This led out onto the catwalk—a railed metal deck three feet wide and built at a slight downward angle, so as to shed rainwater. The thought of having to walk about out there, exposed and unprotected sixty feet above the ground, with that harsh wind pummeling her body, gave Alix a sharp pang of vertigo. She didn't mind heights when she was enclosed like this, or up in an airplane; but out in the open, where one false step could send you plummeting . . . no, thank you.

Jan straightened up finally from behind the lens and switched off his flashlight. The twilight had begun to deepen so that shadows obscured part of his face.

She asked him, "Something wrong?"

"Clockworks don't look good. Bonner could have at least come up here once in a while with cleaners and polishes. It'll take me weeks to put the lens in working order." He shook his head in annoyance.

"Aren't there inspectors?"

"Not for out-of-service lights. No one with any expertise has inspected this one in at least three years. It's a crying shame. I told Channon that, for all the good it did."

"Channon? Oh, the assistant to the State Parks administrator."

"Right. He's also on the Advisory Committee on Historic Preservation, which claims to be satisfied that the light is being maintained and cared for in an acceptable fashion. Channon's an idealist; he's convinced there'll be both state and Federal funding to complete restoration by the end of next year.''

"Don't you think he's right?''

"No,'' Jan said flatly. "I don't.''

She wasn't sure she shared his pessimism. He was such a fanatic on the subject of lighthouses, and such an ardent conservationist, that impatience and anger at the slow-grinding wheels of bureaucracy made him cynical. Other lighthouses along the rugged four-hundred-mile Oregon coast—and along the California and Washington coasts as well—had been restored and turned into historic monuments; some of these were still working lights. There was no reason to believe the same thing wouldn't eventually happen to the Cape Despair Light, even if the lens itself remained dark. It was a matter of funding, that was all. The National Historic Preservation Act of 1966 had saved it from deterioration and ultimate destruction when it had been abandoned by the Coast Guard in the early sixties, after more than a hundred years of continuous service. (It had been rendered more or less obsolete in the thirties, however, when a powerful radiobeacon was installed at Cape Blanco, not far down the coast—a beacon that could be picked up by ships as far as two hundred and fifty miles out to sea. The Coast Guard, which had inherited it after the U.S. Lighthouse Service was disbanded in 1939, maintained it as a standby station until the cost of manning and operating it became prohibitive.) Once the state of Oregon had assumed control of the light, a grant from the Department of the Interior's Historic Conservation and Recreation Service, coupled with funding obtained by the State Historic Preservation Officer, had resulted in partial restoration and the appointment of a full-time caretaker. The Federal grant and most of the state funds had been exhausted three years ago, and budget cuts had prevented the acquisition of additional monies. But it was only a temporary setback. Private conservation groups within the state were working to raise funds that, they had been promised, would be matched by another Federal grant and by state allocations. Channon's prediction that within fifteen months the necessary funds would be available to complete restoration, pave the three-mile access road, establish tourist facilities, and turn the outer reaches of the cape into a state park struck her as likely to come true.

Jan had moved over to one of the west-side windows and was rubbing his eyes—probably because they were strained from the long drive. She hoped he wasn't having one of his headaches. She stepped up beside him and looked out to where the clouds moved restlessly across the horizon, their underbellies stained the colors of saffron and tarnished gold by the sunset's afterglow. "Don't worry, love," she said, slipping her arm around his waist. "It'll work out."

He was silent for a moment, and she sensed a preoccupation in him. Finally he said, "I hope so."

"Meanwhile, there's your book. Number-one priority, remember?"

"Our book."

That pleased her more than anything else he might have said at the moment, and she sensed he was back with her. She hugged herself closer to him. "Your brilliant prose, my stunning illustrations. How can it miss?"

He laughed softly and she felt him relax again. He began to massage the small of her back with his knuckles—a caress that never failed to excite her. "Nice up here this time of night," he said. "Quite a view."

"It's beautiful."

And it was. The colors were gone now on the horizon; the sky was gray-black where the clouds moved, a deep lavender-black in the clear patches. Far out to sea, the running lights of a small ship glistened in the twilight. Closer in, the offshore rocks, some of them as large as two-story buildings, stood above the dark, heavy sea in ominous silhouette. And down below, some two hundred feet away at the base of the headland, the wind-roiled surf churned against the shoreline rocks and sent up fans and geysers of faintly luminescent spray.

To the south, the cliffs fell away to narrow driftwood-strewn beaches and a ragged line of breakers that stretched far into the distance. The wooded slopes of the Coast Range rose to the east, like great blotches of India ink spilled in irregular patterns down the lower half of the sky. Inland to the northwest, from this height, Hilliard Bay was visible beyond the inner headland; the lights of the village bloomed in the gathering darkness.

"Beautiful," she said again. Then she said, "Don't stop. I like that, the way you rub my back."

"I know."

"Mmm, yes, that's nice."

"Any minute now, you'll start purring."

"I'm already purring."

He turned her body against his and kissed her. He knew how to kiss, soft-mouthed, urgent and gentle at the same time; she had never known any man who kissed better than Jan. The heat that his rubbing had kindled in her grew and spread. She ran her fingernails along the side of his jaw, rotated her hips provocatively, and said, "Mm," in her throat when she felt his arousal. It had been almost two weeks since they'd last made love, what with all the preparations for the move. Too long. Much too long.

At length he broke off the kiss. "Why don't we go down and christen our new bed?"

"That's a fine way to put it," Alix said, but she took his hand and they moved across to the open trapdoor.

Downstairs, in the living room, the telephone rang.

It had a loud bell and the acoustics of the tower allowed

them to hear it plainly. Jan said, "Damn. Your father, I'll bet. He always did have a fine sense of timing."

"Could be somebody else."

"Your father," he said. "You'd better go answer it."

"All right. Wait for me in the bedroom."

"Just don't be too long. I'm pushing forty, you know; I can't maintain an erection as long as I used to."

"Hah," she said, and kissed him quickly, and hurried down the three flights of stairs to the living room. She was puffing when she picked up the receiver and said hello.

Her father's voice said, "Alix? That you?"

"Yes, Dad, it's me."

"You okay? You sound out of breath."

"I'm fine. We were up in the lantern."

"The what?"

"The lantern. Top of the tower where the light is."

"What were you doing up there?"

"Jan was checking the lens."

Matthew Kingsley chuckled. He considered Jan's enthusiasm for lighthouses—as well as his scholarly vocation—whimsical, on a par with becoming a poet or running off to join a traveling circus. In Matthew's world, real men didn't teach—they worked with their hands, built, accomplished tangible tasks. He himself had been a twenty-year career man in the Navy, had flown missions in the Korean War, and then had gone on to make a name—and a small fortune—in the aerospace industry. Now he was a successful politician: congressman from California's influential Eleventh District for the past eight years, and a strong contender for the next gubernatorial nomination. Matthew seemed genuinely puzzled by his son-in-law's passion for the classroom and books; but at the same time he was fond of Jan, so what few criticisms he voiced took the form of mild and good-natured kidding.

"Well," he was saying, "just as long as you kids are having a good time."

"Is that why you called—to see if we're having fun?"

"Just wanted to make sure you'd arrived safely and are on your way to getting settled. I have a personal interest in this venture, you know."

There was a note of pride in her father's voice; he'd been remarkably successful in the complicated matter of getting them permission from the Oregon State Parks Department to live in the Cape Despair Light for a year. And he was genuinely pleased to have been of help; Matthew liked using his influence to help others (although he seldom used it in his own behalf).

He'd have been hurt if he knew her gratitude was mixed, that she feared his help in the matter had been obtained at some cost to her marriage. Years before, when Jan had learned—after the fact—that his father-in-law had been directly responsible for his appointment to the Stanford faculty, he'd been angry and resentful. And once that storm was over, they'd mutually decided they would never again allow Matthew to use his influence on their behalf.

Why, then, had Jan broken their vow and gone to her father behind her back to ask for this enormous favor? At first she'd thought it had to do with her own plans to enter into partnership in a Los Angeles graphic arts firm next year. Although she would be establishing the Northern California branch of the company, the work would entail a lot of traveling to L.A. She'd asked him if that was his reason, and he'd said of course it was: "You won't have time for lighthouses after you become a big executive." But he'd said it so readily that she wondered then if it wasn't just a convenient excuse, if there was some other explanation for the puzzling urgency of his request to her father. When she'd tried to question Jan further, he'd become closed off and unreachable, unable or unwilling to talk to her about it.

Her father was saying something. She said, "I'm sorry, Dad, what was that?"

"I said, everything *is* all right, isn't it?"

She hastened to reassure him it was, gave him a brief description of the lighthouse, and promised to call him and her mother when they were more settled. After the conversation ended, she sat on the lumpy, overstuffed couch that, along with two equally lumpy chairs and a couple of end tables, comprised the living room furniture. It was dark beyond the small windows; she peered out at the night, thinking about her family and her home, about Jan's drop-everything need to start writing his history of lighthouses that had brought them so many miles from all that was familiar.

But she didn't sit there for long; there was nothing to be gained by brooding. Besides, Jan was waiting upstairs. And tonight he was all she really needed.

Alix

Late the next morning, they went into Hilliard to buy supplies and propane tank refills.

It was another cold day, overcast and windy; the daylight had a dull, steel-gray quality. Alix drove, bundled up in her pea jacket, a wool scarf, and a pair of gloves. Even with all that clothing, and the Ford's heater turned up high, she couldn't seem to get warm. Last night hadn't been bad, cuddled up with Jan in the big old-fashioned four-poster, but this morning . . . God, the watch house living quarters had been like an icebox when they woke up. The heaters did little to dispel the damp chill, and the woodstove in the living room had started smoking as soon as Jan lit the fire. And of course the stove in the kitchen had run out of propane before the coffee was even hot.

It had not been a good morning for those reasons and because Jan seemed to have lapsed into another of his depressed moods. It was odd, considering how cheerful he'd been yesterday, how exuberantly he'd made love to her last night. The only reason she could find for it was that he was suffering another of his headaches. She knew he was because of the way he moved, the pinched look of his face, the controlled wince she would catch now and then in his expression; but when she had asked him about it, he shrugged it off and refused to talk about it. He hadn't said twenty words to her, and he sat silently now, slouched against the passenger door, rumpling his beard and wincing whenever one of the tires bounced through a pothole.

That's what I get for marrying an academic and semi-genius, she thought, and smiled a little and then sighed. His depressions worried her, as did his headaches. For the past few years he had been seeing their friend Dave Sanderson, a neurologist on the staff at Stanford Hospital, for treatment of them. Dave had pre-scribed a variety of drugs—ergotamine, propranolol, codeine pain relievers, different kinds of tranquilizers—but the head-aches and the depressions continued to recur. When Alix finally suggested he might want to consult somebody else, perhaps even a psychiatrist, Jan's reaction had been negative. More than once she'd considered going to Dave herself, asking *him* to ex-plain the problem to her. But Jan, if he had found out, would have considered it a breach of trust. Just as she considered his going to her father behind her back a breach of trust.

He worried her in other ways as well. While she knew that the dark side of his personality was caused by problems in his past—his mother running off when he was only a baby, the hideous murder in Wisconsin—she couldn't believe they were the only factors that made him so often silent and unreachable.

For one thing, he'd come to terms with those problems; they'd talked them out before they were married. But still there was a part of him that he kept hidden; and even though she knew some of the difficulty was in her inability to understand it, it also seemed that he couldn't or wouldn't let her see that side of him, even after eleven years of marriage. A part he seemed to retreat into more and more of late, so that she seemed constantly to be reaching and tugging him back out of himself.

With the silence heavy in the car, she negotiated a turn near the rise where she and Jan had stopped for her first view of the Cape Despair Light. On the other side of the turn, she was surprised to see an old green Chevvy pulled off on the grassy verge. A youth of about twenty in a plaid shirt and jeans and a teenaged girl—no more than sixteen—were leaning against the Chevvy's hood, staring at the station wagon as it came into view. Then they both seemed to relax and the girl waved casually; she wore a bold-figured blue-and-white Indian poncho, and her thick auburn hair was pulled back with a beaded leather headband.

Alix returned the wave as she drove past, then caught a glimpse of what the young man was holding in one cupped hand and understood the reason for their initial tension. It was a hand-rolled cigarette—marijuana, no doubt. She smiled wryly, glancing sideways at Jan.

"Oregon's not so different from California, is it," she said.

"What?"

"Those kids back there. Smoking dope out in the country just like they do back home."

"I suppose you're right."

The silence resettled between them, remained unbroken all the way to the junction with the county road that looped off Highway 1 eight miles away, became Hilliard's main street, then looped back out to rejoin Highway 1 further north. Most of the terrain here was flattish sheep graze, strewn with prickly

31

broom, small stands of trees, and hundreds of placid black-and white-faced woolies. All the sheep, Alix supposed, belonged to the owners of the big ranch a half mile or so to the south, off the county road. There were no ranches out on the cape itself, no private dwellings of any kind; the land that didn't belong to the one sheep rancher was controlled by the state.

A weathered metal sign, pocked with dents and holes made by kids (adults, too, for all she knew) out plinking with rifles and handguns, loomed to one side of the intersection. Alix glanced at it again as she turned north onto the country road.

CAP DES PERES LIGHTHOUSE
3 Miles
CLOSED
TO THE PUBLIC
NO CAMPING   NO PICNICKING   NO HUNTING

Despite the rather forbidding wording, Alix thought it wouldn't keep adventurous tourists from wandering out there for a look at the lighthouse. Most of them would come in summer, but a few would no doubt show up in the off-season months as well. A few hundred yards to the south of the turnoff was a rest area with public toilets and a pay phone; the lighthouse, clearly visible from there, would attract a fair number of those who stopped. She and Jan would just have to deal as politely as possible with any who grew bold enough to come knocking on the door asking questions.

The county road was reasonably well paved; it hooked downward toward the bay, past a weathered gray Victorian house and ramshackle garage set on a low promontory and a smaller, squarish building in the foreground near the road. The smaller building bore a sign that said *Lang's Gallery and Gifts* in ornate blue lettering.

Alix noted the sign with interest. She wondered who Lang

was, and what sort of artwork Lang's Gallery exhibited. When she came into the village alone she would definitely stop in and find out.

The road dropped down to parallel the shoreline at sea level, and other buildings appeared ahead, some of them flanking the road, others visible among the pines and Douglas fir that wooded the slopes rising above the village to the east. One of the latter, near the road, had a large screened front porch that bore a banner advertising antiques, driftwood, and shells for sale. Antiques, Alix thought wryly, was probably a euphemism for junk. Not that she minded junk; junkshops were a favorite haunt of hers. That was another place she would have to stop in.

They were into the village proper now—two blocks long and deserted-looking, despite the sign on the outskirts that announced Hilliard's population at three hundred and eleven. Mike's Bar & Grill. A launderette. Hazel's Beauty Salon and Bob's Barber Shop, two halves of the same building. Hilliard General Store. Sea Breeze Tavern. The Seafood Grotto, a smallish restaurant built out over the bay on pilings. A-1 Marine Supply. A big cannery at the north end of the harbor, with its name painted in faded black on the sloping metal roof: South Coast Fisheries, Inc. They all seemed to be made of colorless native wood and stone, or of clapboard stripped of paint by the elements and scoured to a uniformly dull gray. Even the cannery and the long pier behind it, the boat slips that stood adjacent, and the two dozen or so fishing trawlers moored there, seemed to possess the same shabby, scrubbed gray appearance. The only buildings of much color were on the hillside. One was a whitewashed church, its steeple rising above the trees; the other was what looked to be a good-sized old schoolhouse painted red, with its bell tower intact. Beyond the Sea Breeze Tavern, an unpaved road led up that way; a wooden arrow at the intersection indicated that the two structures were the Hilliard Community Church and the Hilliard Town Hall.

As she turned onto the gravel parking area in front of A-1 Marine, Jan stirred and spoke for the first time in twenty minutes—an occurrence she took as a positive sign. "Not much to it, is there."

"No. It looks kind of . . . I don't know, depressed."

"It is. Hard times around here these days."

"How come?"

"Commercial fishing is Hilliard's life-support," he said, "and the main catch is salmon. Chinook and coho, the big ones. But the salmon runs have been poor the past three years; the trolling season that ended earlier this month was the worst of them."

"Why?"

"Dry winters, dry rivers and streams. Salmon are anadromous, remember? Thousands of them couldn't get from the sea to their spawning grounds."

"Can't the fishermen go after other species?"

"They do. Groundfish, mostly, but they don't fetch the same high price. And their boats have to be re-outfitted for that kind of fishing."

"What're groundfish?"

"Flounder, perch, lingcod," Jan said. "They use lines and nets to haul them up off the ocean floor."

He opened his door and stepped out into the chill wind; she followed suit. The air had a brackish, fishy smell that was not unpleasant. Gulls wheeled out over the cannery pier and boat slips, shrieking hungrily. A few men moved around out there; a late-arriving trawler was just putting into one of the berths. Across the road, on a flattish strip of raised land, two yelling boys chased each other among six or seven dilapidated trailers—a sort of makeshift trailer park, Alix thought. Otherwise, there was no activity anywhere in the vicinity.

She unlatched the rear door and helped Jan carry the empty

propane cylinders into A-1 Marine. A taciturn man in overalls traded them full tanks, charged them what Jan grumbled was too much, and didn't offer to help them take the full tanks out to the car. Friendly natives, she thought, and the thought depressed her. The whole village depressed her in a vague sort of way. Or maybe she was just reacting—overreacting?—to Jan's moodiness.

They left the Ford where it was and walked down past the Seafood Grotto to the general store. Its interior was cavernous; opaque globes suspended from long metal conduit cast dim light over the rows of shelves, old-fashioned meat case, dark wood checkout counter, and the partitioned-off cubicle adjacent to it, near the door, that contained a barred window and a sign reading *U.S. Post Office, Hilliard, OR*. The look and smell of the place caused a bittersweet wave of nostalgia to wash over Alix. Her corner deli in New York's Greenwich Village had had the same black-and-white linoleum squares, the same aromas. Now, thousands of miles and over a dozen years away, she could still conjure up the warmth and coziness that had made Greenberg's a haven for the twenty-three-year-old artist who had been so eager to take on life in the big city. Eager, yet secretly so afraid. . . .

"Help you, folks?"

The gruff, mannish voice came from a woman sitting on a stool behind the grocery counter. Her hair was short and gray, in a style that Alix automatically labeled "home chop job," and she wore a heavy red-plaid flannel workshirt. The expression on her seamed, weathered face was neither welcoming nor unfriendly.

Alix rummaged in her purse for the list she'd made the night before. "Thanks, we have quite a few things to pick up. We're the Ryersons, the new caretakers out at the lighthouse—"

"Take your time. When you fill a basket, bring it up and leave it on the counter."

There was a stack of vari-colored plastic baskets on the floor next to the produce section; Alix picked one up. Jan had already wandered off toward a far corner of the store that appeared to be stocked with hardware and household goods. The woman behind the counter had picked up a magazine and was leafing through it; her disinterest struck Alix as odd. She didn't seem to care what sort of people had moved into the vicinity, had chosen to live in isolation on Cape Despair. Well, maybe she was a friend of Seth Bonner's. That might explain it. Or maybe she was just plain disinterested—the exact opposite of the stereotypical small-town busybody.

With her list in one hand and the basket in the other, Alix went down the first aisle to the left. That was where the bottled water was; she loaded the basket with that and took it up to the counter. The older woman didn't even glance up from her magazine. Alix was surprised, and mildly amused, to see that it was *Sunset,* a publication whose offices were located in Menlo Park, Palo Alto's neighbor to the north, and for which she occasionally did freelance illustrating. *Sunset* was a glossy paean to the refinements of living in the western U.S.—such refinements including an indulgence in gourmet food and wine, redwood decking and hot tubs in the backyard, and spacious homes with lots of cutely concealed storage space. The magazine's presence in this backwater store was a contradiction that pleased Alix, as life's inconsistencies often did.

She was loading a second basket with meat and poultry when the bell above the door jingled. Alix glanced that way. The woman who came in had stringy brown hair that hung to her shoulders, wore a soiled and stained quilted coat. Despite the bulkiness of the quilting, she looked painfully thin. She went to the grocery counter and began talking to the storekeeper in low tones. Alix couldn't make out the words, only the rhythm. The thin woman had an accent. Texas, perhaps—someplace like that. Her voice faltered and trailed off; then the storekeeper spoke in gruff tones that carried to where Alix stood.

"I told you the other day. No more credit. You and Hod are two months behind."

"I know that, Mrs. Hilliard." The words were soft, helpless.

A pause. Then the Hilliard woman said, "Can you give me something on account? Twenty dollars?"

"Ten is all I have. . . ."

"Oh, hell. What do you need?"

"Milk. Bread. Eggs—a dozen."

"All right. That all?"

"We can get by on it. And I'm grateful—"

"Just give me the ten dollars, Della."

The thin woman, Della, fumbled in the deep pocket of her coat and produced a pair of crumpled five-dollar bills. Alix's basket was full again, so she moved toward the counter. At close range she could see that Della's complexion was sallow, her fingernails nicotine-stained and bitten to the quick.

Mrs. Hilliard took the two five-dollar bills, rang open the old wooden cash register, and put them away. Then she said to Della, "Go pick out your groceries. And take some oranges, too—they're cheap, and good nourishment."

Within a few minutes, Della had finished gathering her meager groceries and was bagging them herself, under Mrs. Hilliard's watchful eye. When she'd finished, the storekeeper held out the copy of *Sunset* to her.

"I'm done with it. You want it, you can have it."

Della started to reach for it, then withdrew her hand and put it into her coat pocket. "Thank you, Mrs. Hilliard, but I don't think I want it."

"I won't charge you for it."

"It's not that. I'd just rather not." Della picked up her grocery sack and quickly left the store.

Now what was all that about? Alix wondered. The woman wasn't averse to buying food on credit, but she wouldn't take a free magazine . . . ? Oh, of course—it would be painful looking at all that rich food, all that affluence, when times were bad.

Della, Alix decided, was a sensible woman.

Jan had emerged from the hardware section carrying a handful of tools, glass cleanser, and metal polish. He motioned at Alix's list. "Help you with that?"

"Sure."

She tore off the bottom half and handed it to him. The faintly surprised look on Mrs. Hilliard's face made Alix smile. The woman might not be curious about their tenancy at the lighthouse, but their domestic arrangements seemed to hold a certain interest for her. Apparently the men in Hilliard didn't share the household duties with their wives.

When the last item on the list had been crossed off, their purchases filled six large cardboard cartons. Jan took the first and went to move the car closer, while Alix counted out twenty-dollar bills into Mrs. Hilliard's square, blunt-fingered hand. Just as she finished, the bell above the door tinkled again and two men—a lean one in a brown parka and a stockier one in a pea jacket similar to her own—came inside. A medium-sized dog—red, like an Irish setter, but obviously of mixed ancestry—followed them, circling and jumping up on its hind legs in an effort to get some attention. The men's faces were ruddy from the cold, and they gave off a faint fishy odor. Fishermen, probably, already done with the day's work.

"Pack of Camels, Lillian," the lean one said.

The lines around Lillian Hilliard's deep-set eyes had tightened. "Mitch Novotny, I told you before about that dog. Get him out of here."

The man brushed limp brown hair off his forehead and smiled disarmingly. "Now, Lillian, Red's not hurting anything."

"Not yet, but any minute he'll have that produce all over the floor. He's too rambunctious for his own good. Yours, too."

As if to prove her point, Red lunged against a bushel basket and sent potatoes flying in all directions.

Mitch rolled his eyes ceilingward. "Okay, okay, you're right as usual." He snapped his fingers at the dog, then pointed toward the door. Red ran over there, and the stockier man held the door open so the animal could go out.

"Now, you pick up after your dog," Mrs. Hilliard said. To the stocky man she added, "And you help him, Hod Barnett. Your wife was just in here wheedling more credit from me, so it's the least you can do."

The man called Hod Barnett—Della's husband?—scowled but bent and began helping Mitch pick up the potatoes. Alix glanced at Lillian Hilliard and saw she was watching him with a smug expression that belied the compassion she had shown earlier for the woman. Probably enjoys dispensing charity because it gives her power over people, Alix thought.

When the two men were done Mitch turned back to the counter, counted out change for the cigarettes Mrs. Hilliard handed him. Then he and Hod went out past Jan, who was just returning.

Jan took the largest carton, and Alix followed him outside with a smaller one. The two fishermen were standing in the gravel parking area nearby, lighting cigarettes in cupped hands. They glanced at Jan and Alix, their expressions neither hostile nor accepting; rather, their looks were ones of apathy and indifference. The dog was once again frisking around, begging for attention, and Jan gave it a nervous look. He was afraid of dogs, the result of a childhood misadventure with a German shepherd in which he'd been painfully mauled. Where larger dogs were concerned, his fear was almost a phobia.

As Jan started to where the station wagon waited with its tailgate lowered, Mitch's dog turned playfully and went after him, nipping at his heels. He pivoted in alarm and shook his leg, trying to push the animal away. The groceries shifted dangerously in the carton; he came near to losing his grip, staggered as he tried to maintain it. Red closed in again, teeth snapping at Jan's calf.

Alix stifled a cry. But Mitch just laughed. "Hey, Red," he called, "don't bite that fella's leg off."

Jan half stumbled to the station wagon and thumped the carton down on the tailgate. The dog nipped at his leg again, this time catching the cloth of his jeans. Jan's face was pale with fear. He swung around in reflex and kicked the dog solidly on its rump—not hard enough to hurt it, but hard enough to make it yip and scurry backward. It stood at a distance, tail down, eyes accusing.

"Hey," Mitch said angrily. "What the hell's the idea?"

Jan had leaned a hand against the Ford's roof. He looked up, said blankly, "What?"

"I said, what's the idea, kicking my dog?"

"It was biting me . . ."

"Red don't bite. Nips a little, that's all."

"How was I supposed to know that?"

Mitch tossed his cigarette onto the gravel and took a step forward, his jaw set in tight lines. Hod Barnett looked uneasy now. Alix felt an uneasiness of her own, one that deepened her concern for Jan. Out of the corner of her eye, she saw that a pair of women who had been approaching the store had stopped to watch.

"You can't just kick a man's dog, mister."

Jan straightened, frowning. "I told you, I had no way of

knowing the dog was harmless.'' He made the mistake of enunciating each word, as if speaking to one of his slower students. ''Why don't you keep him on a leash?''

''That dog never hurt nobody,'' Mitch said.

There was belligerence in his voice, and Alix's fingers tightened on the carton she was carrying. God, he seemed to want to fight! That was the *last* thing they needed as newcomers to Hilliard. And Jan, never a physical person, was in no shape to take on these two; he wouldn't back down—he wasn't a coward—and that meant he might get hurt.

She hurried to the car, set her carton down, caught hold of Jan's arm. ''Come on,'' she said, ''let's get the rest of the groceries.''

''All right.''

But he hesitated, because Red was back near his master, circling again, his tail sawing the air, and both Mitch and the dog were between the station wagon and the store. Another man had joined the two women, Alix saw, drawn from Bob's Barber Shop next door. She also saw Lillian Hilliard watching through the front window of the general store. The woman had been firm with the two fishermen earlier; why didn't *she* do something to defuse this?

Mitch sat on his heels, put one hand on the dog's collar. But his eyes were still on Jan. ''You hurt my dog, damn you.''

''No I didn't. Look at him. Does he act as if he's hurt?''

Surprisingly, as if he felt as Alix did about avoiding a fight, Hod Barnett said, ''He's right, Mitch. Hell, Red's not hurt.''

Mitch was silent, glaring. His hand moved protectively over the animal's somewhat shabby coat. Alix watched him tensely—they were all watching him that way.

The frozen tableau lasted another three or four seconds. Then Mitch let go of the dog and stood up in slow movements. Some of his anger, Alix saw with relief, seemed to have dissipated.

"Yeah, all right," he said to Jan. "But you listen, mister. Maybe where you come from it's all right to kick another man's dog, but not here, not in Hilliard. Don't ever do it again, hear?"

Jan said without inflection, "I hear."

Mitch turned abruptly and went across the street toward the Sea Breeze Tavern; Hod Barnett and the dog followed, Red now nipping at his master's heels. The other three locals also stayed where they were, their expressions watchful, cold—accusing. Lillian Hilliard had vanished from the window of the store.

Alix let go of Jan's arm. He bent over the tailgate and pushed the cartons inside with agitated movements that belied his calm exterior. Then he said, "I'll get the other things," and walked off to the store in a stiff, jerky stride.

Alix went around to the driver's side. The three watchers moved then, too; the man returned to Bob's Barber Shop and the women continued on to the store, their glances sweeping over the imitation-wood-paneled length of the new Ford. When they were past, one of them pointed at the rear license plate and said in a voice obviously intended to carry, "Californians."

Everything was said in that one contemptuous word. Some Oregonians, Alix knew, resented their neighbors to the south, looking scornfully upon the Golden State with its urban sprawl, its fast-paced and often eccentric lifestyles, its prosperity. It had never bothered her before; even the rash of bumper stickers a few years back—DON'T CALIFORNICATE OREGON—had amused her more than anything else. But this was different. This was personal.

When Jan returned with more cartons she slipped in behind the wheel, sat huddled inside her pea jacket. The overcast sky seemed even bleaker now, the village's shabby buildings more uninviting—part of a foreign and incomprehensible landscape. And the wind, gusting in across the bay, was a bitter, icy cold.

Jan

The first lighthouse, a marvel of structural'engineering not incomparable to the great pyramids, was the Pharos of Alexandria, completed under Ptolemy II in approximately 280 B.C. "Admirably constructed of white marble," according to Strabo, it stood for two centuries near the mouth of the Nile; what finally destroyed it is a secret lost in antiquity. No accurate description or representation of the Pharos has survived these past two thousand years, although an imagined rendering appears on many Roman coins. Edrisi, the Arabian geographer, described it in 1154 as "singularly remarkable, as much because of its height as of its solidity. . . . During the night it appears as a star, and during the day it is distinguished by the smoke." The fact that it was one of the Seven Wonders of the Ancient World has nowhere been disputed in

No. Too flat, too pedantic. The Pharos must have been awesome; it deserved better than this. Sparkle. Flair. Make the student—excuse me, the *reader*—see the sun on the white marble, the smoke from its open fire, the glow radiating out to the Mediterranean sailor in his galley.

Jan ripped the sheet of paper from his old Underwood portable, crumpled it, chucked it at the cardboard carton he was using as a waste receptacle, and inserted a fresh sheet. His fingers felt cramped; he flexed them. He still wasn't used to working on a manual typewriter—*any* kind of typewriter, for that matter. He had a secretary at school; she transcribed his dictated tapes on an IBM word processor.

All right. Try it again.

In the Romance languages the word for lighthouse is *pharos,* a word derived from the world's first and most remarkable safeguard for the mariner, the Pharos of Alexandria. Completed under Ptolemy II in approximately 280 B.C., this marvel of structural engineering stood sentinel at the mouth of the Nile for two centuries, by day sunstruck and wreathed in smoke from its slave-tended fire, by night sending out its beacon across the dark waters to the unwary sailor

For God's sake, *no!* Childish. Like a bad freshman composition. No one would publish this sort of drivel.

The pain intensified behind his eyes.

It was no longer sharp; it had modulated into that bulging ache again, as if the pressure might pop his eyes right out, roll them down his cheeks like sunstruck white marbles. Wait it out, that was all he could do. Just when he felt he could suffer it no longer, it would subside and he would begin to feel normal again for a few days. Then it would come back, as it had tonight, after a full week of relative peace, to remind him of what the future held. Sharp and pulsing. Dull and pulsing. Savage. Nagging. Bulging. That was the worst, the *bulging*—

Damn you! he thought suddenly, savagely, and drove the heels of his hands against his eyes. His vision blurred, shifted; he endured a panicky moment until it cleared again. Calm, he thought. Calm. He reached for his pipe, loaded it with McBaren's, set fire to the tobacco.

On one corner of the table that served as his desk, the stack of finished manuscript pages caught his attention. He picked it up. Nineteen pages so far. Not bad, really, considering how much time in the week they'd been here he'd spent on housekeeping matters, on preparations for work on the light, on organizing his notes and research material. Introductory remarks, a prologue comprised of an edited-down version of

Anderson's taped reminiscences about his days as keeper of Washington's Destruction Island Light, and a scant beginning for the general-history chapter. And now he could not seem to get past the Pharos of Alexandria, one of the Seven Wonders of the Ancient World.

The title page seemed to stare back at him, mockingly.

<u>Guardians of the Night</u>
A Definitive History of North American Lighthouses

By Jan H. Ryerson

He replaced the stack, got to his feet, and paced the room. The smoke from his pipe formed an undulant line, like marshy vapor, just below the low ceiling. He felt restless now, disinclined to work, disinclined to do anything and yet in need of movement, activity. After a time he stopped pacing and began to rummage manically through the file boxes of research materials he had brought from home. Photostats of old newspaper, magazine, and book articles. Books and pamphlets of utilitarian value, some of them quite rare—A. B. Johnson's *The Modern Lighthouse Service*, for one, published by the U.S. Government in 1890. Annual reports of the U.S. Coast Guard. Departments of Treasury and Commerce lists of Lights and Fog-signals, 1900–1954. Lighthouse Service Bulletins, 1866–1939, and Lighthouse Board Reports, 1920–1939. Transcriptions of taped interviews with four men who had worked as lighthouse keepers in various parts of the country—one of them Anderson—and two others who had worked under George R. Putnam, U.S. Commissioner of Lighthouses in the 1930s. Copies of the *Journal of American History*, the *New England Historical Quarterly*, the *Oregon Historical Quarterly*, *National Geographic*, and several other publications—all with articles by

him on various lighthouses and aspects of lighthouse history that
he planned to incorporate into *Guardians of the Night*. An extra
copy (why had he brought an extra copy?) of the small-press
edition of his Ph.D. dissertation, *Lighthouses of the Upper New
England Seaboard*, which in revised form would comprise from
one-quarter to one-third of *Guardians*.

He thumbed through some of the material, but the words
seemed to blur together like ink under a stream of water. He
paced some more. He sat down, pulled the sheet of paper out of
the Underwood's platen, rolled in another.

> The Romans built many lighthouses, none of the splendor or
> size of the Pharos. Beacon towers for ships, which appear to
> have been in use long before the Pharos was constructed, al-
> though there is no record of when such lights were first adopted,
> were revived by the seafaring Italian republics in the twelfth
> century. There were few such beacons in the world, however,
> when the first lighthouse in America was erected at Boston in
> 1715 no 1716

Bulging. Bulging.

On his feet again, pacing the room. It seemed to have
contracted, the walls to have bent sharply inward. Claus-
trophobia—a byproduct of the pain, the tension, the restlessness. He had experienced it before; there was no use fighting
it. Open space was what he needed. Fresh air, cold air.

He went out along the hall to the staircase, down into the
living room. The place was still: Alix was in her studio with the
door shut, working on the first of her illustrations for
Guardians—the Pharos, her conception of what it must have
been like. She had shown him the preliminary sketch earlier,
after supper. Good, very good. So much better than the crap
he'd written tonight.

In the middle of the living room, he hesitated. Alix. He felt a sudden need to go to her, talk to her, tell her what was happening to him. It was a need that came over him more and more often lately, and yet one that he could never quite act upon. In the past few years she'd changed so much. Not that he hadn't been pleased about that. When he'd met her she had been at loose ends, not sure of who she was or what she wanted to do—needing someone like him to help give her life direction. She didn't need him anymore; her decision to buy into the graphic arts firm next year proved that. What if she couldn't or wouldn't stay with a man who was totally dependent upon her?

He was afraid, and being afraid angered him and drove him deeper inside himself. He had always been self-reliant, had had to be. Wisconsin farm kids learned early on about the harsh realities of life. The early loss of his mother, the later truth about her disappearance, had taught him about pain; his father's death while he was still at the university had left him completely on his own. He could deal with any sort of crisis alone. Even now. Especially now.

He went to the door, got it open, felt the cold sting of the wind as he walked out into the darkness. He had forgotten to put on his coat, he realized, but he did not want to go back inside yet. He moved away from the watch house, steered by the wind—across the grassy area on its inland side, around past the shed that housed the well, across humped, barren ground toward the cliffs on the north side of the headland. Wind-twisted cypress trees grew along the edge, half a dozen of them; he stopped alongside one, took hold of a low branch to steady himself against the pull of the wind.

Choppy sea, angry-looking in the dark. No lights anywhere, not even starlight. He looked down. The cliffs weren't sheer there; the land fell away in a series of rolls and declivities to the boiling surf and the rocks fifty or sixty yards below. One of the

47

declivities was clogged with driftwood, a whitish mass in the blackness. Bones of old ships, lost off Cape Despair. Old mariners too, perhaps. Dead things. Piles of old bones.

He listened. Blowhole down there somewhere: he could hear the whistling hiss as one of the bigger waves crashed through the cave or crack. Primitive form of fog signal, blowholes. Drill a hole through the top of the rock and mount a real whistle above it, and every time a wave struck the entrance the whistle would blow. *Wheeee-oo! Wheeee-oo!*

The wind had numbed his face, his hands; had caught in his shirt and was billowing it violently, threatening to tear it off his back. But his awareness of these things was peripheral: mercifully, the pain had begun to lessen. He stood quite still, his face upturned to the dark overcast sky, listening to the pound of the surf and its whistling hiss through the blowhole. Better. Not gone completely, some of the pressure still there, but better. He could think and see again with clarity.

He took several deep breaths, raked a hand through his beard, and then through his hair. Cold—now he felt it, the numbness and the chill. His teeth began an involuntary chattering. Idiotic, coming out here like this without a coat. Inviting pneumonia.

He pushed away from the cypress, hurried back to the house. Alix hadn't realized he'd gone out; the same silence told him she was still at work in her studio. He crossed to the old woodburner, fed several chunks of cordwood to the dying fire within, and knelt before its open door until the numbness left him and his skin tingled from the heat. The pressure behind his eyes was mostly gone now, but the restlessness was still in him, the need for movement. As soon as he was warm he stood up, began to pace the room. Back upstairs to work? No, he couldn't face the typewriter again tonight. What then? A drive? He didn't like to drive at night these days, but up here, as isolated as the area was, and if he was careful and didn't stay out long . . .

He went into the cloakroom off the kitchen, got his overcoat, and then entered Alix's studio. He told her he was out of tobacco and felt like a drive anyway; he couldn't tell her the truth. It relieved him when she didn't ask to come along. She was caught up in her sketch of the Pharos.

"What do you think?" she asked, turning her drawing board so he could see it. "Satisfactory?"

"More than that."

She smiled, pleased. "Well, it still needs work. How's the writing coming?"

"So-so. I can use the break."

"You look tired, love. Maybe you should wait until tomorrow to go into the village. There might not be any place open this time of night that sells pipe tobacco."

"No, I'm all right."

"You sure?"

"Driving relaxes me, you know that."

In the doorway he hesitated. The need was there again, the need to unburden himself to her. But the words he wanted to speak were walled up inside him and he didn't have the tools to break down the wall. Might never have the tools; the truth might have to come from Dave Sanderson or one of the specialists.

How do you tell your wife you have atrophying optic nerves and there is nothing the medical profession can do about it?

How do you tell her you're slowly and inexorably going blind?

Driving relaxes me, you know that.

But not this time. He was on the outskirts of Hilliard when it started again.

The bulging . . .

Alix

She set down her pen, adjusted the Tensor lamp, and looked critically at the more fully realized sketch of the Pharos on her drawing board. Not bad, really, given that she had so little factual detail to work with. Or maybe that was what made it good, the opportunity to give her imagination free rein. The image had come to her almost unbidden. Wouldn't it be strange if the shining marble tower of her sketch actually resembled the ancient, vanished lighthouse? How did metaphysicians explain things like that? The collective unconscious? All of mankind's knowledge stored in a pool and available to any given individual should he tap into it. Something like that. She'd have to ask Jan; he'd know.

She raised her head, looked at the slick blackness of the window behind her worktable. She couldn't see much of the cliffs and the sea beyond, but she was aware they were there. Normally she loved the ocean, could sit and watch it for hours, even at night. But tonight the thought of it—cold and turbulent, gnawing insatiably at the rocky shore—filled her with a wrenching loneliness. She wanted warmth, cheerful sounds, companionship—none of which were available with Jan gone. The only sound was the wind, baffling around the lighthouse tower, muttering down the kitchen chimney.

She got up, switched off the light, went into the living room. Jan had apparently fed some wood to the fire before he'd gone out; it still radiated a small amount of heat and the room was somewhat smoky. She debated the two evils—cold or smoke—opted for smoke, and knelt to add a few more chunks of wood to the stove. Then she went into the kitchen, poured herself a glass of red wine.

Back in the living room, she sat on the couch and pulled her feet up, tucking them under the folds of an old afghan. The fire was burning strongly now, the room was warmer, the smoky smell was not unpleasant. She glanced at the table beside her, where the telephone sat. Too late for anyone to call now. And too late for *her* to call her best friend Kay or her mother or anyone else. She didn't feel like reading. Didn't feel like doing much of anything except sitting.

How long had Jan been gone? she wondered. She slipped her left arm from under the afghan and looked at her watch. Ten-twenty. Not that that told her anything. She'd been so absorbed in her sketch when he left that she hadn't noticed the time.

The wind gusted sharply; smoke backed up into the room. Alix coughed, fanned it away. North wind tonight—and its gusts seemed to spiral around the lighthouse from top to bottom, bottom to top, in an unrelenting assault. It made her feel very much isolated and alone, more so at this moment than at any time since their arrival.

A bittersweet memory struggled to the surface of her consciousness. Boston, twelve years ago. Jan's apartment on the shabby back of Beacon Hill. Winter. Ice slick on the steeply slanting sidewalks, newly fallen snow covering it deceptively. And wind, freezing wind off the Charles River that threatened to batter the flimsy building into rubble.

The apartment had been on Russell Street, in a row of tenements soon to be condemned. The buildings on either side had already been vacated, but the stubborn residents of Jan's building had insisted on their right to stay until spring and the arrival of the wreckers. The combination of the fresh snow and the empty shells of buildings gave the area a hushed, unreal quality, muting even the wail of an ambulance on its way to nearby Massachusetts General Hospital.

She had entered the apartment as stealthily as a burglar, knowing she was an interloper and probably unwelcome. But even the most unwelcome of guests have their ways of gaining access; in her case, she'd known where Jan hid his spare key. Her flight bag in hand, she stood in the tiny living room with its threadbare carpet, brick-and-board bookcase, Salvation Army couch and coffee table. She hadn't packed much before leaving New York. She didn't expect to be permitted to stay.

She went into the bedroom. It was dominated by the narrow built-in bunk that they'd often shared—never mind the discomfort—and the bunk was neatly made up. Trust Jan to rise early and perform his household chores before leaving for Boston University, where he'd taught history after receiving his Ph.D. from Harvard two years before. Setting her bag on the bed, she glanced around to see if anything had changed since the last time she was there. It didn't appear that much had. Then, feeling like a sneak, she opened the closet door and peered inside. Jan's clothes, nobody else's.

Relieved, she went back through the living room and into the bathroom and kitchen that opened off its far end. Both were tidy and contained only his few possessions. He'd even washed his egg cup and spoon, which also didn't surprise her. There was some brandy in the cupboard over the sink, kept mostly for visitors. She poured a couple of fingers into a glass, for courage, and then returned to the living room to wait. And as the wind howled and the underlying quiet assailed her, she practiced what she would say when he came home.

I will not allow you to just walk away from me without an explanation.

No, too pushy. It would only anger him.

How can you turn your back on me, push me out of your life, without telling me what's wrong?

Too pitiful. Tears would come to her eyes, and that would force him to feel sorry for her—something she didn't want.

Jan, let's discuss our relationship in a straightforward, adult fashion.

God, if anyone approached her like that, she'd throw up!

I love you and I don't want to lose you.

Better, but there was so much more that needed to be said. . . .

She had formed no definite conclusion when, twenty minutes later, she heard Jan's key in the lock. He came in, wrapped in his too-large tweed overcoat, blinking in surprise at the light. His eyes, behind the horn-rimmed glasses, were startled and wary until he saw her curled up on the couch; then they brightened—briefly. The sudden spark of pleasure dimmed and the corners of his mouth pulled down in what might have been displeasure and might have been resolve. He came all the way into the apartment, set his shabby briefcase on the coffee table, and struggled out of the coat (which could easily have held two of him).

"What are you doing here?" he said.

Not a promising beginning. "Obviously I came to see you."

"I told you not to."

"I had to come, Jan."

His eyes shifted away from hers, to the glass on the floor beside the couch. "Well, I see you've made yourself at home."

"Yes. Can I get you a brandy?" God, she sounded assured. And all the while she was like jelly inside.

His mouth twitched: the ghost of a smile. He wasn't put off enough not to appreciate what he often referred to as her "sassiness." He said, "No, I'll get it. You want another?"

"Yes." For courage.

He returned after a minute with the drinks, then went back to the kitchen and brought out a straight-backed chair. So he wasn't even going to sit on the couch beside her. Another bad sign.

"Why are you here?" he asked again.

"Oh, Jan, you know why I'm here. Let's not play games with each other."

He was silent, looking down into his glass.

"I love you and I don't want to lose you," she said. "But I don't know how to keep that from happening because I don't know what's wrong, why you've . . . changed toward me all of a sudden. Was it something I did?"

No response.

"I don't think it was," she said. "First you told me not to come to Boston; you were busy, you'd drive down to New York at the end of the semester. Then you had to work on an article over semester break. I offered to come up here; you didn't think that was a good idea. Next you promised you'd meet me in Connecticut for the weekend, but you cancelled at the last minute. You haven't written or called in the last three weeks. Jan . . . is there somebody else? Is that it?"

He looked up. "There's no one but you, you know that."

He had spoken the words softly, apologetically, but they only served to anger her. "How can you say, 'There's no one but you'? There isn't even *me* anymore! You've forced me out of your life and I want to know why."

"I'm trying to do what's best for you—"

"What's best for me? Don't you think *I* have the right to make that decision?"

He sighed and finished the rest of his brandy. Then he leaned forward with his elbows on his knees, rolled the empty glass between his big hands. He said slowly, "Look, Alix, I'm not an easy person to be around all the time. Not an easy person to be close to. I tend to brood—"

"I know that—"

"No, hear me out. This past year you've seen the best side of me. I've been happy and that's allowed me to open up to you in a way I never have to anyone else."

"So why should that change now?"

He went on as if he hadn't heard her question. "What you didn't see this past year was the other side of me. I'm prone to periods of depression—severe depression. I wouldn't ask anyone else to suffer through one of those periods, least of all you."

"I don't understand. What brings on this depression?"

"I'm not sure. I mean, it isn't as if something goes wrong at the university, or I have a bad day otherwise, and I get the blues for a while. It's not that simple. My depression is chronic and cyclical."

"Why? What causes it?"

"There are things in my past," he said. He spoke even more slowly, still rolling the glass between his palms.

"What kind of things?"

When he met her gaze again his eyes, even with the protection of his glasses, revealed a vulnerability that touched her deeply. "I told you my mother died," he said. "And it's true; she died over ten years ago. But what I didn't tell you was that years before that, when I was only three, she left my father and me, ran off with another man."

"Oh, Jan, I'm sorry."

"His name was Petersen, he worked for the creamery in Baraboo that bought most of our milk. He was from Minnesota, some town up by Duluth; that was where he and my mother went."

"Did your father try to get her back?"

"No. He disowned her completely, would never even mention her name. I was twelve before I found out the truth. A kid on one of the neighboring farms told me. He laughed about it; I thought at the time that everyone must be laughing and I felt humiliated. Indirectly, that's one of the reasons I became interested in lighthouses: I spent most of my time with books, after that.''

She wanted to say something comforting, but no words came to her. None except, "But that was such a long time ago. . . .''

"No, listen. I know it's irrational, but all my life I've felt that the people I cared most about were going to abandon me, just as my mother did. And they have: my father died when I was in college. The only other woman I've loved besides you broke off our two-week engagement to marry someone else. I can't even keep a cat. They get sick and die or run off.''

"So you're afraid I'll leave you too, eventually.''

"Yes. Somehow, in some way. Tragedy of one kind or another has plagued me all my life, Alix.'' He paused, looked away from her again. "I didn't tell you about the murder, did I.''

A small chill settled between her shoulder blades; she sat up straighter. "Murder?''

"It happened during my senior year at Madison. There were several of us—all history majors—who shared a house near campus. Outcasts who couldn't afford a fraternity or couldn't get into one. In a way we formed a fraternity of our own. We had parties, of course. And there was a regular crowd of people who would come—most of them outcasts, too, I suppose.

"One Saturday night in October, one of the regular girls brought a friend to the party. Sandy. Sandy Ralston. *She* wasn't an outcast; she was blond and quite beautiful. We all took a turn at trying to impress her. Maybe one of us or someone else at the party succeeded; maybe not. There were a lot of people there— loud music, plenty of beer. Everyone was at least a little drunk, and afterwards no one could remember when Sandy left, or with whom.''

"She was the one who was murdered?"

"Yes. She didn't come home that night—she roomed with another coed—and when she still hadn't returned or called by noon the next day, the roommate got worried and called the police. A search was organized; most of the fellows in my house joined in. She had been raped and strangled and her body left in a wooded area only a few blocks away." He was silent for a moment, and when he spoke again his voice was raw with emotion. "I was the one who found her."

"How awful for you!" She reached over, put her hand on his arm. Almost convulsively, he set down his glass and twined her fingers with his.

"We were all suspects, of course, everyone who'd been at the party. We were questioned over and over again. None of us remembered much about that night—it was all a blur. At first we talked about it, but it wasn't long before things got strained among us. We began to look at one another differently. Could one of *us* have strangled Sandy Ralston? Rob had been dancing with her about ten. Kevin kept bringing her beers. She talked to Neal for a while. And so forth. After a while, along with wondering if one of your friends was a murderer and a rapist, you began to wonder what each of them was thinking about *you*."

Jan's fingers were gripping hers so hard he was hurting her. She pulled her hand free, as gently as she could. "Did they . . . did they ever find out who *did* kill her?"

"Yes. Inside of two weeks they arrested the fellow who had the room next to mine—Ed Finlayson. He claimed he didn't do it, but they had a strong circumstantial case and eventually he was convicted and sent to state prison. All of us in the house wanted to believe in Ed's innocence, but at the same time it was a relief to think the murder was solved; even before the trial we had more or less abandoned him. I didn't even go to visit him in jail."

He paused, and then said softly, "I'm not proud of the way I abandoned Ed. And I've often wondered if he wasn't telling the truth. The others must have felt the same way, because by the end of the term our group had disbanded and we'd all gone our separate ways. Ashamed to face one another as well as Ed, I suppose."

She came off the couch, knelt beside him, held his hand in both of hers. "Jan, you were young then. And afraid. It's hard to do the right thing when you're inexperienced and frightened."

He nodded slowly, looking down at their clasped hands. "I know, and the incident in itself isn't important. It's that it's part of a pattern in my life: people going away, people dying. And me letting down the people I care about, too. If I let you into my life, I'm afraid the same sort of thing will happen. And I couldn't face that. . . ."

He had always seemed so strong and self-sufficient; now that he needed *her*, she felt totally ineffectual. Every phrase that came to her mind seemed trite: *It will be all right. Maybe you should see someone, get some counseling. I won't leave you, I won't go away, I promise you I won't.*

And then something warm and wet touched the back of her hand. A tear. And when she glanced up at his face, others had squeezed out from under his glasses and were sliding down over his cheeks. Silently, very silently, he was crying.

His tears washed away her inadequacies. The pain was no longer only his, but a wrenching emotion she shared with him. She reached up, removed his glasses, set them aside. Then she pulled him off the chair, into a kneeling embrace with her face close to his, and held him until their tears mixed together in one healing, strengthening flow.

"I love you," she said. "That's all that matters. I love you, I love you."

It was later that night, after they'd made love, that Jan had asked her to marry him.

Now she sat staring at the still-smoking woodstove, her wine untouched beside her. She had no regrets about marrying Jan. Good God, no. By and large they'd been happy. His periods of depression had been relatively few, and certainly no tragedy had befallen her or anyone close to them in the past eleven years.

Oh, there had been difficult times, but they were the kind that surfaced in most young marriages. When they'd been in such dire financial straits in Boston because funding had been cut back and Jan was on half salary and she could find no work. And later, when he'd been humiliated after discovering her father had finagled his position at Stanford for him. Her two miscarriages, and the realization they'd never have a child of their own. The formalized ordeal of his application for tenure.

But through it all there had been love to anchor them, love and Jan's steadiness—a calm, often wryly humorous strength that had helped them weather the very worst of it. It was what Alix loved most about him, beyond his good looks, his quick intelligence, or his confident sexuality. It was a strength that came of self-knowing, an acceptance of what he was, his good points as well as his limitations. Other people whom Alix cared for and admired had the same quality—her father, her mother, her friend Kay—and she sensed that over the years she had developed a measure of it herself. She had even coined a term for it: character. A simple word that said much about an infinitely complex and desirable quality.

The strength was still there in Jan, but lately the ability to laugh at himself seemed to be vanishing. It hadn't been long, only these past few months, when the depression had returned with such frequency and Jan had been subject to moody silences and brief rages. Only these past several months that he had begun a frantic work schedule, begun acting in other ways that puzzled and concerned her.

She consulted her watch again. Quarter of eleven. Where was he? Well, Hilliard was a place where everything but the taverns probably shut down with the setting sun, even on a Friday night, and taverns might not stock pipe tobacco; it wouldn't be unlike him to have gone as far as Bandon, especially if he planned to start work early in the morning. Jan always worked better when he could smoke his pipe.

Restlessly, still fighting off the loneliness, she went upstairs to see what he'd accomplished tonight. She was eager to get on with her sketches, and if she read his pages now they might give her an idea for the next in the series of drawings. In his study she sat down and picked up the typescript that lay beside the old Underwood portable in a neat pile. But as she did, she noticed something on the desk next to Jan's pipe rack: his oilskin tobacco pouch. Frowning, she reached out and felt it. Half full. Now why had he told her he was going out for tobacco when he still had plenty here?

Why had he lied to her?

Hod Barnett

Hod was shooting pool in the Sea Breeze with Adam Reese. Mitch was supposed to be there too—the three of them had taken to chalking up every Friday night—but he must have got hung up at home or something because he hadn't come in yet. Didn't look like he was going to, either. It was after ten o'clock.

They were playing Eight Ball, nickel a ball, dime on the

eight, and Adam was winning. He kept hopping around the table, right foot, left foot, hippity-hop like a damn rabbit; he made Hod nervous. Little guy, not much meat on his bones, looked like a stiff wind would blow him halfway to Coos Bay— but Christ, he had more energy than anybody Hod had ever known. Never sat still a minute. Worked harder than two men, always off doing something, hippity goddamn hop.

Hod watched him move around the table, left foot, right foot, lining up a shot. "Three ball, side pocket," Adam said, and stroked, and the three dropped clean. He hopped around on the other side of the table and stopped long enough to drink some of his beer. That was another thing about Adam: his capacity for suds. Hod had seen him put down close to a dozen bottles of Henry's without getting a heat on and without having to piss. Little guy like that, it just wasn't natural he could hold twelve bottles of Henry's without having to take a leak at least *once*.

He came hopping over to where Hod was, lined up another shot, said, "Four ball, corner pocket, kiss off the six," and stroked and made that one clean, too. Then he said, "So how about it, Hod?" in a low voice so the other three customers and Barney Nevers behind the plank couldn't hear. "What do you say?"

Hod knew what he was talking about; they'd been talking about it the past hour, off and on. "Hell, I don't know. It's a hell of a fine if you get caught. I can't afford a fine like that. And you can't pay it, they put your ass in jail."

"They got to catch you first," Adam said. "Nobody's caught *me*, have they?"

"First time for everything."

"Shit, Hod, I'm trying to do you a favor here."

"Sure, I know. I appreciate it, don't think I don't."

"You got a family to feed. Wife and kids like venison, don't they?"

"You know they do."

"Well, then? We go out around two, maybe three o'clock, out on the cape. No game wardens around there at that hour."

"Not so far, maybe."

"I never saw one yet. Come on, Hod, what do you say?"

"Take your shot, that's what I say."

"Hod . . ."

"I'm still thinking on it, all right?"

Adam shrugged and hopped around, lining up his next shot. Hod watched him and *did* think on it, and it still made him nervous. He had nothing against jacklighting deer, not on principle. These were lean times and a man had a right to eat, a right to feed his family the best way he could, and to hell with a lot of stupid-ass laws. He'd bought a side of venison from Adam once, traded him ten pounds of fresh sablefish fillets for some venison steaks another time; he didn't mind doing business that way. But going out himself, running the risk of getting caught, getting fined . . . he just didn't like the idea of it. What would Della and the kids do if he wound up in jail? Go on welfare? He had them to think of, four other mouths to feed beside his own. Four for now, anyway; Mandy probably wouldn't be around much longer, the way she was carrying on now that she'd quit school. Get herself knocked up by that long-haired jerk from Bandon she kept sneaking off with, that was what would happen to *her*. What could he do about it? She wouldn't listen to him or Della, you smacked her one and she just looked at you. He knew that look, he'd seen it often enough before. The old fuck-you look . . .

". . . shot, Hod."

"What?"

"I said it's your shot. You dreaming or what?"

"Thinking. I told you I was thinking, didn't I?"

He lined up on the fourteen ball, an easy cut into the side

pocket—and missed it. Shit. How could he miss a shot like that? Nervous, that was how. Adam hippity-hopping around like Bugs Bunny, all this talk about jacklighting deer, it was a wonder he didn't miss every time.

He had left Adam wide open; he saw that and knew it was over. Adam tapped in the six, tapped in the seven with just enough English to give him position, and then tapped in the eight. "My game," he said, grinning. "Beer's on you, too, right?"

"Yeah, right." They'd had a beer side bet on this one and Adam always seemed to win when they had a side bet. Not that Hod figured he was being hustled; Adam wasn't *that* good. Just lucky. That was why he'd been able to go out jacklighting and not get caught. Pure luck. Hod didn't have that kind of luck; first time *he* went out, game warden would be hiding in the bushes ten feet away when he fired his first round.

There were two stripes still on the table, his last two balls. He gave Adam twenty cents—five for each of the stripes, ten for the eight ball—and went to the bar and called to Barney Nevers for two more Henry's. Two stools down from where he stood, Seth Bonner was nursing a highball; old Seth must have come in while they were playing the last game.

"Hey, Seth," he said, "how's it going?"

"Hell of a question to ask a man just lost his job."

"Tough about that," Hod said sympathetically.

"People from California," Bonner said. "Goddamn college professor. Mr. Jan Ryerson, he says the first time he come around. What kind of name is that for a man? Jan?"

"Man can't help the name he's given."

"Comes all the way up here, takes my job away from me, and for what? Write some damn book. Bookwriter with a name like that, he's probly queer."

"Not with a wife like he's got. She's a looker, Seth."

"Don't mean nothing," Bonner said. "Lots of 'em go both ways, down there in California. Besides, he probly married her for her money. Her father's some big mucky-muck politician. That's how they got hold of the lighthouse."

Hod shook his head, paid Barney for the two Henry's, and carried them back to the pool table. Queer—that was a laugh. What did Bonner know about queers? Or anything else, for that matter? He was half cracked, and living alone out at the lighthouse the past three years had only widened the crack. Maybe it was a good thing those people had come up from California. Now Seth had a decent place to live and his sister Emma to take care of him, whether he liked it or not.

Another thing, too. Hod remembered the way that big blond Ryerson had kicked Red the other day, and how he hadn't backed down from Mitch afterward. Never mind that he was a college professor; he had guts. Probably tough when push came to shove—that quiet type could fool you. Mitch must have sensed the same thing, because he hadn't tried to push it with Ryerson, hadn't said much about the incident afterward. Queer? Not that one. No way.

Adam was still hopping around, right foot, left foot, cradling his cue stick across his body like it was that Springfield 30.06 he kept in his van. "Losers rack," he said, and Hod said, "Yeah, yeah," and fished the balls out of the return slot and racked them for Adam's break.

That was when Mitch came in.

Hod knew right away something was wrong. It was the way Mitch moved, hard and angry, and the way he was banging his fisted hands against his thighs. One long look at his face, when he got close enough, and Hod could tell that whatever it was, it was bad. Real bad.

And it was. "Red's dead," Mitch said.

"Dead? Christ, Mitch, what—?"

"Run down in the road not far from my place. An hour ago."

"Chasing cars again?"

"No. Wasn't any accident."

Adam said, "It wasn't? What was it?"

"Murder, that's what it was. Son of a bitch ran him down deliberate."

Hod said, "Jesus, who did?"

"That bastard from California, the one out at the lighthouse. Ryerson."

"How do you know? You see it happen?"

"Enough of it. I was just coming out of the house, getting ready to come over here." Mitch slammed his hands against his thighs in a hard, steady rhythm. "Red screamed," he said. "When Ryerson hit him . . . he screamed. You ever hear a dog scream?"

"No," Hod said. His throat felt tight.

"Just like a woman. Knocked him into them bushes alongside the road, screaming all the way. Big car like that . . . he never had a chance."

"That new Ford wagon?"

"That's the one," Mitch said. "No other like that around here. It was Ryerson, all right."

"He didn't stop?" Adam asked.

"Didn't even slow down. I told you, he done it on purpose. Saw Red out running the way he liked to do, swerved over, and picked him off like a jackrabbit. Poor old dog was dead when I got to him, head all bashed in. Poor old dog. He never hurt nobody in his whole life."

Hod said, "But why? Why would Ryerson do a thing like that?"

"Red nipping at him last week; words we had over it. He seen in his headlights it was the same dog and let him have it."

"That's no damn reason . . ."

"Not for you and me, it ain't."

Mitch hadn't been trying to keep his voice down; everybody else in the Sea Breeze had heard him too. Seth Bonner got off his stool and came over halfway and said, "Plain dirt meanness, that's what it was. Looked at me once like he wanted to kill me, too. Crazy California queer. We don't want his kind around here!"

He was getting himself worked up, but Mitch wasn't paying any attention to him. Nobody was except Barney Nevers. Barney said, "Pipe down, Seth, will you?"

"Don't have to do what you tell me," Bonner said.

"You want me to ring up Emma?"

Old Seth said, "Wouldn't do that," but he went back to his stool and sat down.

Adam said, "What'd you do, Mitch? Go after him?"

"No. Too late for that."

"What, then?"

"Took Red up to the house and called the sheriff."

"What'd he say?" Hod asked.

"Said there wasn't much he could do. Said I didn't see the whole thing, said it was dark and easy to make a mistake about intent. Said Ryerson could claim he didn't know he hit Red and that was why he didn't stop, and you couldn't prove otherwise." Mitch whacked his thighs again and his next words came out bitter. "Said it just ain't much of a crime to hit-and-run a dog."

"You could swear out a complaint anyway," Barney Nevers said from behind the plank. "Malicious mischief or something."

"Sheriff said that too."

"You going to do it?" Hod asked.

"No. No damn point in it. Law ain't worth a shit when it

comes to this kind of thing." Mitch sat heavily against one corner of the pool table. "Hod," he said, "get me a drink, will you? Double shot of sour mash."

"Sure. Sure thing, Mitch."

Hod went to the bar, paid Barney Nevers for a double Jack Daniel's—cost him his last dollar but the hell with that—and brought it back. Mitch drank it off neat. Then he made the shot glass disappear inside his big fist; squeezed on it, real tight, like he was trying to break it. His face had a funny dark look, a look Hod had never seen before.

"That son of a bitch," Mitch said. His voice was funny and dark like this face. "He ain't going to get away with murdering Red."

Adam was cradling his cue stick again, rifle-like. He asked, "What're you gonna do, Mitch?"

"I don't know yet," Mitch said. "But I'll do something, you mark me plain on that. Ryerson just ain't going to get away with it."

Alix

Lang's Gallery and Gifts housed one of the worst collections of pseudo-art Alix had ever seen.

The space itself was pleasant: a large rectangular room with white walls and polished wood floors. Natural light poured in through a huge central skylight. But the cool simplicity of the place was spoiled by the objects offered for sale.

To the left of the front door was a three-foot-high raised platform, also painted white, displaying a group of driftwood birds. Each was composed of a single piece of wood, perched on spindly coathanger legs. Beady eyes, which were actually bits of broken glass, stared blankly. The beaks were made of bluish-black mussel shells; the wings of seagull feathers, several of which made the birds look as if they were molting. Alix shook her head and turned to the right, where a similar platform held a collection of items made from shells. Some of these weren't bad: simple, gracefully formed nautiluses and conches—undoubtedly ordered from a supplier rather than plucked from the hazardous local beaches—mounted on plain wooden bases. Others, however, were standard tourist fare: coasters and trays with shells laminated under plastic; abalone-shell ashtrays; oven-proof dishes made from what a clam had once called home. A larger, taller central platform directly under the skylight held other grotesqueries: driftwood lamps with hideous pleated shades; ceramic sea lions and brass whales; redwood burl clocks. Above all this, suspended from hooks around the edges of the skylight, were garishly glazed pottery windchimes. The breeze that had followed Alix inside caught them, making them clank and jangle.

The place was deserted. But after a few seconds, a slender, wiry woman with long dark hair pulled back in a severe knot appeared in an open doorway behind the sales desk. "Be with you shortly," she called.

"Don't hurry. I just want to browse."

Alix moved to the wall at the left as the woman disappeared again and examined the paintings there. They were of different types: standard seascapes, poorly done, almost of a paint-by-the-numbers quality; cutesy depictions of birds, seals, and sea lions that imparted almost human qualities to the creatures; photographs of the neon-light school, sentimental iridescent scenes of lovers wandering the shoreline. But interspersed among these were occasionally startling canvases, abstract oils that were close to being good—good enough to make her stop in front of one and then another.

True primary colors. Crisp lines. Hard-edged forms. Slick, sophisticated Cubism, reminiscent of the work of American abstractionists of the twenties. Too slick, though. And there was something else wrong with them too. . . .

She moved on to a third canvas, a study in red, yellow, and blue, with occasional stiff intrusions of black and white. Something disturbing about this one, too. But what? On the surface, sterility. Too strict an adherence to color and form. Didn't express anything. But underneath . . . yes, strong emotion tightly reined. It made her wonder what the work would be like if he—she?—really let go.

Alix leaned forward to read the small signature at the bottom of the canvas: *C. Lang.* Lang's Gallery and Gifts. Most likely the work of the owner. She wondered if the dark-haired woman who was working in back—she could hear vague sounds coming through the open doorway—was C. Lang, or merely an employee. It would be interesting to find out—to perhaps talk shop with someone who had at least a measure of talent.

She owed herself some pleasure this morning, which was the reason she'd stopped here in the first place. She'd been on her way into Hilliard with a load of dirty laundry when she'd spotted the gallery and decided to stop in and put off her chores a little longer. Not that anything she experienced today would be truly pleasurable; she was tired and had one of those scratchy headaches that come from a restless night. Jan had not returned until almost midnight, long after she had crawled into the four-poster; and when he'd come in he had tiptoed around, obviously thinking her asleep and trying not to wake her. If she could have asked him why he'd lied to her, perhaps found out that he'd simply overlooked the half-full tobacco pouch, then she might have rested better. But somehow she had preferred uncertainty to the prospect of a long middle-of-the-night confrontation. And now she was paying for it with a headache.

Ignoring the pain, she stepped back and studied the canvas

from a different angle. No, it wasn't really good, but she had to admire the artist's raw talent. She herself had that talent, a compulsion to translate her perceptions and thoughts into lines, shapes, and colors. Once, when she'd first moved to New York after graduating from Stanford, she'd thought she might become a serious painter. But there had been a semi-famous painter (married) under whom she had studied (in more ways than one). He had claimed to understand and appreciate her talent, but what she had taken for professional ardor had in reality been simple middle-aged desperation and need for sexual reassurance. When their affair had ended (back to wife, reassured), she had emerged wiser and a touch cynical. She had set aside her dreams of serious work, studied and learned the craft of a commercial artist. She was good at it, too, she'd always known that, even if it had taken her a long time to become established.

The years they'd spent on the East Coast had been lean ones professionally. Jobs were few, commissions for free-lancers even scarcer. But once they'd returned to California, her career had taken an upward turn. Over the years she'd done whimsical watercolors and bold sketches for children's books; botanically accurate pastels of regional plants and trees for a series of textbooks; pen-and-ink drawings for a special edition of a Jack London novel; illustrations for trade magazines and house organs. Once she'd even illustrated a crochet book—endless diagrams of wool being manipulated with a hook, until she could have crocheted an afghan in her sleep. And next there would be the partnership in the design firm, and the new challenges that would bring. But first there were the drawings for Jan's book—a challenge also, if not a particularly difficult one. What appealed to her about the project was the chance for the two of them to work together, bringing one of Jan's dreams to fruition. They'd never had anything they could work together on before. . . .

Alix turned as the dark-haired woman reappeared and came around the sales desk. She was about forty, handsome in a strong-featured way, and the lines of her face spoke more of worldly experience than of age. In spite of her wiry appearance, she had large breasts and gracefully curved hips that were evident even though she wore a loose brown tunic top. Alix noted her full figure with a certain envy; she'd always wished she'd been better endowed.

"Sorry to keep you waiting," the woman said. "I was wrapping a painting for shipment. A couple from Washington bought it this morning, for their daughter."

"Sounds as if business is good."

"Not really. Even the summer is slow. Trouble is, I'm too far off Highway One." The woman shrugged and then smiled. "Is there something I can help you with?"

"Yes and no. I'm not a customer. Actually, I'm one of your new neighbors. My name's Alix Ryerson; my husband Jan and I moved into the lighthouse last week."

"Oh, of course. You're from California, aren't you?"

"Palo Alto. My husband teaches at Stanford."

"Stanford," the woman said. She sounded impressed. "Well . . . don't you find living conditions out on the cape awfully primitive? I mean, compared to what you're used to."

"No, it's surprisingly comfortable. Not an interior decorator's dream—challenge is more like it—but quite liveable."

"I'm surprised, what with old Seth Bonner living there the past three years. Nothing against Seth," she added at Alix's inquiring look. "He's all right once you get used to him. But he's mildly retarded and I wouldn't guess much of a housekeeper. But I'm being rude. My name's Cassie Lang, I'm the owner of this place."

Alix clasped the hand extended to her and found it strong, almost sandpapery in texture. "Nice to meet you."

"Same here." Cassie seemed to mean it, which was a relief. "Look, why don't we have a cup of coffee? Or tea, if you'd prefer?"

"Coffee sounds good."

"I have a pot going in back. We can sit and talk back there, if you like."

"Fine."

Cassie led the way through a door behind the sales counter, into a narrow back room half-full of shelves piled with cardboard cartons. A worktable cluttered with tools, pieces of driftwood, and other items took up most of the remaining floor space; but at the back, next to a window that gave a good view of the nearby Victorian house and garage and the bay beyond, was a table supporting a Mr. Coffee. A yellow paisley armchair flanked the table and matching curtains were hung in the window. Cassie motioned for her to sit, then bustled around collecting cups, inspecting them for cleanliness, pouring and serving.

Alix asked, "You *are* the C. Lang who did the paintings out front?"

Cassie set her cup down and pulled a swivel chair, the kind secretaries use for typing, over from the worktable. Her expression was guarded as she said, "Yes, they're mine."

"I found them very interesting. They grab your attention." Alix paused, then decided to lie for kindness' sake. "I like them."

Cassie relaxed and smiled, pleased. Like many artists of modest talent, she had probably been hurt many times by casual and thoughtless criticism. "Thank you. They're the main reason this gallery exists. All the rest of the stuff—well, you've seen it."

"Where do you get your seascapes?"

"A fellow up the coast. He turns them out to order."

"And the shell things?"

"Most are from a mail-order house in Portland. The nicer ones come from Florida." She gestured at the worktable. "I do the driftwood birds myself. They're awful, but easy to make; and they sell better than anything else I stock."

Alix shook her head sympathetically and sipped her coffee. Her headache had lessened, and she felt warmed by both the hot drink and the company. "You're somewhat isolated here," she said. "Do you live alone?"

"Yes."

"Doesn't it worry you sometimes?"

"Not really. I have a handgun and I'm a good shot."

"Oh. I'm afraid of guns myself."

"I grew up handling them. My father belonged to the NRA." Fortunately for Alix—who was pro-gun control—Cassie did not want to discuss the subject any further. She said, "But tell me about you. Are you interested in art?"

"Actually, I'm an artist myself."

"You are? For heaven's sake!" The woman seemed genuinely pleased. "What kind of work do you do?"

Alix told her, describing some of her more interesting projects and mentioning both her sketches for Jan's book and her future business venture. When she had finished, Cassie looked so impressed and wistful that she quickly said, "But that's enough about me. Tell me how you came to start this gallery. Have you always lived in Hilliard?"

The other woman looked startled, almost shocked. "Oh no! I was born in Eugene, lived there most of my life."

"When did you move here?"

A certain reticence had come into Cassie's expression, a kind of closing off. "Only a year ago. I . . . I was divorced, and I'd always liked this part of the coast. Hilliard seemed like a good place to start over." She smiled wryly. "Too bad I didn't know about the lack of tourist trade."

"You're making ends meet, though?"

"Just barely. I own the house and the gallery outright—I bought them with my divorce settlement. And it doesn't cost much to live here."

"Have you made many friends among the locals?"

"Acquaintences, yes. I know almost everyone in the village. But no, I'm not friends with anyone."

"Are they such hard people to know?"

"Oh yes. Hard to know, hard to talk to. Particularly when you don't have much in common with them—and I don't. Hilliard's a cultural wasteland. High culture to the people here is watching the Super Bowl on the widescreen TV at the Sea Breeze Tavern."

"I'd gathered as much." Alix looked down into her coffee cup, thinking of her last visit to Hilliard. "Tell me, do you know a couple of local fishermen named Mitch Novotny and Hod Barnett?"

"Yes. Why?"

It didn't seem as though Cassie had heard about Jan's run-in with Novotny, and Alix didn't care to enlighten her. "My husband and I saw them at the general store last week," she said. "I've been curious about them."

"Oh. Well, Mitch's family has been in Hilliard for generations, and as far as I know they've all been fishermen. It's a funny thing about villages like this."

"What is?"

"People just keep on doing the same things, generation after generation," Cassie said. "I don't suppose Mitch's way of life is much different than his father's or grandfather's, except now they have TV. And higher taxes, of course."

"Is the same true of Hod Barnett?"

"No. He moved here several years ago from Coos Bay, I gather. He owned his own boat for a while but lost it just after I moved into town; couldn't make the mortgage payments. Now he works as a deck-hand for Mitch, not that that makes him a living wage. Mitch can barely make ends meet himself. The fishing all along the coast has been poor the past three seasons."

"Yes, that's what my husband told me."

"Hod lives in a little trailer in that encampment on the north end with his wife and three kids. Must be awful to have to live like that. There are no utility hookups, and they have to haul water from a central faucet. Adam Reese has made some improvements since he moved in, most of them for free, but the conditions are still primitive."

"Adam Reese?"

"The local handyman. Lillian Hilliard has him building shelves in her storeroom these days; she's the only one in the village with any money. You've met her, I'm sure?"

"Yes," Alix said.

"I guess you could say Lillian epitomizes the spirit of Hilliard—if it has any. She's the last living member of the founding family, and so proud of it that when she married she insisted on keeping the family name. There's a consensus in the village that the husband—Ben Gates, I think his name was—died young because it was the path of least resistance, certainly easier than standing up to Lillian. I wouldn't be surprised if that was true."

"She does seem to rule that store with an iron hand."

Cassie smiled, not warmly. "Oh, she does. Collects gossip, dispenses charity—when she feels like it—and pronounces judgment on everything that goes on in town. If there's ever anything you need to know about anyone in Hilliard, just see Lillian."

Alix nodded, vaguely uncomfortable, thinking that Cassie—given the chance—might rival Lillian Hilliard in the gossip department. She hoped she hadn't been too candid about herself, imparted too many personal details to a virtual stranger.

She finished her coffee and then looked at her watch. "Oh, it's getting late. I've got to get moving—laundry day."

"Please stay. Have another cup of coffee—"

"I'd love to, but I do have to go. Perhaps we can get together soon, though. Have you ever been to the lighthouse?"

"Out near it, but never inside."

"I'll show you around, then, if you'd like to come out."

Cassie smiled. "I'm already looking forward to it."

As she got into the station wagon, Alix realized her headache was gone. It had been more from tension than from anything else—a tension that probably stemmed from too much worry and introspection. Inconsequential chatter—and even gossip— over coffee had proved good for her, and she resolved to call Cassie soon and reemphasize her invitation to visit the lighthouse.

Alix

She lifted her sopping laundry from the washing machine and dropped it into the wire cart, then pushed it toward the dryer and began unloading. The Hilliard Launderette was completely deserted. Two of the other dryers were in operation, wisking a bright assortment of clothing round and round, but the owner of that laundry was mercifully absent. Alix was grateful for the solitude, glad there were no villagers to cast curious glances at her, the stranger from California.

She set the dryer in motion and sat down with the paperback novel she'd brought along. It was one of those thick imperiled-

children sagas that were so much in vogue, and had begun to
bore her after the first chapter. Now she set it aside and merely
sat, watching the clothes whirl hypnotically, still feeling
warmed by her visit with Cassie Lang.

The visit had brought a sense of normalcy into her day; it was
much the same sort of thing she would have done at home.
There she often met with other free-lancers for morning coffee;
at noon there were luncheons with clients; and in late afternoon
it was not uncommon for someone to stop by for a glass of
wine. Perhaps a friendship with Cassie would provide a needed
balance to her life here in Hilliard. . . .

The door opened, letting in a gust of cold air, and Alix
glanced up. Della Barnett came in and walked to one of the
still-turning machines. The woman wore the same soiled quilted
coat she'd had on in the store the week before, and her hair, if
possible, looked even more greasy and stringy. An auburn-
haired teenaged girl in a bold-figured blue-and-white poncho
and jeans followed behind her; Alix recognized her as the one
she'd seen smoking grass on the road to the lighthouse that first
morning they'd driven into Hilliard. Della's daughter? The girl
was attractive; when she shed the last of her baby fat, she might
even be pretty. Hard to believe Della and Hod Barnett could
have produced her.

The girl saw Alix and her blue eyes registered recognition.
She glanced at Della, then looked back at Alix. Fear molded her
expression briefly; then it modulated into a look of defiance and
challenge that seemed to say, ''I don't care if you know I was
smoking dope that day. Go ahead and tell my mother if you
want to. I'll just call you a liar.''

Della had opened the dryer door; she felt the laundry inside,
then shut the door again and went to sit on one of the chairs at
the end of the row. The girl wandered around the room, being
very casual and aloof and humming a rock tune under her

breath. Every now and then she would glance slyly at Alix. Della sat staring straight ahead, puffing on a filter-tipped cigarette; Alix might not have been there, as far as she was concerned.

After a minute or so Della said in an irritated Southern twang, "Mandy, for heaven's sake sit down. You're making me nervous."

The girl sighed elaborately but went to sit beside her mother. "Isn't it time for that stuff to be dry?"

"Soon."

"Why does the damn dryer always have to take so long?"

"Don't swear. You know I don't like that."

"Oh, all right." Mandy sat fidgeting for half a minute; then she was on her feet again. "I'm going to the store for a Coke."

"No you're not," Della said. "We can't afford for you to be buying Cokes all the time."

"Oh, Mom . . ."

"No Coke."

Mandy stamped her foot in a little-girl gesture. Her Indian headband had a cluster of bead-tipped leather thongs at the back and they clicked together with the movement. When her mother merely looked at her, unperturbed by her little tantrum, she glared back and then began pacing as before. And casting the same sly looks at Alix as before.

Alix managed to absorb herself in part of a chapter. Then she realized Mandy had come over near where she was sitting; she looked up, saw the girl watching her.

"You're the lady from the lighthouse," Mandy said.

"Yes, that's right."

"You going to live out there long?"

"For the next year."

"That long? I sure don't envy you."

"No? Why not?"

Della had got up and was at her dryer again. "Mandy," she said, "stop bothering the lady and get over here and help me. Laundry's dry now."

The girl went reluctantly, began stuffing clothing into pillow cases her mother held open. When they were finished, Della started away with the two heavy cases; Mandy stopped her and relieved her of both, saying, "No, Mom, let me take them. You'll hurt your back again."

Not a bad kid underneath it all, Alix thought. At least she looks out for her mother.

Della went out. Mandy followed, but paused in the open doorway and said over her shoulder to Alix, "I don't envy you for a lot of reasons. *I* wouldn't want to be married to a dog murderer."

"A *what?*"

"A dog murderer. After last night, you people aren't going to be—"

"Mandy!" Della called from outside.

The girl shrugged and was gone without another word.

Alix sat openmouthed. By the time she had recovered from her surprise and hurried outside, they were pulling away in an old Nash Rambler, Della at the wheel. Neither mother nor daughter looked back.

Feeling a little stunned, Alix went back inside the launderette. Dog murderer. What did that mean? It hadn't sounded like a joke or some sly teenager's game; Mandy had been serious. Something must have happened last night, something involving Jan and a dog . . . Mitch Novotny's dog?

Oh God, she thought.

She caught up her pea jacket from where it lay on one of the chairs, shrugged into it, grabbed her purse. Ignoring her laundry, she hurried out again into the wind-chilled street. The Hilliard General Store was opposite the launderette on a slight diagonal; according to Cassie, if anyone would know exactly what had happened last night, it would be Lillian Hilliard.

Alix barely noticed the rush of warm air and homey smells that greeted her when she stepped inside. Mrs. Hilliard was in her accustomed place behind the grocery counter; opposite her stood a tall, thin man in a brown overcoat and a short, wiry man in workclothes. They had been talking, but they all stopped when they saw her. Both men gave her their full attention— more attention than anyone in the village except Cassie Lang and Mandy had displayed thus far.

Alix stopped a few feet away, near the post-office cubicle. For a time none of them moved; the silence that followed the tinkling of the entrance bell struck her as heavy and a little tense. The short man was the first to move and speak; he swung around to face Lillian Hilliard again and said, "So what should I do about the shelves?"

"Well, Adam, if you can't fit six in, I'll have to settle for five."

Adam was holding a hammer in his right hand; now he began to slap it against the opposite palm, shifting his weight as he did so from his left foot to his right, his right foot to his left. He had longish blond hair and a wispy mustache, and was wearing a toolbelt around his waist. "I didn't say I couldn't fit six. I just meant I'll have to do 'em closer together."

"Won't do. They have to hold tall packages."

"Okay, then. Five it is." He started toward the back of the store in a peculiar hopping gait. When he reached the end of the canned-food aisle he turned, gave Alix another long speculative look.

The tall man pulled a knitted cap from the pocket of his overcoat and put it on over his pale thinning hair. Still peering at Alix through his wire-rimmed glasses, he said, "You must be Mrs. Ryerson, our new neighbor out at the light."

Such a direct overture from anyone in the village was surprising. "Yes, I am."

The man extended a slender, well-manicured hand. "I'm Harvey Olsen, minister of the Community Church. Welcome to Hilliard."

"Thank you, Reverend . . . it is Reverend?"

"Yes. The ministry is Methodist, but we like to think of ourselves as nondenominational. So we can better serve the community, we encourage parishioners of all faiths to participate. But please call me Harvey—everyone does."

"Well, thank you . . . Harvey."

He continued to peer at her; behind his glasses, his eyes were as pale as his hair. "I hope we'll be seeing you and your husband at services soon," he said.

This was absurd. She had come in here to find out if there was any truth to Mandy's claim that Jan was a dog murderer, and here she was being urged to attend Sunday church services. For a moment she was at a loss for words. Neither she nor Jan was particularly religious, although she had been raised Episcopalian, he Lutheran. Still, she didn't want to offend the one person aside from Cassie Lang who had tried to make her feel welcome in Hilliard.

She finally managed to say, "I hope so too."

Harvey Olsen nodded, smiled, and then picked up a sack of groceries and a copy of the Portland *Oregonian* that was lying on the counter. To Lillian Hilliard he said, "You'll be chairing the ladies' organizing committee for the fall bazaar tonight?"

"I will. Someone's got to keep those hens in line so it doesn't turn into one big coffee klatch."

The minister smiled again, vaguely this time, lifted a hand to Alix, and went out.

Now that she was alone with Alix, Mrs. Hilliard assumed an odd, guarded expression. "Help you with something?"

"Yes." But she didn't know where to start.

The storekeeper plucked a wilted celery leaf off the counter, then reached underneath for a rag and began wiping the worn wooden surface. From the back of the store came the staccato sound of hammering.

"Well?"

"Mrs. Hilliard . . . did something happen in the village last night? Something involving my husband and a dog?"

"Mean you don't know about that?"

"No. I wouldn't ask you if I knew, would I? All I know is what Mandy Barnett said at the launderette."

"What was that?"

She didn't want to repeat it. "Mrs. Hilliard, will you please tell me—"

"Lord knows I didn't like that dog," the storekeeper said. "Mitch was always bringing him in here and he was always upsetting something. But Mitch was fond of Red, treated him like one of his kids—better, some might say."

"It's dead? Mitch Novotny's dog?"

"Run down in the road right out front of the Novotny house. Run down on purpose, according to what Mitch says."

Alix suddenly felt sick to her stomach.

"Didn't stop, didn't even slow down," Lillian Hilliard said. "Pretty cold-hearted, you ask me."

"I don't believe it."

"Well, Mitch wouldn't lie. I'll say that for him."

"Then he must have made a mistake. How could he be sure it was my husband?"

"Wasn't any mistake. That big new car of yours is the only one like it around here. And Mitch says he saw it happen."

Alix stood still, her hands clenched, fingernails biting into her palms. It just wasn't possible. Jan was a gentle man, he had often spoken out against blood sports and other cruelties to animals. . . .

Mrs. Hilliard said, "Seems to me if it was just an accident, he'd have stopped afterward. And told you about it after he got home. Now wouldn't you say?"

She didn't know what to say. She just shook her head. Not a word to her last night; and this morning, he'd gotten up before she had and locked himself in his study and started working as if nothing had happened. Working hard: she'd heard the steady beat of the typewriter keys and hadn't wanted to disturb him; had left him a note saying she was going into the village to do the laundry.

The storekeeper bunched up her rag and tossed it back under the counter. "Maybe you better go back to the lighthouse and ask him about it," she said almost gently. Her expression now was one of pity. "Maybe he's got an explanation that'll satisfy everybody."

"Yes. Yes, I'm sure he does."

Numbly, she turned her back on the other woman's pity and left the store. The station wagon was parked nose-in to one side of the launderette; she crossed the street and walked around to the front of the car. She hadn't looked at it up close this morning, hadn't had any reason to. Now she did.

The bumper was dented, scratched. And there was a thin smear of something on it that might have been blood.

Alix

Jan was at his worktable, aligning the stack of manuscript pages next to his typewriter, when she came into the study. His fingers moved quickly—*tap, tap, tap*—bringing the papers into neat order. When he heard her he looked around. His color wasn't good, his face pale and pinched, but he seemed in reasonably good spirits.

"There you are," he said. "I've just finished the introductory chapter on lighthouse history and I want you to—"

"Jan, we have to talk. Right now."

He frowned. "What's wrong?"

On the drive back to the lighthouse she had decided on an indirect approach, one that wouldn't be too accusing or threatening. Give Jan the opportunity to tell her what had happened. "Last night," she said, "you told me you were going out for tobacco."

"Yes?"

"But you're not out of tobacco. There's a half-full pouch on your desk. Why did you lie to me?"

He let out his breath in a tired sigh. "Alix, I'm sorry. I had one of my headaches and I thought a drive would relax me. But I wanted to be alone, and I didn't feel like explaining. I didn't want to upset you while you were working."

She felt her anger rising; forced it down. She was determined to handle this in a way that would damage them the least. "Jan, why didn't you tell me about the dog?"

"What dog?"

"Mitch Novotny's dog—Red. Everyone in the village is talking about it."

"Still? My God, that was over a week ago."

"They're not talking about last week, they're talking about what happened last night!"

For a moment Jan seemed honestly bewildered; then an uneasiness—and something that might have been fear—crawled into his eyes. "I don't know what you mean," he said.

Alix sat heavily on the extra chair, a mate to the lumpy ones in the living room. "Someone ran down and killed Mitch Novotny's dog last night. He claims it was you. And that you did it deliberately because you didn't stop, didn't even slow down.''

''Oh, God.''

Now Jan looked ill. He shook his head, winced, pressed thumb and forefinger against his eye sockets.

''You did run down that dog, didn't you?''

''I . . . don't know.''

''What?''

''I don't know!''

''My God, how can you not know? Even if you didn't see it, you'd have to have felt the impact. Or heard it. The front bumper is dented, there's blood on it. . . .''

He got convulsively to his feet, went to the window, stood staring out. ''The headache wasn't so bad when I left here,'' he said in a low, pained voice. ''But it'd worsened by the time I got to the village, got so bad I could barely see. I turned around, drove back a ways, and then I couldn't see at all and I stopped—somewhere out on the cape—and just sat there, a long time, until it eased enough so that I could make it back here. I was afraid of hitting something or somebody, that's why I stopped. I . . . I didn't know I'd already hit the dog.''

Conflicting emotions moved through her: relief, concern, fear, even a small doubt. She stood and went to him, caught one of his arms and turned him gently until he was facing her. The deep pain etched in his face was frightening.

She said, ''Jan, those headaches of yours seem to be getting worse, more intense. They worry me. You've got to do something about them. Call Dave Sanderson or something. . . .''

''I've already called him. He gave me a referral to a doctor in Portland. I'll be seeing him on Tuesday.''

''I'll go to Portland with you—''

''No, somebody has to stay here and take care of things.''

"I don't like the idea of you driving all that way alone, not after last night."

"I won't drive if a headache starts."

"Promise me that? Never again?"

"I promise. God, do you think I want to hit anything else with the car? Just the thought of that poor dog . . ." He shuddered. "Novotny must be pretty upset, must think I'm some kind of criminal. Everyone else in Hilliard, too."

"They'll get over it when they hear the truth."

"Will they?"

"Maybe if you call Novotny and apologize, explain what happened . . . maybe he'll listen."

"It's worth a try. But I remember when Thud was killed—the driver of the car that hit him apologized and we still suffered for weeks."

Alix remembered too—all too well. Thud had been their big, solid yellow cat, named for the noise he made when lesser cats would have jumped off the furniture soundlessly. Years later she still felt his loss, still expected at odd moments to find him lurking in the kitchen next to his food bowl, or to hear him thudding through the house.

Jan forced a smile that was meant to be reassuring, squeezed her hand; but the fear still crouched in his eyes. She wondered if her own fear showed in her eyes, too, for him to see. His explanation hadn't quite banished it, and neither had her sense of relief.

What if his headaches were no longer just the product of tension? What if something was seriously wrong with him?

Jan

Sitting morosely in front of the old wood-burner in the living room, he could hear Alix moving around the kitchen. She was making a lot of noise—thumps, bumps, clatters. Working off her anxiety at the same time. That was a trait he had always admired in her. Whenever she was upset or angry, she found some sort of physical labor to engage in; attacked it with a determination that bordered on the obsessive. And when the job was done, or when she had exhausted herself, her emotions were back in sync again. No grudge-holder, she. She could forgive anything in less than twenty-four hours.

Almost anything.

His pipe had gone out; he relighted it. He watched his hand as he did so, watched it tremble. An indicator of how overwrought he was today. How afraid.

The pain had been bad last night—that awful bulging. But that wasn't the worst part. He'd lied to Alix about the worst part, his second lie to her in two days, because the truth was too painful. And the truth was, he didn't remember the drive into the village proper, what had happened there or afterward, nor most of the drive back here. His memory ended with the bulging as he neared the county road, picked up again as he jounced along the cape road a half mile or so from the lighthouse.

Blackout. More than two hours of lost time. That sort of thing had never happened to him before . . . or had it? It *could* have; that was what made it so terrifying. You blacked out, you did things during that blank time, and then afterward you not only couldn't remember what those things were, it was possible you didn't even realize you'd *had* a blackout.

But no, this was the first time—it had to be. It was all somehow connected to the atrophying of his optic nerves, his imminent blindness, even though Dave Sanderson had been carefully noncommital when he'd called Dave earlier and told him about the blackout (but not the details of it, not that he'd been out driving and killed a dog).

"Blackouts aren't common with the type of eye disease you have," Dave had said. "But that doesn't mean they can't happen or won't happen again. Your condition is rare; we just don't know enough about it. I think you ought to see another ophthalmologist, find out if the degenerative process has speeded up any, or if there are any new complications. There's a good one in Portland; I'll call him for you right away."

Then Dave had paused. And then he'd asked, "Have you told Alix yet?"

"No."

"When are you planning to?"

"I don't know. I haven't decided yet."

"Doesn't she suspect you're having vision problems?"

"Not yet, no."

"She will before much longer. Jan, I really think you're making a mistake by not confiding in her. She's your wife, she has a right to know. Why do you insist on hiding the truth from her?"

Because I'm afraid, he'd thought. Damn you, I'm *afraid!*

He'd gotten in touch with the Portland ophthalmologist, Dr. Philip R. Meade, and made an appointment for early Tuesday afternoon. And he didn't want to go, because he was afraid Meade might tell him the degeneration was accelerating and he would be blind sooner than the year or two the others had projected; afraid he wouldn't be able to stay here the full term, wouldn't be able to finish his book; afraid he would experience more blackouts. Afraid of everything these days, that was Professor Jan Ryerson, eminent authority on beacons in the night.

Abruptly he stood, went to the stove, added fresh lengths of cordwood to the blaze inside. His pipe had gone out again; he laid it in the ashtray alongside the telephone, reclaimed his chair. God, he thought then, that poor dog. But it's not possible I deliberately ran it down last night, even in a blackout state. Novotny's wrong. It *had* to have been a freak accident.

Try calling again, he told himself. Whoever had been occupying the Novotny line the past hour—he had called three times in those thirty minutes, busy signal each time—had to hang up sooner or later.

Sooner: the line was clear this time. Three rings, four. And then a man's voice said, "Hello?"

"Mitchell Novotny, please."

"You're talking to him. Who's this?"

"Jan Ryerson. Out at the lighthouse."

Silence for several seconds. Then, coldly and flatly, "What the hell do you want?"

"To tell you how sorry I am about your dog."

"Yeah? Then what'd you run him down for?"

"I didn't, not deliberately—"

"I seen you do it."

"No, you're mistaken. It was an accident. I don't remember seeing the dog; I didn't know until just a little while ago that I'd hit anything."

"You trying to tell me you didn't hear him scream?"

Jan winced. "I'm sorry, Mr. Novotny. Believe me, I—"

"Bullshit," Novotny said. "You didn't stop. You didn't even slow down."

"I had a headache, a bad headache. It's a chronic condition—"

"That's no damn excuse."

"I know that. I know I shouldn't have been out driving. I'm

not trying to excuse myself, I'm only trying to tell you how badly I feel about the accident.''

"Sure you do."

"Worse than you can imagine. I'd like to make it up to you somehow, if you'll let me. Perhaps buy you another dog, any kind you—"

Novotny hung up on him.

Jan sat holding the receiver for a time before he cradled it. Then he got up again, went into the kitchen. Alix, wearing a pair of old jeans and one of his old shirts, her hair tied back with a scarf, was up on a stepladder scouring the smoke-grimed ceiling with abrasive cleaner and a sponge. Her face was flushed and shiny with perspiration.

"I talked to Mitch Novotny," he said.

She stopped her scrubbing and looked down at him. "What did he say?"

"He doesn't believe me that it was an accident. He hung up when I offered to buy him a new dog."

"Maybe you should try talking to him in person."

He nodded. "But not today. After he's had a chance to cool down."

"Whatever you think best."

She returned to her cleaning, still with that vehement determination. He watched for half a minute, wondering if he should offer to help. No. Any other time she would have been pleased if he had, but not now. She needed to be alone a while longer, needed to finish regrouping.

He left her and climbed the stairs to the second floor. The idea of physical labor, the kind Alix was doing which didn't require thinking, appealed to him too; perhaps it would help *him* regroup. He continued up to the lightroom. In one corner was the lighthouse's diaphone, removed from its mounting halfway down the westernmost cliff wall when the Coast Guard abandoned the station in 1962. The air compressor that had operated it was also there, along with most of its four-inch air line.

Diaphones fascinated him; he intended to do a full chapter on them in *Guardians of the Night*. Large or small, they produced an amazing amount of noise and vibration—one high-pitched note that could be heard during most kinds of weather for a distance of seven miles, one low-pitched note, or "grunt," that could be heard much farther away. The volume of compressed air that passed through the instrument, even at a pressure of thirty pounds, was so enormous that the actual operating time of the diaphone was seldom more than eight seconds per minute. He had had the pleasure (if you could call it that) of standing within fifty feet of the big diaphone at the Point Reyes Lighthouse, near San Francisco, when it was in operation; any closer than that and it would have damaged his eardrums. He had literally been able to *feel* the noise and vibration all over his skin.

He assembled his tools and began to dismantle this one, taking time and care so as not to damage its working parts. Inside the cylinder, the brass reed—shaped somewhat like an automobile piston—that was the diaphone's heart looked to be free of corrosion, and it moved freely enough when he tested it. When you pumped compressed air past the reed, it vibrated back and forth in short strokes, rather than rotating as the reeds in the air sirens that had preceded diaphones as the preemptory fog-signal had; that produced the high-pitched note. You got the grunt by rapidly diminishing the quantity of air being fed to the reed.

He cleaned the reed and the other interior parts, reassembled the instrument, and cleaned and polished the outer brass casing. Then he examined the compressor and its air line. The line looked to be in reasonably good condition, considering its age; the compressor was dusty and needed cleaning, but he thought it would probably work well enough. He tinkered with it for a time, confirming his suspicion—and then found himself wondering if the diaphone *would* actually work after all these years. If he could *make* it work. Mount it outside somewhere away from the lighthouse, run the lines, see what happened. A test, an experiment—why not?

The thought intrigued him. A-1 Marine in Hilliard would probably have compressed air tanks. Better yet, he could pick them up while he was in Portland next week.

There was nothing more to occupy his attention in the lightroom; he went from there into his study. He felt somewhat better now. His labor with the diaphone and the prospect of operating it had temporarily crowded the death of Novotny's dog, all his other fears, into the back of his mind. More work on the book? Yes, while he was still in a productive mood. He sat down before the Underwood, loaded and fired another of his pipes, and plunged into work without any of his usual mild procrastinations.

Lighthouse construction. Basic design of the modern lighthouse originated by John Smeaton in 1757—famous Eddystone Light in the English Channel near the town of Plymouth (where tallow candles served to light its beacon for more than fifty years). Stone tower in place of wood. Huge blocks of granite weighing upwards of a ton each, cut so that they interlocked—not only on the flat first course but from one course to the next above. This pattern of construction used as a model for future lighthouses worldwide. . . .

It went well. Eight and a half pages. And all of the material, he felt, incisive and informative without being dry or pedantic. He lost all track of time, so that when Alix appeared at his side, startling him slightly, to announce that dinner was ready, he said, "Dinner? My God, is it that late?"

"Almost eight."

He glanced over at the window. Dusk had fallen without his

having noticed it. He rolled his head, stretching the tightened muscles in his neck and shoulders. After a moment Alix moved over behind him and began to massage the tight area, her thumbs kneading along his fourth cervical vertebra. That, and the weariness that had replaced the anxiety and anger in her expression, told him that it was all right between them again. At least for now.

He said, "Wasn't it my turn to cook tonight?"

"I came up earlier, but you were so involved I decided not to disturb you."

"Thanks. I'll take mess duties tomorrow and Monday."

They went downstairs. Pan-fried chicken, asparagus, a small salad. Beck's for him, white wine for her. He ate with some appetite; Alix picked at her food. They made small talk at first—neutral topics. Then he told her about the diaphone, and they discussed her next illustration (the Eddystone Light), and after that they were no longer awkward with each other. They cleaned up the dishes together, went upstairs, she read his pages, they went to bed. And during all of it he felt almost relaxed, normal, as if nothing ugly had happened last night, as if their life together weren't about to change so radically that neither of them would ever be the same again.

But the feeling of normalcy was an illusion, a lie erected by his mental defenses. It was his body that told the truth. He had the desire to make love, once they were in bed, and Alix was willing, but there was no physical response in his loins; it was as if he had gone dead from the waist down. Alix's touch, always electric, did nothing for him. He had never had this kind of failure, no failure at all except for the one time he'd gotten a little too high on champagne punch at the faculty New Year's Eve party.

"It's okay," she murmured against his ear, "don't worry about it," but it wasn't okay. It was another thing that frightened him. What if this wasn't just an isolated instance? What if he became permanently impotent as well as permanently blind? Pain, deterioration both physical and mental—unmanned in every way.

What if I did hit that dog on purpose? I don't remember, I don't remember. . . .

He held her tight and began to stroke her slowly, gently, concentrating his caresses on her clitoris, concentrating his thoughts on her instead of himself. In the dark she whispered, "You don't have to," and he thought, Yes I do, and said, "I want to," and after a while she came shuddering against him, with her face turned sideways against his chest. And even her orgasm did nothing to arouse him. Nothing at all.

Her face still pressed to his chest, she whispered, "Oh, Jan, I love you."

"I love you too," he said, and thought: That's enough, isn't it? Even at the end, when the darkness comes, it'll be enough.

He went to sleep holding her, loving her, and not believing any of it.

Jan

The first rifle shots woke him immediately.

He sat up in bed, groggy at first, but as always when he was jerked out of sleep the disorientation passed in a few seconds and he was alert. Next to him Alix stirred, came half-awake, mumbled something incoherent. He looked past the shape of her, at the red numerals on the Sony digital clock radio. 3:18.

He had no idea at first what the noises were, didn't identify them as gunshots until something made a metallic spanging sound outside—close outside, on the lighthouse grounds—and then he heard the hollow echo of the third shot. He thought: Jesus! and swung his legs out of bed, fumbled with hands and feet for his slippers. He was aware, now, that the room was not fully dark, that there was whitish moonlight coming through the window.

Glass shattered, faintly but unmistakably. And the reverberation of the fourth shot rolled like a small thunderclap, died away into a heavy silence.

Alix was awake now, sitting up; her voice reached out for him, frightened and confused, as he stood and groped for his robe. "Jan, what is it? What's happening?"

"I don't know. Stay here, I'll find out."

He ran out into the hall, pulling the robe around him, and half-stumbled down the stairs into the living room. The windows, like the one in the bedroom, faced seaward; there was nothing for him to see in that direction. The kitchen, then. He ran in there, leaned up to peer through the curtained window above the sink. The moonlight was bright out on the grounds: the cloud cover had broken up sometime earlier, leaving the sky clear and hazed with stars. The patch of grass that separated the lighthouse from the garage had a whitish cast, as if it had been dusted with talcum powder; the walls of the garage, the fence farther down, showed faintly luminous. He could see beyond the gate, all the way along the rutted cape road to where it jogged inland and disappeared into a hollow.

Nothing moved anywhere.

No sounds, either—no more shots. Just that intense silence, like a noise in his ears pitched too high for him to hear.

The breaking glass, he thought then. Window in the garage? But the station wagon caught and held his attention. It was parked thirty yards away, at the edge of the grass, swung around at an angle to the north; he could see that the front end was listing his way, that the left front tire was flat.

He swung away from the sink, hurried up the steps into the cloakroom for his coat, came back down and through the kitchen to the front door. Alix was standing at the foot of the stairs, clutching her old quilted housecoat around her. She had turned on the lights; they revealed the pallor of her face—the same color as the moonshine outside.

"Jan, those were shots. Was somebody—?"

"They shot the car," he said grimly.

"What? They what?"

His head had begun to ache; he could feel the pressure starting to build again behind his eyes. "I'm going out there," he said. "You stay here."

"Jan, don't—"

"Lock the door after me. Watch through the kitchen window."

"No, wait . . ."

But he didn't wait; he opened the door and walked outside.

The wind had died down to a murmurous breeze; it occurred to him peripherally that that was why he had been able to hear the shots so clearly, the ricochet and the breaking glass. But it was still cold, not much above forty degrees. There was a crystal-like quality to the air, so that every object stood out in sharp relief.

He stopped five feet from the door, holding his coat bunched shut at his throat. Still nothing moving. The only sound was the gentled-down coupling of surf and rocks at the base of the cliffs. After a moment he began walking again. There was an awareness in him that he made a perfect target out here in the moonlight, that if they were still nearby they could shoot him as easily as they had shot the car. He fought down an impulse to turn back, kept moving forward instead at a slow walk. Never show fear. Never let anyone see how afraid you might be.

When he reached the Ford he saw that the right headlight had been blown out. That explained the breaking glass. He moved around the front of the car to determine if there had been any other damage. Furrow along one fender where the one bullet had ricocheted; that was all.

He turned to look back at the lighthouse. He couldn't see Alix's face behind the kitchen window but he was sure she was there. He lifted his hands, gestured to her that everything was all right. And it was—for now. They were gone, long gone, like the cowards they were.

He walked back across the grass at the same slow, measured pace. Alix had the door open for him; he entered and shut it and threw the bolt.

"One flat tire and one broken headlight," he said. "I'll put the spare on in the morning. Get the damage fixed while I'm in Portland."

She gripped both his arms. "Jan, you shouldn't have gone out there. Suppose—"

"They're gone, don't worry."

"We'd better call the sheriff."

"In the morning. There's nothing anybody can do tonight."

"But who *were* they? Who'd do a thing like that?"

"Kids," he said. "Just kids."

But he was thinking: Mitch Novotny, that's who.

Mitch Novotny

After church on Sunday morning, Mitch went down to the boat slips to do some work on the *Spindrift*. It was a nice day, clear, ten degrees warmer now that the clouds had blown inland, and Marie had wanted to drive down the coast to Port Orford, where her sister lived. Sister knew somebody who had setter pups for sale, she said. But he wasn't in the mood for a drive or looking at any damn setter pups. It was too soon; Red was still on his mind. Red, and that asshole out at the lighthouse. He'd snapped at her some, made her cry—Christ, you looked cross-eyed at a pregnant woman and she was like as not to bust out in tears. (Number three on the way, due in two months. He could barely provide for the five of them now; how the hell was he going to provide for a sixth? Should have had himself fixed, that was what he should have done. But Marie wouldn't hear of it. Wasn't natural, she said. Natural. Shit. *She* didn't have to earn the money to pay the bills, did she?)

So then he'd left and come down here where it was quiet, where a man could have a little peace of a Sunday morning. Who could blame him? Marie bawling, her mother crooning to her and glaring at him like he was some kind of ogre—dried-up old bitch, he didn't know why he let her keep on living with them; he should have sent her packing a long time ago— Tommy and Nita glued to the TV, sound up loud as hell so you couldn't hear yourself think, some silly-ass cartoon show. Madhouse, that was what it was up there half the time. Damn madhouse.

He finished hosing down the worn decking, shut off the pump, and watched the last of the water run out through the scuppers. Thirty-two years old, the *Spindrift,* almost as old as him; his father had bought her new in Coos Bay. Good worker in her day, but out-of-date now and starting to rot. Outriggers too small, hydraulic winch too undependable. Old Jimmy diesel had developed problems, too; if it broke down so he couldn't fix it, what would he do then? Bank in Bandon had already turned him down for a loan. Hang on, that was all he could do. Bust his ass hauling rockfish off the in-shore reefs—too many fishermen and not enough fish, except for perch and you couldn't even make grocery money off perch. Yeah, and pray the god-damn salmon started running right again next season, a big run that fetched high prices from the cannery; then he could pay off enough of his debts to float a loan for an overhaul on the *Spindrift,* if not for a new boat altogether. New boat. Jesus, one of those fiberglass jobs with good refrigeration, an automatic depth-finder, maybe even a Loran navigation system and a hydraulic winch with an automatic trigger that pulled in a fish as soon as it hit the line—that was what he wanted, what he dreamed of owning. Never get it, though. All his life he'd had shitty luck, never got anything he really wanted. Born to lose, that was him. Just like the song.

He started to haul up the engine housing for a look at the Jimmy. What stopped him was somebody legging along the board float toward his slip. He straightened—and then he recognized who it was and he could feel his gut tighten up. Ryerson. Now what the hell? he thought. More crap about buying him a new dog?

Ryerson came down to the *Spindrift*'s aft gunwale and stopped there, a couple of feet from where Mitch was standing. Mitch didn't move. Bastard's hairy face was set tight, white around the nostrils, and his back was board-stiff. Pissed off about something. What did *he* have to be pissed off about?

"You and I need to talk, Mr. Novotny."

"We got nothing to talk about," Mitch said. "Unless you come to admit you ran Red down on purpose."

"It was an accident, I told you that. And I'm sorry it happened. But that doesn't mean I'll put up with any retaliation on your part. I want that understood right now."

"You don't make any sense, Ryerson. Go on back to the lighthouse, why don't you? Leave me the hell alone." Mitch put his back to the bastard and yanked up the engine housing.

Behind him Ryerson said, quiet, "You'll talk to me now, or you'll talk to the sheriff later."

Mitch faced him again. "What's that supposed to mean?"

"You know what it means, Mr. Novotny. Your little shooting spree last night."

"Shooting spree?"

"You're good with that rifle of yours—one smashed headlight, one ruptured tire, and some minor damage to one fender. By my estimate the repairs will cost at least two hundred dollars."

"You're crazy," Mitch said. "I don't know what you're talking about."

"I'm willing to pay for the repairs myself, because of the accident with your dog. But if anything like last night happens again, I won't put up with it. Do you understand?"

Mitch stared at him in disbelief and gathering anger. "I don't understand none of this."

"I mean what I say, Mr. Novotny. Stay away from the Cape Despair Light. No more nocturnal target practice, no more harassment. I called the sheriff this morning and told him about the shooting. I didn't give him your name but if there's any more trouble I will give it to him. I'll swear out a complaint against you and have you arrested."

Mitch had no words now; they were choked up in his throat. But Ryerson nodded as if he'd said something that had no answer, matched Mitch's stare for a few seconds, then turned his back and stalked off. Mitch watched him go. He was so worked up inside, his hands started to shake when he lit a cigarette.

It took him a while to get his thoughts clear. All that shit about a shooting spree last night—crazy talk. Or was it? No, maybe not. Maybe somebody actually *did* shoot up his car. And Ryerson thought it was him, on account of Red. But who'd do a thing like that? Hell, nobody, not even kids with hot pants, went all the way out to the lighthouse at night—

Nobody except Adam Reese.

Out there on the cape lots of nights late, Adam was, looking to jacklight deer with that 30.06 of his.

Aloud, Mitch said, "Ah, for Christ's sake." He tossed his cigarette into the bay, coiled up the hose, put his tools away, and climbed off onto the float. He went straight from the cannery pier across the highway and up the hill to the trailer encampment.

First trailer he came to was Hod's. Run-down old white thing with a green lattice border around the bottom and a cheap canvas awning rigged on one side—hell of a place for a man to have to live with a wife and three kids. He felt for Hod, losing his boat the way he had; but he felt for himself, too, and more. *Six* mouths to feed in another couple of months, not just five. And now this Ryerson coming around and threatening to have him arrested for something he hadn't done. Jesus Christ!

Hod's two boys, Tad and Jason, were tossing a half-flat football back and forth in the weeds out back. In front his oldest, Mandy, was sitting in the sun in a canvas-backed chair with her Sunday dress hiked up so far on her thighs you could damn near see her twat. She didn't pull it down when he came by, either. Pretty little tease. Get herself knocked up for sure one of these days, just like Hod was always predicting.

"If you're looking for my dad, Mr. Novotny, he's back at Adam's trailer."

"Looking for Adam, thanks."

"Sure is a nice day, isn't it?"

"If you don't catch a draft."

She knew what he meant; she grinned at him bold as hell. Good thing he was Hod's friend. Good thing he wasn't the kind to chase around after tail, young *or* old . . . even with Marie all swollen the way she was and not wanting him to touch her in the last couple of months. A man could get himself in a lot of bad trouble over one like Mandy Barnett.

He went on past the other trailers, to the small humped old house trailer that Adam lived in. Adam had built a workshed on one side of it and a kind of covered areaway made out of wood and tin that connected it with the trailer. There was a table under the areaway, and some chairs, and Hod and Adam were sitting there with bottles of Henry's, playing cribbage and listening to the 49er game on the radio.

Adam said, "Hey, Mitch. You want to sit in on a little crib?"

"No."

"Beating me as usual," Hod complained. "'Niners are winning, though. How about a beer?"

"No." Mitch's hands were steady now; the walk up here had put him back in control again. He said, "Ryerson just showed up down at the *Spindrift*. Says somebody shot up his car with a rifle last night. Did two hundred dollars' worth of damage."

Hod said, "The hell!" Adam didn't say anything; he had his eyes on the cards he was shuffling.

"Accused me of it," Mitch told them. "Said if it ever happened again he'd call in the sheriff and have me arrested."

"You do it, Mitch?" Hod asked. "Shoot up his car?"

"Hell no, I didn't do it." He said his next words to Hod, too, but he was looking at Adam. "You go out on the cape last night with Adam? After deer?"

"No. Overcast breaking up and all that moonlight . . . just didn't seem like a good idea."

"How about you, Adam? You go out?"

Adam popped the cards down on the table, got up in that bouncy way of his. "I went out. No damn deer, though."

"What'd you take? That thirty-ought-six of yours? The one with the scope sight?"

Adam hopped around a little, let out a breath, and then said, "All right, Mitch, I done it. I put a couple of rounds in Ryerson's car."

"Well what the hell *for*?"

"I didn't plan it. It was just there wasn't any deer and it got me frustrated. I was out near the lighthouse, nobody around, that big Ford station wagon sitting there in the moonlight . . . hell, I don't know. I remembered what you said Friday night and it just seemed like the thing to do."

"What *I* said?"

"About not letting Ryerson get away with murdering Red. About making him pay for it."

"I didn't mean by shooting up his goddamn car!"

"What'd you mean, then?"

"I don't know, not yet. But nothing like that."

"Hell, Mitch, I'm sorry. I only meant it as a favor to you. I liked Red too, you know that."

"Yeah."

"I just never figured he'd come down on you for it."

"Suppose he changes his mind, decides to sic the sheriff on me? Or tries to sue me for the damages? What then, Adam?"

Adam was silent for a couple of seconds. Then he said, "That ain't going to happen. None of it."

"Oh it ain't?"

"No. Ryerson can't do nothing to you for what happened to his car, any more'n you can do anything to him for killing Red. Not legally. He's got no proof who fired those rounds last night. If there was anything he could do, it'd have been the sheriff talking to you this morning, not him."

"Maybe," Mitch said, but he wasn't so sure.

"If he did swear out a complaint against you," Hod said, "you could do the same thing to him, couldn't you?" He'd been watching with round eyes and looking nervous. Hod was always nervous when things shifted off an even keel. "On account of Red, I mean?"

"No. I already told you the sheriff said I couldn't."

"Well, couldn't you sue him for false arrest or something?

You could get Gus Brooks, up in Bandon. He's the best lawyer on the coast.''

"Hod, you talk like a man with a paper asshole. I can't afford to hire Gus Brooks or any other goddamn lawyer. I can't afford to get arrested or go to court or miss any damn time at all out on the boat. I can't hardly make ends meet as it is.''

"Ryerson don't have time for it either," Adam said. "He's out there writing some book—got a year to do it and no more. He ain't going to make trouble no matter what happens. Putting the sheriff or some lawyer on you don't buy him nothing but headaches he don't want.''

Mitch didn't say anything. He was still mad as hell, but now he didn't know who he was mad at. Yes he did: it wasn't Adam, it was Ryerson more than ever. Adam was his friend; Ryerson was a damn radical from California who'd murdered Red just because Red nipped him a little. Adam was stupid sometimes and didn't use good sense; Ryerson was a dog-murdering son of a bitch.

"Whole damn year of him out at the light," Mitch said finally. "Sitting out there all high and mighty, killing a man's dog when he feels like it, threatening people. It ain't right.''

"No," Hod said, "but what's there to do about it?''

"Plenty.''

"Like what?''

"Like send him to hell back to California. Pry his ass out of the lighthouse before *this* year's out.''

"You mean force him to leave?''

"Isn't that what I just said?''

"How you going to do that without him running to the law?''

"There are ways," Adam said. He looked relieved that Mitch wasn't pissed at him anymore. "Ain't there, Mitch?''

"Yeah," Mitch said. "There are ways.''

Alix

Jan left for Portland at eight o'clock Tuesday morning. Even though there had been no repetition of the shooting incident, no trouble of any kind, he'd seemed reluctant to leave her alone at the lighthouse. It had crossed her mind that in spite of what he claimed, he didn't really believe it was kids who had been responsible, that he thought it had something to do with the accidental death of Mitch Novotny's dog and was afraid of further reprisals. But when she voiced the thought to him, he had only repeated what the county sheriff had told him: This was the country; youngsters were made familiar with firearms at an early age, and unfortunately they sometimes misused their weapons by plinking at signs, buildings, even automobiles, in much the same way their urban counterparts spray-painted walls and subway cars. She preferred that explanation herself, rather than believe it was malicious mischief on the part of a grown man or men who ought to know better, and had let the matter drop. She wasn't afraid to stay alone. And she had enough on her mind as it was—those headaches of Jan's above all—without cluttering it even more with vague fears that their neighbors were out to get them.

After Jan was gone, she tackled the kitchen again. She'd started painting it on Sunday, and had finished it yesterday with Jan's help. All that remained to be done was some touching-up work and a general cleanup; then, this afternoon, she could get back to work on her preliminary sketch of the Eddystone Light.

By noon she had managed to scrape off most of the paint that had slopped over onto the window, counters, and floor. There were a few stubborn spots but they would come out with turpentine. She set down the single-edged razor she'd been using and surveyed the room with satisfaction. The white semi-gloss enamel had brightened the space considerably; the kitchen even *smelled* clean and fresh. Now turpentine—and then she would be done.

She went through the little cloakroom—still gray and dingy, but she didn't intend to expend any energies on it—and into the pantry, where the painting supplies were. The pantry was good-sized; the staples they had purchased in Hilliard, plus the few supplies they'd brought from home, barely filled its shelves. Obviously, lightkeepers had had to keep much more on hand in the days before the modern automobile made trips into the village both simple and convenient.

She was reaching down for a can of turpentine when she thought she heard a noise. She froze, listening. There was nothing to hear. You're getting jumpy, Ryerson, she thought. Imagining things. But then she remembered the old well, the one under the trapdoor in the pantry floor. Just thinking of it gave her the creeps. Which was silly, of course; but she couldn't help disliking that dark, dank cavity filled with God knew what kind of refuse. And—rats, too? Rats would make a rustling sound.

She looked down at the metal ring that served as the handle for the door. She ought to check. If there *were* rats down there she'd have to buy poison, get rid of them. She wasn't about to live with disease-carrying rodents just a few feet away from their stored food.

Decisively, fighting off a shudder, she bent and grasped the ring and pulled upward. The door yielded, creaking. It was heavy; she drew it up halfway, warily, ready to let it fall again if anything came scurrying out of the darkness. But nothing did. She eased it back as far as it would go on its hinges, left it canted there at an angle to the floor and the well opening it revealed.

The air that rose up from inside the cut-out space was musty, like an old cellar that has gone too long unused. She took their big Eveready flashlight from where it sat on a nearby shelf and shone it down inside the well. Nothing moved in the sweep of light; thank God for that. The cavity was about three feet in diameter, at least a dozen feet deep, with rusted metal rungs mortared into the stone walls. The debris at the bottom was mounded unevenly: unrecognizable metal shapes, some broken china, pieces of dusty glass, a dented tea kettle, even an old (twenties?) automobile hubcap. But no rats. Not even droppings indicating their presence.

Reassured, she shut off the flashlight and lowered the trapdoor. Dusted off her hands, got the turpentine, and started back toward the kitchen with it. But at the entrance to the cloakroom something made her turn and glance back at the trapdoor. It was irrational, but she wished the damned well wasn't there. Or at least that she didn't have to be reminded it was every time she entered the pantry.

Then she remembered seeing some carpet remnants out in the garage, leftovers from the carpeting in the living room. One of the bigger pieces ought to cover the trapdoor. And they could use it as a mat to wipe off their shoes when they came in through the pantry in wet weather.

An hour later the trapdoor was not only carpet-covered, but she had tacked the remnant down at its four corners to make sure it stayed in place. She had also finished cleaning up the kitchen, had polished her blue enamel cookware and hung it on the new hooks on the wall, and was feeling rather pleased with herself. Hungry, too. A tuna sandwich, she thought, and maybe a glass of wine.

She was mixing up the tuna at the drainboard when she saw,

through the window, that she was about to have company. Mandy Barnett, of all people, had just come through the gate and was walking toward the lighthouse.

Frowning, Alix put the tuna salad into the refrigerator, went into the living room, and opened the door just before Mandy reached it. The girl was dressed in the same Indian-style poncho, jeans, and beaded leather headband; she grinned at Alix and said, "I didn't see the car and I was afraid you wouldn't be home."

"Well, this is a surprise. How did you get all the way out here?"

"A guy I know brought me. He's waiting down the road."

"The boy in the green Chevvy?"

"That's right. Aren't you going to ask me in?"

Alix hesitated; but she was curious about why the girl was here. "All right, come ahead."

Inside, Mandy said, "It's not too bad here."

"We like it."

"Nicer than where I live, that's for sure. You know the trailers up on the north end of town?"

"Yes."

"My mom, dad, two brothers, and me live in one of them. We don't even have running water."

Alix didn't know what to say, so she kept silent.

"We take turns hauling water from the faucet," Mandy said. "I sleep on the couch. Last week we had egg sandwiches for supper four days."

"Mandy, why are you telling me all this?"

"I just want you to know where I'm coming from." The girl began to pace around the room the way she had at the launderette, examining things and humming a vaguely recognizable rock tune. The lyrics, Alix recalled, had something to do with wanting to "get it on all night." At Mandy's age she wouldn't have even *considered* getting it on all night, much less sung about it. Mandy was obviously much more precocious; she had a tough, put-on assurance that might have been amusing if she hadn't been so serious.

She said, "Suppose you tell me why you're here."

Mandy stopped pacing. "I wanted to talk. You're from California, right? Someplace near San Francisco?"

"Yes."

"Nice there."

"Yes."

"What do you think of Hilliard?"

Alix debated an answer, but took too long for Mandy's liking; the girl answered her own question.

"Well, I *hate* it!"

The outburst cracked her tough-girl veneer. Alix took advantage of it and asked her, "Why, Mandy?"

"It's ugly and cold, and everybody's poor. There's nothing to do but go to church or to the fucking Bingo games at the community center. I hate living in that trailer. We used to rent a house, but when my dad lost his boat we couldn't even afford that. My mother used to have a dream that someday we'd own our own house, somewhere nice like Bandon or Coos Bay, but that'll never happen. She doesn't dream about anything anymore."

"Don't you have friends in the village? At school?"

"I dropped out·this year."

"Why?"

"Why not? Sitting in school wasn't getting me anywhere and I had a chance to go to work at a boutique in Bandon. But that fell through. Besides, my dad's got a high school diploma and look what it's done for him."

"What about your friend in the green Chevvy?"

"Him? He's just my connection for dope. That's about the

only other thing there is to do around here—smoke dope. And get it on on weekends. But that doesn't mean he's my friend.'' She met Alix's eyes defiantly; the tough veneer had hardened again.

Alix kept her expression neutral. ''Okay, now I know where you're coming from. What do you want?''

''I've got a business proposition for you.''

''Oh? What sort of business proposition?''

''I want to get out of Hilliard. Go to California. L.A., maybe.''

''And do what? Try to get into the movies?''

''God, no! I may live in a hick town but that doesn't mean I'm stupid. Nobody goes to Hollywood and gets rich and famous anymore; that's a lot of shit. But I figure I could get by down there, and at least it's sunny and warm.''

''How would you 'get by'? By turning tricks?''

''What?''

''Prostitution, Mandy.''

''If I have to. That's no big thing.''

Alix sighed.

''Anyway,'' Mandy said, ''I've got it figured out—the price of a bus ticket and enough money to keep me going until I can find a job or something. And what I've got to sell is worth just about what I'll need.''

''Sell?''

''To you, Mrs. Ryerson.''

''Now what could you possibly have to sell to me?''

''Information. Something I heard.''

''What would that be?''

''Come on. If I told you, I wouldn't have anything to sell.''

''Look, Mandy—''

''Five hundred dollars,'' Mandy said. ''Cash.''

''Five hundred—! That's ridiculous!''

"You think so? Well, you'd better think twice, Mrs. Ryerson. What I heard could be important to you. Very important."

The girl's nerve was appalling. But Alix sensed a desperation underneath her hard demeanor; even though Mandy's stance and tone of voice were aggressive, her fingers clenched and unclenched spasmodically. When she saw Alix looking at them she hid her hands in the folds of her poncho.

"Mandy," Alix said, "do you know what the name for this sort of thing is?"

"Blackmail, so what?"

"Not blackmail. Extortion. You can be put in jail for it."

"Don't give me that. You're not going to call the sheriff on me."

"I could call your parents."

The girl laughed. "Good luck. We're so poor, we don't even have a phone."

"You just don't realize what you're doing to yourself, do you? In the first place, I'm not about to give you five hundred dollars, no matter what you think. In the second place, even if you did manage to get to Los Angeles, you'd probably live to regret it. There are men down there who prey on young girls like you—"

"Stop talking down to me! I know all about pimps and pushers, I know all I need to know. I'm not some stupid hick kid you can feel sorry for!"

Mandy's face had reddened with this new outburst; for a moment Alix thought she was going to stamp her foot as she had in the launderette when her mother told her she couldn't have a Coke. Instead, she spun away and stormed across the room to the door.

"Mandy—"

"No, you listen to me, Mrs. Ryerson. If you don't get that

money for me you'll be sorry, you and your husband both. Real sorry." And then she was gone, slamming the door behind her.

Alix went into the kitchen, stood uneasily watching the girl half-walk, half-run down to the gate. What could Mandy have heard that would lead her to hatch such a fantastic extortion scheme? What sort of "information" was worth five hundred dollars, even in her immature mind?

If you don't get that money for me you'll be sorry, you and your husband both. Real sorry.

What could she possibly know?

Jan

It was late Wednesday afternoon when he finally left Portland.

He had intended to leave much earlier, around two, but the garage where he'd taken the Ford to have the damage repaired had failed miserably in their promise to have the car ready by one; he'd spent most of the afternoon wandering through secondhand bookshops, looking for (and not finding) unfamiliar lighthouse material, and it was almost four by the time he finally ransomed the station wagon. Then he stopped at a place on S.E. 3rd that sold and serviced air compressors and picked up a tank for the one that operated the diaphone. It was rush hour by the time he finished there; it took him almost an hour to get out of the city and ten miles down Highway 5.

Freeway driving usually relaxed him, but not this evening. He felt tired, tense, grouchy, and the monotonous flow of miles did nothing to ease any of those feelings. He kept fiddling with the radio—not looking for anything but noise, yet not satisfied with call-in shows, news programs, or music of any kind. None of it kept him from thinking.

Yesterday's examination by Dr. Philip R. Meade was one of the things that kept replaying in his mind, the primary thing. According to Meade, his condition—atrophying optic nerves in both eyes, aggravated by a form of "systemic choroiditis," or disease of the middle layer of tissue deep inside the eye— had not advanced to any marked degree. But neither had it improved, of course. Prognosis: still negative. Meade had administered a cortisone treatment, even though the last ophthalmologist he'd consulted in California had told him the condition had advanced beyond the help of such treatments. The good doctor had also administered bland professional sympathies, the usual recommendations as to what the patient should and shouldn't do, and a stronger codeine prescription to relieve the pain of his headaches.

Jan had asked him about blackouts, if they could become a symptom of his condition; he was careful not to admit that he had already had one, saying only that he "understood" they might be a by-product of intense eye-related headaches. Meade said blackouts were possible—given the rarity and seriousness of Jan's particular eye disorder, many symptomatic complications were possible—but his professional opinion was that Mr. Ryerson need have no fear of "memory impairment," especially if he avoided undue stress.

So much for Dr. Philip R. Meade.

He drove straight down Highway 5, mile after mile, mile after mile. *And many more miles to go before I sleep.* Traffic was thinning out, at least, now that rush hour was over; he could drive at a steady sixty-five, ten above the speed limit, but nobody observed the speed limit on Highway 5. Salem, Albany, Eugene, coming up on Cottage Grove. Coming up on nightfall, too, and still a hundred and fifty miles left to drive. Maybe he should stop for the night in Cottage Grove, or on down the road in Roseburg. Pack it in early, get an early start in the morning. No, he didn't want to spend another night in a motel. Four strange walls, closed in and alone, and worse when he shut off the light. The dark. It was like being a child again—afraid of the dark.

Country-and-western music blaring at him from the radio. "She Got the Gold Mine, I Got the Shaft." For God's sake. Was that supposed to be amusing? He rotated the knob, found a classical station. Something heavy, ponderous—Bach fugue? Terrific, just what he needed. The knob again. Sports-talk program out of Eugene, somebody complaining about the Oregon Ducks football team being perennial losers and poor competition for Pac-10 powerhouses like USC and UCLA. Fine, good. Complain away, my friend, all your worries should be confined to ducks, Oregon or otherwise.

Pretty country on both sides of Cottage Grove, mountains rising, farms tucked away in the folds of the hills. But he couldn't enjoy it. Roseburg next—and full dark when he got there. He turned off on Highway 42, the two-lane state road that connected Roseburg with Coos Bay on the coast. Sixty miles to Coquille, then a dozen miles on winding Highway 42-S to Bandon, then another twenty miles or so from there to Cape Despair. Close to a hundred miles altogether, part of it mountain driving, and already he felt fatigued and gritty-eyed.

Headache starting up, too. Just a small one, but he kept monitoring it, gauging its intensity, trying by force of will to prevent it from worsening. If it did get worse, if the bulging started, then he'd *have* to stop somewhere for the night. No more driving when he was suffering that way. Too dangerous—and he'd promised Alix.

Better take a rest stop soon, get some coffee and something to eat; no food since a small breakfast, and his stomach had set up an insistent growling. Call Alix, too. Eight-thirty now; she'd be wondering why he wasn't already back. Worrying, and he didn't want her to worry.

A truck stop's neon sign swam up out of the night ahead, blue and red and yellow; the colors looked watery at the edges. He pulled into the parking lot, drove past a couple of drawn-up semis, and found a place to park. At the upper end of the lot, where another driveway connected with the main road, two kids were trying to thumb a ride. They never learn, he thought. Don't they know it's dangerous to hitchhike these days? Don't they care? No, it wasn't that. It was just that they were young, and when you're young you never think about death, you never think it'll happen to you.

The diner was half full, hot and noisy, the air thick with the smell of fried food. There was an empty stool at the far end of the counter; he sat down and, without looking at a menu, told a waitress he'd have coffee and a burger, no fries. A corridor ran past the kitchen nearby, to the restrooms in back. He went along it, found a telephone on the wall between the restroom doors, found some change in his pocket, and called the lighthouse number collect.

The line hummed seven times, eight, making him nervous, before Alix answered and accepted the call. "Where are you?" she asked. Relief was plain in her voice. "I was starting to worry."

"Diner outside Roseburg. I got a late start."

"I wish you'd called earlier."

"I should have, I'm sorry."

". . . How do you feel?"

"Not too bad. A little tired, that's all."

"You're not having one of your headaches?"

"No. Don't worry."

"It's still a long drive from Roseburg, isn't it? Are you sure you're not too tired . . . ?"

"Positive. I should be in by eleven."

"Well, if you're sure . . ."

"I'm sure," he said. "Everything all right there? You took a long time answering."

"I was working on the Eddystone sketch."

"No problems or anything?"

"Jan, you asked me that this morning when you called. And last night. Do you expect something else to happen?"

"No, no. I guess I'm still a little spooked after Saturday night, that's all. I'll see you around eleven."

"All right. Take care."

"I will."

He went back to the counter, sat down, drank coffee while he waited for his hamburger. Why didn't he tell her the truth about Saturday night? Didn't want to frighten her. Not that there was anything to be afraid of now; it was finished. Wasn't it? Yes, he'd handled Novotny just right on Sunday—forceful, without being belligerent or unreasonable.

Still. He'd feel better once he was back at the Cape Despair Light with Alix. He hadn't liked the idea of leaving her alone; he wouldn't do it again.

But will she leave me *alone when she finds out?*

He couldn't get the possibility out of his mind. In his more optimistic moments he believed the fear was irrational; they'd been together so many years, been through so much together, and nothing had yet weakened the bond between them. And yet the fear was still there. And the fear kept him from telling her what he faced, what they both faced, in the very near future. So many people had left him in his life, some of them for reasons beyond his comprehension; was it really so irrational to think she would too? That graphic design company meant so much to her . . . no way could she undertake a job like that, with all its travel and other demands, when she had a blind husband to look out for. How could he even expect her to? He couldn't; he wasn't that selfish. Yes, he was. He didn't want to lose her, and he wouldn't, but he was terrified he would. Irrational . . .

His headache was just a little worse now.

He pressed both eye sockets with thumb and forefinger. Food might ease it. If not, one of the codeine capsules nestling in his coat pocket. Meade had warned him against taking the medicine while he was driving, but if he took just one, with plenty of coffee . . .

His hamburger arrived. Tasteless, but he ate all of it, even ate the orange slice that came with it. And he was still hungry. He ordered a slice of cherry pie a la mode and ate that and drank three more cups of coffee.

None of it did his head much good. The pressure remained—constant, but muted and tolerable. All he had to do was hold it at this level and he wouldn't have any difficulty driving; his thoughts were still perfectly clear. He shook out one of the codeine capsules, swallowed it with the last of his coffee. His nerves felt jangly from all the caffeine, but at least that would help keep him alert. He paid for his meal, left a tip, went out to the station wagon.

The hitchhikers were gone; he wondered vaguely who had picked them up. He wouldn't have, even if they'd still been there. Bad idea, picking up hitchhikers; dangerous on both sides.

He began to drive again. Radio blaring rock music, all dissonance and shrieks that scraped like a file across his nerve ends. He spun the knob, found a station that was playing excerpts from old comedy albums. One of Shelley Berman's routines, the one about fear of flying. Bill Cosby telling a Fat Albert story. Newhart on merchandising the Wright Brothers. Jonathan Winters spoofing old horror movies. He laughed a couple of times; most of the material was still funny and it felt good to laugh. The codeine had muted the pressure behind his eyes.

The road climbed up over Camas Mountain, down through the village of Camas Valley. Not much traffic; dark night—cloudy again, no moon. Mort Sahl clip on the radio now; he had never liked Mort Sahl. Sharp twists and turns in the road, climbing again into the Klamath Mountains. Concentrate on the white line. Headlights coming at him, blinding for an instant, gone. Tom Lehrer next, one of his favorites. "They're Rioting in Africa." God, how that song brought back memories. His college days. Madison, the protest marches, the parties—

The murder. Sandy Ralston. Ed Finlayson—guilty or innocent?

He spun the knob again, quickly. Something loud, something fast and catchy. Static instead. Not many stations coming through up here. Damn, there must be something . . . there. One of those "Golden Oldies" stations. The Beatles doing "Yellow Submarine." Silly song. Did we really get excited over songs like that?

Headlights coming at him, blinding, gone. Twists and turns, twists and turns. Town of Remote, aptly named. Headlights, blinding, gone. Climbing again, damn switchbacks all through here, right and left, left and right, back and forth. Headlights behind him this time, coming fast, some damn fool tailgating him on the sharp turns. Get off my ass, you fool, what's the matter with you? And then suddenly swerving around him on a half-blind turn, so that he had to jam on his brakes and veer over; taillights shining bloodily in the dark—and gone. Gone.

But the pain wasn't gone, it was still there. Worse than before.

Credence Clearwater Revival doing "Lodi."

Headlights, blinding, gone.

Town of Myrtle Point. Splashes of neon against the dark. Gone.

The Animals. "House of the Rising Sun."

Twisting, turning.

Hurting.

How far now? Almost to Coquille. Forty miles.

Hang on.

The Beatles. "Paperback Writer."

Coquille. 42-S. Twisting and turning, turning and twisting. Dark, no lights anywhere. Dark.

Eyes burning so bad they were leaking water.

"To Know Him Is to Love Him." The Teddy Bears. My God. The Teddy Bears, what kind of name was that . . . ?

Headlights, blinding, gone.

Shouldn't keep driving, headache getting worse, vision starting to blur a little. The dog, Novotny's dog—don't want anything like that to happen again. Can't risk another blackout, another accident.

Was it an accident?

Almost to Bandon. Not much farther. Twenty miles—

"Twenty-Six Miles Across the Sea."

So dark out there . . .

Somebody up ahead, walking along the road.

Out here at this time of night? Another hitchhiker? Mindless. Don't they realize how dangerous it is?

This fucking *pain*—

Don't they realize—

Bulging.

Oh God, better pull over—

Bulging.

Bulging.

Dark.

Alix

It had been almost three A.M. when Jan finally got home.

She had been frantic by then, still up and debating whether or not to call the state troopers, and when she'd heard the car she had rushed outside to meet him. Was he all right? Where had he been? He hadn't had another accident, had he?

He had seemed exhausted, a little disoriented; but he'd answered her questions, at least, given her some measure of relief. No, he hadn't had an accident, it was nothing like that. One of his headaches had come on suddenly outside Bandon. He'd pulled off on the side of the road, taken a codeine tablet for the pain, and the next thing he knew it had been two A.M. The codeine must have knocked him out. The headache had been gone when he'd awakened and he'd driven the rest of the way without incident.

Well, what about the headaches? she'd asked him. What had the specialist said?

Nothing more than what Dave Sanderson had already told him, Jan said. He was to avoid stress, take codeine when necessary. According to the doctor, it wasn't a serious problem.

Then he had gone straight up to bed, and by the time she'd put out the lights and followed him, he'd fallen asleep. But there had been very little sleep for her—just a couple of hours of fitful dozing near dawn. Most of the time she'd lain awake, staring into the darkness.

And now that she was up and dressed and in desperate need of a cup of coffee, she'd discovered that they were out of coffee. She stood in the kitchen peering into the big ceramic jar where they kept the beans, wondering how she could have forgotten to replenish them. Was there any instant in the pantry? Yes, but she didn't want instant, she wanted *real* coffee. She had hardly slept all night, she felt like hell, she deserved real coffee. At the very least.

What time did the Hilliard General Store open? Eight, wasn't it? Earlier than most of its type, but then Hilliard was a fishing village and fishermen and their families got up early.

She rummaged in the drawer under the drainboard and found the pad she kept there for grocery lists. No sense going all the way into the village just for coffee. They were out or almost out of other things as well. Orange juice, Ry-Krisp, beer. Was there any margarine left? No. Low on mustard, tuna, cheese . . . anything else? Eggs, better get some eggs. Now what about dinner tonight? Chicken? Fish? Hamburgers?

She realized her hand was shaking and set the pencil down. The house was silent, almost hushed—at least to her ears. Jan would sleep for hours; she knew his sleeping habits well enough to predict that. Best to keep busy with mundane chores like shopping until she could talk to him again about last night.

She gripped the pencil again. Make it hamburger for tonight. And fresh vegetables. They could use some milk, too, and Diet Pepsi for her. . . .

Five minutes later she scribbled a note to Jan, on the chance he might awaken before she got back, and left it on the kitchen table. Then she bundled herself into scarf, cap, and pea jacket, and left the lighthouse. The fine weather of the past few days was gone, replaced by a heavy, lowering overcast that promised rain before midday. As she walked to the car she glanced up at the menacing gray-black clouds—and shivered. Better hurry. It looked like a full-fledged storm was brewing, and she didn't want to get caught in it when it broke.

The station wagon was angled in near the garage, even though Jan had insisted after the shooting incident that it always be put inside. When she reached it she hesitated, then went around to the front and examined the bumper, grill, headlights, fenders. He had had the previous damage repaired in Portland; there was no new damage, not even a scratch. That made her feel better. It wasn't that she doubted his word; it was just that he had been so disoriented when he came home, so strange. . . .

She got into the Ford, started the engine, sat there waiting for it to warm up. Had Jan always acted strangely when he was suffering one of his headaches? When he was mired in one of his depressions? A few days ago her answer would have been an unqualified no, but now she wasn't so sure. When you lived in a given situation you tended to normalize it no matter how odd it might seem to an outsider. And the illusion of normalcy was easy to sustain when you were in familiar surroundings, going about your day-to-day business. But if you removed yourself from those surroundings, set yourself down somewhere totally different, you saw things from another perspective. What she was seeing now was more than a little unsettling.

The engine was warm. She reminded herself of her earlier resolve: stick to mundane chores—and mundane thoughts—for the time being. She let out a sigh, put the car in gear, turned it around, and drove down through the open gate onto the cape road.

The ominous clouds followed her, putting intermittent drops of rain on the windshield—more a mist, really, that didn't require the use of the wipers yet. To the south the barren rocks and beaches looked cold, forbidding; the rough sea made her think of the shipwrecks off Cape Despair, and of all the lives that had been lost off the perilous coast. She entered a dark copse of fir trees, with its thick ferny groundcover, and thought of the evil forests of Grimm's fairy tales. Not a good morning for her to be out. Not a good morning for her to be alone at all.

In the open fields beyond, the sheep seemed to huddle together in little flocks; even their thick coats were not enough protection against the icy wind. If it hadn't been for the sheep, she could have imagined herself alone in a wilderness hundreds of miles from the nearest human being. It was that desolate out, that empty.

But it was only an illusion, and it was shattered moments later when she came around a bend in the road past another stand of trees. A hundred yards ahead, near a gully flanked by clumps of prickly broom that cut a jagged line through the south-side sheep graze, several vehicles were drawn up along the road and a small knot of men stood near a flattened section of fence. Alix braked automatically, frowning in surprise and bewilderment. The vehicles were two state police cars, a Curry County sheriff's cruiser, a farm truck, and an ambulance. Most of the men wore uniforms of one kind or another.

They all looked her way as she approached, and one of them—dressed in the state troopers' smoke-gray outfit and broad-brimmed hat—detached himself from the rest and moved onto the road, holding up his gloved hand for her to stop. She obeyed. Rolled down the window as he came ahead to her side of the car. The wind that blew in was cold and misty and smelled of ozone.

The trooper bent down to look at her and glance around the car. She asked him, "What's the trouble, officer?"

"May I see your identification, please?"

She reached for her purse, handed him her driver's license. He studied it solemnly.

"California," he said. "Mind telling me what you're doing out here?"

"I live at the lighthouse."

"That so? Your license gives your address as Palo Alto."

"Yes. But we're staying here for a year."

"We?"

"My husband and I. He's writing a book on lighthouses. Officer, what—?"

"Did you travel this road last night?"

"No."

"Did your husband?"

"I . . . well, yes, he did, he was up in Portland—"

"Where is he now?"

"At the lighthouse. He's sleeping, he didn't get home until late."

"How late?"

"Around three o'clock."

"I see. And you were at the lighthouse alone until then?"

"Yes."

"No visitors?"

"No."

"Did you happen to notice anything out of the ordinary?"

"No, nothing." She was alarmed now; fear, like a small wormlike thing, crawled through her. "Officer, can't you please tell me what's happened?"

He didn't answer for a moment. He had averted his face and was watching two white-uniformed men carry something black over the flattened section of fence and into the gully. Something that looked like a black plastic bag. When he returned his attention to her his face had set into grim lines.

"Young girl—apparently a hitchhiker—was murdered last night. Strangled and her body dumped here." Beneath the wide brim of his hat, his eyes were hard and angry. "Looks like the work of a psycho," he said.

Part Two

Early October

Where there is much light, the shadows are deepest.

—GOETHE

Alix

When she was stressed and preoccupied, she often experienced two totally contradictory moods: she would become indifferent to her surroundings, all thought focused inward on whatever bothered her; but at the same time she would have vivid flashes of clarity, and whatever she was looking at would stand out in almost painful detail. It was the way she felt when she was beginning one of her design projects: at first groping her way, uncertain how to start, then in an instant it would all become clear—how to approach it, how to convey what she wanted others to see. But when it happened in connection with her work, she felt good, elated. Her current preoccupation called up no good feelings at all.

It was during one of those flashes, three days after the murdered girl's body had been found, that she caught herself studying the Hilliard General Store with intense concentration. Half an hour earlier she'd left the lighthouse for the first time since that tragic morning, driven out by a lack of food and even instant coffee. The intervening days had had an unreal quality. A state police detective named Sinclair had questioned her and Jan on two separate occasions about what they'd seen and done the night of the murder; he seemed to find something suspicious about Jan's account of his return from Portland, about the headache that had forced him to pull off the road and spend the night in the car. As a result Jan had retreated further and further into a moody silence. At first she had tried to draw him out of it, but when that hadn't succeeded she had felt the same sort of brooding silence descend on herself, and found it difficult to cope with more than the basic details of living.

She hadn't been able to work in such a state. When she tried, her sketches came out looking like mechanical drawings, lifeless and stiff. An attempt to break the impasse by doing sketches of the interior and exterior of the lighthouse and of the cape itself, with the idea of sending them to her family, had also failed; those, too, had the quality of being mere exercises in technique, and eventually she'd thrown them out. Finally she'd given up and read instead, but her concentration was poor: she found herself rereading the same pages over and over again.

This morning she'd taken herself in hand, added to the grocery list she'd made three days ago, and driven into town. But now she felt a strange lethargy that prevented her from getting out of the station wagon. She sat behind the wheel, hands gripping its familiar surface, staring at the store. Scoured gray wood siding. Dirty plate glass window with the name inscribed in cracked black letters. Sagging shingle roof with rusted gutters. It all stood out in such minute detail.

A gull was perched on one of the utility lines that ran in under the eaves. She watched until it spread its wings and lifted off into the bleak sky. Then she shook her head, reached for her purse, and pushed herself out onto the graveled roadside.

The sense of clarity was still with her when she entered the store. Boxes of detergent, cans of vegetables, bottles of pop all stood out in red, blue, and yellow relief against the drab brown of the shelves. The cracks and worn spots on the black-and-white linoleum floor were sharply visible. Each potato in the big bushel basket near the door seemed to have a uniquely individuated shape. It was only when she moved her eyes to the staring faces of two elderly women at the counter, and then to the impassive countenance of Lillian Hilliard, that she noticed the silence.

It hung heavy, tangible, like that following a sudden explosion. The three women's immobility complemented it; they stood frozen, their shabby monochromatic clothing and faded hair reminding Alix of an old photograph. For a moment she froze too, her hand still on the door. Then she let go and it closed with a bang that shattered the stillness and prodded the women into jerky motion. Lillian Hilliard pushed a button on the cash register and counted change into the outstretched palm of the heaviest of the elderly women. The thinner one gathered up two grocery bags, glancing furtively at Alix as she did so. When her companion had placed a handful of dollar bills inside her purse, she picked up the third sack. Then, with another sly glance, their seamed mouths slightly agape, they bustled from the store.

Alix watched with a curious detachment, one that also permitted her to see herself as she stood there: a slender young woman in a pea jacket, knit cap pulled down over her hair, body held straight and steady, face as blank and calm as that of the storekeeper. She nodded at Mrs. Hilliard, felt a grim pleasure when the older woman's gaze shifted toward the window.

She took a basket and started down one of the aisles. The entire time she was filling it she was aware of an undercurrent of activity in front. Lillian Hilliard moving on her stool, casting quick glances Alix's way. The bell over the door jangling, customers coming in, greeting the storekeeper. Mrs. Hilliard answering in low tones and the voices of the customers lowering to match it. None of those who came in stayed more than a minute, as if they couldn't bring themselves to do their shopping in the presence of the outsider.

At last her basket was full. She took it to the counter, set it down, and watched Lillian Hilliard reach for it with motions that were brusque, uncourteous. Alix thought she detected a glint of malice in the woman's previously bland eyes, felt a strong stirring of dislike. And out of some perverse desire to annoy the storekeeper, she said, "How are you today, Mrs. Hilliard?"

Without looking up Lillian Hilliard said, "As well as I deserve to be," and went on ringing up the groceries as if there had been no interruption.

Alix watched the woman's stubby fingers as they moved over the cash register keys, mentally calculating along with the machine. Coffee, $4.55—higher than at home. Chicken breasts, $1.79 a pound—about the same. Soup mix, 89¢. The lettuce didn't look very good, not at 59¢ a head. And the cheese . . . hadn't Jan said there was a good cheese factory in Bandon?

Mrs. Hilliard finished and silently handed Alix the register receipt. While she put the groceries in bags, Alix studied the column of figures. The coffee was the third item, after the laundry soap and box of kitchen matches—she was sure she had remembered the order correctly—but the price was $5.55, a dollar higher than the one stamped on the can. The price of the soup mix had been entered as $1.89. At least half of the other items were higher, too. All in all, the bill had been padded by more than twenty percent.

"Something wrong?" Mrs. Hilliard asked. She had bagged the last of the groceries and was watching Alix with a faint smile tugging at the edges of her mouth.

Alix didn't answer immediately; she was afraid the anger building in her might make her voice shake or crack. She drew a deep breath before she said, "Yes, something's wrong."

"Well?"

"These prices . . . they're too high."

Lillian Hilliard shrugged. "This is a small store, a small town. Prices are bound to be high. We can't give you the kind of deals your big-city California stores do."

"That's not what I'm talking about and you know it." Alix held out the receipt. "I'm not stupid, Mrs. Hilliard—I know what your prices are and I remember the order you rang things up in.''

"You don't like what I charge, you can shop someplace else.''

"I don't like being cheated—"

"Lord knows I don't want your kind in here anyway.''

"I said I don't like being cheated. Do you pad all your customers' bills, or only those of outsiders like my husband and me?''

"Now hold on a minute—''

"No, *you* hold on a minute! I didn't say anything before when you were unfriendly to us. Or later, when you made accusations against my husband without bothering to listen to his side of the story. But when it comes to outright dishonesty—''

"What I do ain't nothing compared to murder.''

"Murder?'' Alix stared at her. "What are you talking about?''

"Don't you know?''

"No, I don't.''

"Lots of murderers down in California,'' Lillian Hilliard said. "All kinds of crazies running around loose. Pick up the paper and read about it every day. One could be living right next door to you and you'd never know it until he gets caught. One could even be living in your house, maybe.''

The full implication of the woman's words registered. Alix's first reaction was shock. Then her anger flared, turned to rage coupled with a fierce defensiveness. Her fingers bit into her palms as she struggled to calm herself.

"Are you trying to say my husband had something to do with that girl's murder the other night?''

"If I am, I'm not the only one.''

"Damn you, I—''

"Don't you curse me in my own store.''

Alix could no longer control her rising fury. She said, "You're a disgusting woman, Lillian Hilliard. Your mind is small and your morals even smaller. I wouldn't have anything you've touched in my house!" And she grabbed the nearest bag of groceries, shoved it violently across the counter.

The storekeeper almost fell backward off her stool as she clutched at the bag. It slipped through her hands, crashed to the floor. Alix shoved the other two bags after it and then turned toward the door. Lillian Hilliard shouted after her, angry words that she didn't listen to and that she cut off by slamming the door.

She was at the car, fumbling in her purse for her keys, when she became aware of a man coming toward her. It was the wiry little workman who had been installing shelves in the store several days before—Adam something. This morning he was wearing a red headband to hold back his longish blond hair, and there was a smile on his sharp-featured face that did not reach his eyes.

"Morning, Mrs. Ryerson."

I don't know you, she thought. I don't want to know you. She gave him a vague smile and continued to rummage in her purse for her keys.

The man was not put off by her silence. He maneuvered between her and the door of the station wagon, directly in her path. His grin was broader now, showing yellowed teeth, a chipped incisor.

Alix faced him in annoyance. "Is there something I can do for you?" she asked.

"Why, I'm just being neighborly, Mrs. Ryerson. My name's Adam Reese."

"I'm sorry, Mr. Reese, but I really have to be going." She tried to edge around him, but he bounced over to block her again.

"This is a real neighborly town," he said, still smiling. "Just thought I'd stop and ask how everything's going out there on the cape."

"Everything is fine."

"Sure about that?"

"Just what is it you want, Mr. Reese?"

Reese kept smiling, but it was a smile that meant nothing—a mere reflexive stretching of mouth and facial skin. "Now, Mrs. Ryerson, like I said, I was just being neighborly—"

"Is that what you call it?"

"Sure thing. It's just that out there at the light, you're pretty isolated. Things can happen to people who live in lonely places like that."

She could feel her rage rekindling. "Things such as somebody shooting at our car in the middle of the night?"

Reese's eyebrows rose, meeting the wispy fringe of hair that escaped from his red headband. "Well, now, why would anybody want to do a thing like that?"

"You tell me."

"Can't say. Seems a waste of good ammunition to me."

Alix tried to step around him again. And again he moved into her path. "'Course, that's nothing," he said, "now there's been a murder practically in your front yard. Found that dead girl's body no more'n a couple of miles from the light, wasn't it?"

She said nothing, just glared at him.

"Not that that means you folks know anything about it. Or had anything to do with it. Sure is funny, though. I mean, you folks move in out there at the light, my friend Mitch's poor old dog gets run down, and next thing there's this poor young girl found strangled in a ditch—"

"Get out of my way, damn you!" She pushed around him and yanked at the door handle.

"Hey," Reese's amused voice said behind her, "don't go away *mad*."

She got into the car, ground the starter, finally got the engine going and the transmission into reverse. Once on the road she slammed the gearshift into drive and accelerated with such force that the tires threw up a spray of gravel. When she looked into the rearview mirror, Adam Reese was still standing there, hands on hips, the grin splitting his face like a wound.

It wasn't until she turned off onto the cape road that she slowed down, and when she pressed on the brake pedal, her leg began to shake. She pulled onto the verge, switched off the ignition, and leaned forward against the steering wheel, spent by her rage.

God, how I hate those people! she thought. Small-minded, insular, suspicious of anyone who's not like them. As if anyone would *want* to be like them.

She sat there for what seemed a long time, forehead against her folded arms. After a while, when the last of her anger was gone, a new feeling rose, one of unease.

Why was she letting them get to her this way? She'd lost control in the general store, and she would have struck that handyman if he hadn't let her past him. And over what? Nasty innuendo that she should have laughed off as small-town rumor-mongering.

Still . . . when a person allowed gossip to upset her like this, it was usually because she felt there might be some truth in it. Underneath was she afraid that Jan *might* be a murderer?

Instantly she rejected the notion. It was ridiculous. Jan was her husband, the man she had lived with every day of the past eleven years. She might suspect him of minor faults but never of a crime, much less one as monstrous as cold-blooded murder.

She raised her head and looked out at the flat gray joining of the bay and sea that lay beyond the barren reach of the headland. In spite of herself, her thoughts went back to that night in

Boston, the one and only time Jan had spoken of the murder of the girl in Madison. Had he been unduly traumatized by finding the body of someone he'd known only a few hours? Horrible as the experience had been, had his reaction and subsequent depression indicated a deeper involvement in the crime? No, she refused to believe that. The real trauma came later, from the way he and his friends had treated Ed Finlayson and the inevitable disintegration of the group.

Then her thoughts shifted back to the present . . . to Mitch Novotny's dog. It had been an accident; Jan hadn't even known he'd hit the dog because he'd been having one of his headaches . . . just as he'd had one of his headaches the night the hitchhiker was murdered and her body left on the cape. The hit-and-run killing of a dog, the strangulation murder of a young woman. Hardly equivalent, and yet . . .

Those headaches and his sudden mood changes over the past year—it was almost as if he had undergone a personality change. And the way he seemed to be keeping something from her. At times it was like living with a stranger, someone she really didn't know or understand. And all because of those headaches.

He'd minimized them upon his return from Portland, had claimed the doctor there had found no organic cause. But now she began to wonder if he might have been lying to her. No, not lying . . . trying to protect her from some kind of disturbing knowledge. She *had* to find out more about those headaches, for her own peace of mind. But their own doctor—and close friend—had refused to discuss them with her; and if Dave Sanderson wouldn't reveal the nature of the problem, surely the Portland specialist would be even more reluctant to do so. Perhaps if she called Dave, explained the urgency of the situation. . . .

And if he still refused? If he didn't even *know* how serious the headaches were because Jan hadn't told him?

Over the past few years she'd become accustomed to keeping

her problems to herself, taken pride in her ability to cope with and solve them on her own. But now she wished she had someone to confide in, to give her advice. Her best friend, Kay? No, theirs wasn't that intimate a relationship. Alison, her future business partner? Impossible. Her mother? It would merely frighten her; Mom was strong in her way, but she didn't deal well with emotional issues. Her father? God, no. If she alarmed him, he'd want to fly up here and take over. Alix shuddered at the thought of the chaos that would result.

No, she'd have to deal with this on her own, too, in her own way. And the first step was to call Dave Sanderson. She wouldn't be able to do that from the lighthouse, of course; even though Jan had taken to spending most of his time up in the tower, sound carried so easily in the place that he'd be certain to overhear every word of the conversation. The best thing would be to drive to Bandon—they still needed groceries and she would never go back to the Hilliard General Store—and make the call from a pay phone.

She reached for the ignition key, started the engine again. A plan of action always made her feel better, more in control of a situation and of her own emotions. And now more than ever, until she found out what was causing Jan's headaches and was able to rid herself of her nagging doubts, she needed to maintain control.

Mitch Novotny

Mitch stubbed out his cigarette and gestured down the bar. "Another bottle of Henry's, Les."

"Kind of early, ain't it?"

"You my goddamn wife or something?"

"Don't get sore, Mitch. I was only—"

"Yeah, you were only. Another Henry's."

"Sure. You're the boss."

That's a laugh, Mitch thought moodily. I'm not the boss of anything these days, including my own frigging life. Not enough of a catch this morning to pay for another tankful of diesel; barely enough this week to buy groceries and pay the mortgage on the house. Old Jimmy engine acting up worse every day, quit on him any day now; he felt it every time he cranked the son of a bitch up for another run. Things weren't bad enough, he'd come in at nine-thirty, hungry and drag-ass tired, and Marie and her old lady had started in on him. Hadn't even let him pour himself a cup of coffee, get a bite of toast. Just started right in on him soon as he walked in the door.

"Doctor says I might have to have a cesarean, Mitch. How are we going to pay for that?"

"Can't you get another job, Mitch? You got to take better care of Marie and my grandkids."

"There's no milk in the house, Mitch. Kids are crying for milk."

"Mrs. Hilliard looks at me with pity, Mitch. You think I like people to look at me that way?"

"Mitch, what are we going to do?"

"Mitch, you better do something."

"Mitch, Mitch, Mitch . . ."

Jesus, it was enough to drive you crazy. He'd got out of there. Hadn't even had his breakfast; they took the appetite right out of a man, harping, all the time harping. It wasn't his fault. He was trying, wasn't he? Doing all he could?

He lit another cigarette as Les Cummins, the Sea Breeze's day bartender, set down the fresh bottle of Henry's. Fifth beer since he'd come in, and it was only ten-thirty. Keep this up, he'd be shit-faced by mid-afternoon. No sense in that. What

good did it do? You sobered up, you still had the same problems and a hangover on top of them. He couldn't *afford* to get
drunk, that was another thing. Couldn't afford the five bottles of
Henry's he'd had already. Or the ten cigarettes he'd smoked.
Half a pack and it was only ten-thirty and he was supposed to be
rationing himself to a pack a day. Pretty soon he'd have to give
up smoking and drinking altogether. Then what would he have?
Nothing, not a frigging thing. Couldn't even get laid, with
Marie all swollen up like a balloon. Maybe wouldn't get any
nookie for *months,* if she had to have a cesarean and took a long
time to mend.

What the hell was the use? Man had to have some hope, see
some light at the end of the tunnel; man had to have something
to live for. What did he have? Nothing. Not a goddamn thing.

Mitch poured his glass full and drank half of it. Les was
down at the other end of the bar, reading the Coos Bay paper;
he knew Mitch didn't feel like talking—he damn well better
know it. There wasn't anybody else in the Sea Breeze this early.
Or there wasn't until half a minute later, when the door opened
and Seth Bonner blew in.

Shit, Mitch thought. He knew Bonner would come straight
over and start babbling at him, and sure enough, there he was
perched on the next stool, saying, "You're early today, Mitch.
How come? You got something to celebrate?"

"Go away, Seth."

"What's the matter? You don't want company?"

"You're smarter than you look."

"Huh?"

"Go bend Les's ear. He likes it; I don't."

"Hell, Mitch . . ."

"You want me to shove you down the bar?"

Bonner got up and went down to where Les was, looking
hurt. Well, fuck him, Mitch thought. He drained his glass, re-
filled it with what was left in the bottle.

"What's in the paper?" Bonner asked Les. "Anything new about the murder?"

"If there is, it ain't printed here."

"No story at all?"

"Short one. They identified the girl—Miranda Collins, student up at the U. of Oregon."

"What was she doing down here?"

"They don't know. No family in this area or anywheres else in the state. She's from up in Idaho."

"Hitchhiking to California, maybe," Bonner said. "Everybody wants to go to California, seems like."

"Not me. I like it here."

"Me too. California's full of queers and weirdos."

"Miranda," Les said. "I knew a girl named Miranda once. Pretty little thing."

"This one wasn't pretty, not when they found her."

"Yeah? You see her, Seth?"

"Seen her picture, the one they printed in the paper."

"Can't tell much from that kind of picture."

"Tell enough," Bonner said. "She wasn't pretty dead and she wasn't so pretty alive, neither. Maybe that was why she wasn't raped."

"How do you know she wasn't raped?"

"Talked to Deputy Frank Pierce over to the café last night. He stopped by for coffee while I was having dinner and I asked him and he said she wasn't raped. Just strangled, that's all."

"Pierce tell you anything else?"

"Well," Bonner said, real sly, "she was pregnant."

"The hell she was."

"That's what Frank Pierce said. Four months pregnant."

"Wonder who the father was."

"Some college kid. Who cares?"

"Maybe he's the one killed her."

"Way over here on the coast?"

"Why not? Maybe she wasn't hitchhiking at all. Maybe he brought her down here and strangled her because she got herself knocked up."

"Wasn't any college kid strangled her," Bonner said. "I told Frank Pierce who I think done it, but he wouldn't listen."

"Who do you think done it?"

"Ryerson, that's who. Out at the light."

"Why'd he do a thing like that?"

"He's crazy, that's why. One of them homicidal maniacs. He run down Mitch's dog, didn't he?"

"Big difference between running down a dog and strangling a woman, Seth."

"We never had no murder around here before he come," Bonner said. "No murder in thirty-seven years, that's what the papers said. Thirty-seven years and then Ryerson shows up and now Red's dead and we got us a girl strangled right here in Hilliard, not more'n two miles from the Cape Despair Light."

"Seems funny, sure. But that don't necessarily mean Ryerson killed the girl."

"Does as far as I'm concerned. Hey, Mitch, you think I'm right, don't you? You think Ryerson killed that little girl?"

Mitch didn't say anything. He was tired of all this talk—all morning, ever since he'd brought the *Spindrift* in, nothing but talk, talk, talk. His head was pounding: the beer and the cigarettes and the talk. He needed some air, some peace and quiet. He could get that much, by Christ, if he couldn't get anything else.

He climbed off his stool, told Les to put the beers on his tab, and went out with Bonner calling something after him that he didn't listen to. It was a cold day, cold and gray; the sky had a dead look, like the way he felt inside. He walked down along the bay, away from the boat slips and the cannery because he didn't want to run into Hod or Adam or any of his other buddies. They'd ask him what was wrong, try to cheer him up. He didn't want that; it would only make things worse.

He walked out near the southern headland. Where the thin strip of beach began to curve, he stopped and sat down on a driftwood log and looked out to sea. There wasn't anybody else around. The wind lashed at him, but he didn't mind that. Didn't mind the cold either. Out here his head didn't hurt nearly as much as it had in the Sea Breeze.

After a time he found that he wasn't looking at the ocean anymore; he was looking out at the rocky shore of the cape. You couldn't see the lighthouse from here, but he was seeing it inside his head. Ryerson, too, out there all smug and satisfied, like some king in his little private castle. What did *he* have to worry about, the bastard? He had plenty of money—he had everything a man could want. Red's blood on his hands and he had everything and you couldn't touch him, a man like that, couldn't touch him at all. It wasn't right. It just wasn't right.

Hey, Mitch, you think I'm right, don't you? You think Ryerson killed that little girl?

Talk, that was all. Bullshit talk. Or was it? Ryerson had killed Red, run him down that way, in cold blood; man who'd do a thing like that was capable of murdering a human being, wasn't he? Maybe old Bonner was right. Maybe Ryerson *had* strangled that girl.

But then why hadn't the state troopers arrested him? Didn't know what the hell they were doing, could be. Hamstrung by a lot of legal crap. That was why they hadn't arrested him for murdering Red, wasn't it? Man was a killer and they hadn't done anything about it. Weren't *going* to do anything about it, way it looked. Just let him keep on sitting out there, smug and satisfied, safe, until he felt like killing somebody else's dog—somebody else's kid, too, maybe.

Something ought to be done, by God. He'd been going to do

something himself, even before that girl turned up dead. Wasn't that what he'd said to Hod and Adam? That bastard won't get away with it, he'd said. I'll see to that, he'd said, I'll fix his wagon. There are ways, he'd said.

But what had he *done?* Nothing, that's what. Only one who'd done anything was Adam, shooting up Ryerson's car the way he had—*he'd* taken some action, even if it hadn't done much good. Good old Mitch, though, he hadn't done anything except blow off at the mouth. Story of his life: talk, talk, talk. Big plans, big talk, but when it came down to the crunch . . . nothing.

But it didn't have to keep on being that way. He didn't have to keep on being a blowhard, a loser. Things could change. Yes, and by Christ they were *going* to change! He was tired of being pushed around, sick and tired of it. He couldn't do much about the bad fishing or Marie or her mother or all his debts, not right now he couldn't, but he could do something about Ryerson.

He sat there a while longer, letting the wind rip at him, letting his anger build to a high, hot flame that insulated him against the cold. Then he got up and walked back along the beach and went into Mike's Café. There was a public telephone back by the johns; he made sure nobody was around and then got the number of the lighthouse, put a quarter in the slot, put his handkerchief around the mouthpiece as he dialed.

"Hello?"

"Ryerson?"

"Yes? Who's calling?"

"Get out of Hilliard, if you know what's good for you. You got twenty-four hours."

Silence for four or five seconds. Then, "Who is this?"

"You heard me, you prick. Twenty-four hours, or we'll come and drag you out. You and your wife both."

Mitch slammed down the receiver, hard, before Ryerson could say anything else.

Alix

She brought the station wagon to a stop in the parking area of Lang's Gallery and Gifts and looked with dismay at the CLOSED sign in the window. Then she glanced past the squarish building to the shabby gray Victorian house that stood some twenty yards beyond it. Through the sheer-curtained front window she saw the glow of a chandelier. Cassie Lang was probably taking the day off at home.

Alix sat drumming her fingers on the steering wheel, wondering if she should bother the gallery owner. She herself hated unexpected visits at home, but not everyone was as jealous of her privacy. And on her prior visit to the gallery, Cassie had seemed glad, even eager for company. At length she nodded decisively, got out of the car, and made her way across the overgrown lawn toward the Victorian.

Her trip into Bandon had been disappointing. Dave Sanderson, she'd been told when she reached his office in Palo Alto, was unavailable: he was attending a medical convention in Atlanta and wasn't scheduled to return until next week. His nurse had offered to put her in touch with the colleague who was covering for Dave, but Alix had declined and hung up without leaving a message.

Rather than give in to her disappointment, which would only have led to depression, she'd taken her crumpled grocery list to a nearby supermarket. There, among the familiar boxes and bottles and cans, selecting familiar merchandise with practiced motions, she was able to create a semblance of normalcy, concentrating on such mundane questions as what to have for dinner that night and whether the food in the cart was enough to hold them for a full week. She was able to make the sense of normalcy last all the way back to Hilliard, wrapping herself in a comfortable cocoon, and when she'd seen the sign for Cassie's gallery, she'd decided on impulse to stop and prolong it. She just didn't feel like returning yet to the bleak landscape of Cape Despair.

In the center of the house's front door was an old-fashioned brass knocker, shaped like a gargoyle's head. Using such things always made her feel foolish. She looked for a doorbell, found one, and pushed it. Chimes rang loudly within the confines of the house, but no one answered them—not the first time and not when she pushed the bell again a second time.

But she could clearly see that the chandelier was burning in the front parlor, and that had to mean Cassie was home. Why didn't she answer the door? Because, Alix thought then, she saw me coming and doesn't want to talk to me? Because she's heard what the villagers are saying about Jan and she believes it too?

The possibility made her feel hunted and alone. If Cassie had turned against her, too, it meant that Hilliard was completely hostile territory—a place she didn't dare set foot in again as long as she and Jan remained at the lighthouse.

The wind gusted in off the bay, seemed to blow away the illusion of normalcy that she'd carried with her from Bandon. Now she *was* depressed. How could she live this way for a full year, treated like an outcast? The answer was, she couldn't. Something had to be done and done soon.

She started back toward the car. And as she approached it, she saw Mandy Barnett pedaling along the road toward her on a bicycle painted an electric blue, the same color as her Indian poncho and headband. The girl's face was flushed with exertion and her red curls streamed out behind her. When she glanced up and saw Alix she braked abruptly, seemed about to swing her bike around in a U-turn, then changed her mind and got off and walked it forward.

"Hello, Mandy," Alix said when the girl turned into the graveled parking lot.

Mandy nodded curtly, kept moving toward the gallery.

"It's closed today."

The girl stopped and turned, the beads on her headband clicking with the motion. "Where's Mrs. Lang?"

"I don't know."

"Oh. Well, I guess I'll have to come back tomorrow, then."

"Did you want to buy something?"

"Birthday present for my mom. Something nice on account of everything being so shitty this year."

"The merchandise here is pretty expensive, you know."

"Sure, I know. I've got the money."

"Where'd you get it?"

"That's none of your business. I've got it, that's all."

"From selling information to someone else?"

"What's that supposed to mean?"

"You know what it means, Mandy."

"Oh, come on, Mrs. Ryerson!" Mandy's laugh was false, made shrill and then shredded by the wind. "You don't think I was serious that day, do you?"

"Yes, I do. You said you had something to sell me. Well, now I might be in the market." The words came out without conscious thought, and Alix surprised herself further by adding, "I can't pay you five hundred dollars, but I'm willing to work something out."

For a moment Mandy's green eyes glittered calculatingly. Alix was about to reinforce her offer when the girl said, "What is this, anyway—some kind of trick?"

"No trick, Mandy."

Mandy's face twisted into a sneer that was incongruous with its baby-like plumpness. "Right. You probably got the state troopers hiding in the bushes. I say yes, and you have me arrested for—what'd you call it?—extortion."

"You know that's not possible. How could I have known I'd meet you here? I'm perfectly serious. I want to know what you're selling."

"I'm not selling anything. Not anymore."

"Why not?"

"Because I'm not."

"Look, Mandy—"

"No." The girl made her characteristic foot-stamping gesture. Then the sneer returned, and Alix had an unpleasant vision of the woman Mandy would one day become. "All of that is past history, okay? I've got nothing to sell you, Mrs. Ryerson. Nothing at all."

Alix said the girl's name again, but Mandy turned away from her, mounted her bicycle, and pedaled off across the parking area to the road.

Staring after her, Alix thought: Damn her, what does she know? Or what does she think she knows?

She got into the car. She felt even more depressed now. A year of living here, among people like Mandy and Lillian Hilliard and Adam Reese, among circumstances of doubt and distrust, and she'd be a basket case. She couldn't face eleven more days of it, much less eleven more months.

Why do you have to? she thought then.

Why don't you leave now, you and Jan? Leave Cape Despair, Hilliard, the state of Oregon, and go home to Palo Alto?

But even as she thought it, she knew Jan would never agree. For years he had planned this lighthouse sabbatical, this time in which to set down on paper the fruit of all his research and study. He would never allow circumstances, no matter how grim, to cheat him out of the fulfillment of his dream.

All right, then. But why couldn't they leave temporarily, for a week or two, until the furor over the murder died down? Detective Sinclair had told them to check in if they planned to leave, but he hadn't confined them to the area. They could drive up the coast into Washington; Jan had a colleague in Seattle with whom he'd corresponded for years, and they had an open invitation to visit, had always intended to but never gotten around to it. Seattle was supposed to be an interesting city; the new environment would take their minds off the events here, allow them both to relax, regain some perspective.

It wouldn't be easy to convince Jan to make the trip, would, in fact, take a good bit of maneuvering; but right now the method didn't matter. She'd think of something. And while they were away, she'd contact Dave Sanderson as soon as he returned from his convention and find out about those headaches of Jan's. And when they came back to Cape Despair, enough time would have passed so that the rest of their stay would at least be tolerable for her.

Adam Reese

Adam parked his battered Volkswagen van in a copse of trees just off the cape road. He didn't have to shut off the headlights; he'd been driving dark the past couple of miles. Taken him fifteen minutes to cover those two miles, as dark and foggy as the night was and as slow as he'd had to drive, but it was the only way. Ryerson and his woman might still be up, even though it was after three A.M. You never knew with people like that, city people, California people. And light was visible a long way out here, particularly moving light.

The lighthouse was maybe three hundred yards away and he could see it plain. This was where he'd parked the other time, when he'd shot up their car. There'd been moonshine that night, plenty of it; it was just like sighting in daylight, with that four-power Bausch & Lomb scope of his. He'd of had trouble if he'd been shooting tonight, though, because he didn't have no sniper scope. There was a nightlight on the front wall up there, a small spot that threw an irregular patch of mist-blurred yellow across the lawn for maybe fifty feet, but it didn't reach the garage or the pumphouse or anything else in the yard. Not hardly enough light for clear shooting, not unless your target was standing right in the middle of the yellow patch. Well, it didn't matter. He wasn't going to do no shooting tonight.

Their car wasn't out; he wondered if they were even home. Probably. Taken to putting the car in the garage, probably, on account of him shooting it up. The windows he could see didn't have any light showing. Good, good. He'd give odds, now, that if they *were* home, they were both asleep in their bed.

He reached behind him to where his Springfield 30.06 was clipped to mounts anchored to the van's deck. Hell of a piece, that Springfield. Accurate—you couldn't ask for no more accurate center-fire rifle, even with the 180-grain ammo he was using for better energy and trajectory. He ran his fingers over the smooth, silky wood of the stock. Fiddleback maple, made by an outfit back east, polished to a high gloss. Jesus, he liked to touch it. It was like touching a woman's flesh. That woman up in Lake Oswego . . . no, better not think about her. Inviting him into her house, drinking his liquor, and then yelling rape when he tried to love her up. He should of given her something to yell about, instead of running like he had. Lucky thing he hadn't told her his real name; otherwise the cops would of got him by now, and then where'd he be? In the goddamn state pen in Salem, that's where. That bitch. But they were all bitches, weren't they? Guns were better for you than women. Rifles like this baby. You took care of them and they took care of you. Nobody ever heard of a Springfield 30.06 yelling rape when you put your hand on its butt.

That Ryerson woman was worse than most. Snooty. Had her nose in the air all the time, like her shit didn't stink. He knew *her* kind, he'd been around. City people—he'd never met one who treated him halfway decent. Met damned few anywhere who'd treated him decent, for that matter, until he came here. Hilliard . . . hell, it was the home he'd never had growing up. Been on his own since he was twelve, riding freights, taking any job he could get, back and forth across the whole damn country and never once felt like he belonged anywhere. Then he'd come here. Hilliard. Met Mitch and Hod, and they'd taken him right in like he was some long-lost kin. Not only treated him decent, treated him equal. No, sir, they weren't just friends, they were family—the family he'd never had. Do anything for them. That was why he'd come out here that other time and shot up the Ryersons' car, on account of what Ryerson had done to Red, that poor dumb dog. That was why he was out here tonight. Mitch had asked him to do it this time, told him the way things stood, told him maybe Ryerson had killed that little bitch of a hitchhiker they'd found back along the cape. We got to get those people out of the lighthouse, Mitch had said. Got to get rid of them before Ryerson hurts somebody else. Well, Mitch was right and that was why Adam had volunteered to do the job alone. He'd do anything for a real friend.

Adam felt himself fidgeting, kind of vibrating like the van was still bouncing over the rough cape road. He couldn't help it; he always twitched and jerked when he was worked up. Drove Hod crazy. He knew it did, but he couldn't stop it. That was just the way he was. He quit stroking the rifle—he'd of liked to take it with him but he only had two hands and there wasn't no point in it, since he wasn't going to do any shooting—and got out and went around to the back. He'd oiled the latch on the van's rear doors, but it was so quiet here, what with the fog, that you could hear it snicking open. Wind had died down for the time being. Damned cold, though. Cold enough to freeze the balls off a brass monkey. He laughed to himself, inside. He'd always liked the sound of that, the image it put in his mind. Cold enough to freeze the balls off a brass monkey.

He opened one of the doors and dragged out the first of the burlap sacks. There were three of them, twenty-five pounds each, and that meant three trips. But he didn't mind. It was the least he could do. Mitch thought this stuff would do the trick, but Adam wasn't so sure. Might, and then again it might not; you just never knew with city people. If it didn't . . . well, like Mitch had said, there were other ways. And one of the best was right there in the van, all shiny and waiting on its mounts. He wouldn't mind doing some more shooting if he had to. Wouldn't mind it at all, no matter *what* the target was.

He hefted the first sack onto his shoulder, got a tight grip on it, and set out through the fog and shadows toward the lighthouse.

Jan

They were just starting to make love when the telephone rang downstairs.

"Oh, *damn*," Alix said. "Isn't that always the way?"

He said, "I'll get it."

"Let it ring. It's probably a wrong number anyway. Who'd be calling us at seven-thirty in the morning?"

He managed to keep the tension out of his voice as he said, "No, I'd better get it." He disentangled himself from her arms and legs, slid out of bed, and shrugged into his robe.

Alix rolled over to watch him. Playfully, she said, "You've got something sticking out of your robe there."

It wasn't funny. Once it would have been; not these days. But he laughed anyway, because she expected it, and said, "Don't go away, I'll be right back."

He left the bedroom and went downstairs, not hurrying. In the living room, in the stillness of early morning, the ringing telephone seemed louder than ever before—a shrill clamoring that beat against his ears, set his teeth together so tightly he could feel pain run along both jaws. He caught up the receiver with such violence that he almost knocked the base unit off the table. He said nothing, just waited.

"Ryerson?" the muffled voice said. "That you, asshole?"

He didn't answer.

"You packed yet? You better be if you know what's good—"

He slammed the receiver down with even greater violence; the bell made a sharp protesting ring. He stood with his hands fisted, his molars grinding against each other, his eyes squeezed shut. Every time something like this happened, he was terrified the tension and pressure would bring on one of his headaches. It had been days now since the last bad one, since the night he had come back from Portland . . . that hideous night. He was overdue. The word seemed to echo in his mind, flat and ominous, like a judge's pronouncement of sentence: overdue, overdue, overdue.

He opened his eyes, moved to the nearest of the windows. The glass was streaked with wetness: tear tracks on a cold blank face. Fog coiled and uncoiled outside, thick and gray and matted, like fur rippling on the body of some gigantic obscene creature cast up by the sea.

God, what an unbearable week. That nightmarish drive from Portland, the second blackout, waking up on the side of the county road half a mile north of Hilliard with no recollection of having driven there from Bandon. Then the murdered hitchhiker, found near here of all places, and the troopers coming around with their questions, and the little lies he'd had to tell that detective, Sinclair, to keep the questions from becoming accusations. (Hitchhiker . . . there was something about a hitchhiker on the dark road outside Bandon, something he couldn't remember. But it hadn't been the same one, the girl who'd been strangled; he had a vague recollection of a boy, a boy with long hair. *Couldn't* have been that girl. If he let himself doubt that for a minute, it would be like standing on the edge of madness.) And now these damned threatening calls. Three of them in less than three days. Novotny—who else? He'd taken each of them, so Alix didn't know yet. He couldn't tell her. She was on the verge of abandoning the light as it was. She'd been trying to get him to leave "just for a week or two," go up to Washington; she was insistent about it, so insistent that he was afraid she'd eventually make up her mind to go alone, and not just for a week or two. And if she did . . . would he try to stop her? Not if Novotny tried to make good on his threats; the last thing he wanted was to subject her to any real danger. And yet he would do anything to stave off the inevitable separation—anything except to run away from here himself.

Neither Novotny nor anyone else was going to drive *him* out, take away this one last refuge before the curtain of darkness came down. It wasn't stubbornness, it wasn't pride; it was something deeper than either one, more profound. Ryerson's Last Stand. He was staying no matter what. They would have to come for him with guns and burning torches, like the villagers in the old Frankenstein movie.

"Jan?" Alix, calling from the top of the stairs. "Is everything all right?"

"Fine. Go back to bed, I'll be up in a minute."

He walked into the kitchen, poured himself a glass of milk, drank it slowly. Through the window he could see the closed doors to the garage. No more driving for him; he'd promised Alix that. Just the thought of getting behind the wheel again made his hands moist, his heart beat faster. If he suffered another blackout it would not be behind the wheel of a car, where he might endanger another life, a human one this time.

When he went back upstairs and re-entered the bedroom, Alix was in bed with the covers pulled up to her chin. She said, "Who was that on the phone?"

"Nobody. Wrong number."

"I heard you bang the receiver . . ."

"People ought to be able to dial the right number," he said. "It's a damned nuisance."

He felt her eyes probing at him as he unbelted his robe, got into bed. But after a few seconds she fitted her body to his, held him, and said, "Now where were we?"

He wasn't sure if he could make love now. But when he blanked his mind, the heat of her body and the stroking of her hands gave him an erection almost immediately. But it wasn't good sex, at least not for him. She put herself into the act with passion and intensity, as if she were trying too hard to please him, or trying too hard to escape from whatever thoughts and fears crowded *her* mind. For him it was detached and mechanical. All body and no soul, brain still blank, lost somewhere inside himself, in a place untouched by the sensations of physical pleasure.

They lay in silence afterward. Alix broke it finally by saying, "I'd better get up. My turn for breakfast today. Are you hungry?"

"Ravenous," he lied.

"French toast and bacon?"

"Great." It was his favorite breakfast.

She got out of bed and let him watch her walk naked into the bathroom, moving her hips more than she had to for his benefit. It didn't give him as much pleasure as it should have. He might have been watching her through someone else's eyes. Was this the way schizophrenics felt? Detached, yourself and yet not yourself? Those blackout periods . . . what exactly did he do during one of them? The thought of his body in the control of some other self, some stranger, was terrifying. Why couldn't he remember . . . ?

He heard the rush of water as the shower came on—and half a minute later, he heard Alix cry out.

The sudden horrified shout jerked him out of bed, sent him stumbling across to the bathroom door. He threw it open, and she was out of the tub, bent over and scrubbing frantically at her body with a towel. Her bare skin was streaked with an ugly brown. The shower was still running and the cold water that came out of it was the same brown color; more brown stained the tile walls, the tub, the floor at Alix's feet. The stench in the room made him gag.

Manure, cow shit. The water pouring out of the shower head smelled like the inside of a barn.

The significance of it didn't register fully at first. He caught Alix's arm with one hand, a second towel with the other, and pulled her out into the bedroom. Slammed the door to barricade them against the stench and then helped her wipe the brown filth off her body. She said in a choked, bewildered voice, "I just turned on the cold water, all I did was turn on the cold water. . . ."

The towels weren't doing any more good; he got the comforter off the foot of the bed, wrapped it around her, made her sit down. Then he hurried back into the bathroom, managed to get the shower turned off without letting much of the tainted water splash on him. He found the catch on the window, hauled up the sash. Breathing through his mouth, he pivoted to the sink and rotated the porcelain handle on the hot-water tap. It ran clean. But when he tried the cold tap, the water that came out was filthy.

He understood then. Novotny had fouled the well. Sometime during the night, with sacks of manure.

Rage stirred through him, but it was like no other rage he'd ever felt. Cold, not hot. And it did nothing to him: caused no tension, no pressure and pain behind his eyes. He felt no different than he had before Alix's cry, except that most of the detachment was gone. He was very calm, very much in control of himself.

Alix was on her feet again, moving around in a stunned way, when he came out. "I've got to wash this off," she said. "I'll be sick if I don't." She started past him to the bathroom.

He stopped her with his body. "No, don't go in there. You'd better clean up downstairs."

"The water . . . what . . . ?"

"It's polluted. Somebody dumped manure into the well."

She stared at him for a moment, then shook her head—a gesture of incomprehension, not denial. The movement seemed to let her smell herself; she made a small gagging sound. "I can't stand it, I've got to wash . . ."

"Use the hot-water tap in the kitchen," he said. "What's stored in the tank is still clean." He reached for his pants, pulled them on.

"What are you going to do?"

"Go out and look at the well. Go ahead, go on down. Take your robe so you don't catch cold."

She went out without saying anything else. He buttoned his shirt, sat on the edge of the bed to tie his shoes. He wasn't thinking at all now. He didn't trust himself to think just yet.

Downstairs, he took his jacket out of the coat closet. He

could hear Alix in the kitchen, filling a pan with hot water. When he stepped outside, the fog was still swirling in over the cliffs from the sea, turning the garage and the woodshed and the pumphouse into wraith-like shapes in the dull morning light. But the smell of it was moist and salt-fresh, cleansing.

He opened the door to the pumphouse, looked inside. Flakes of spilled manure littered the floor. They'd carried the rest of the evidence away with them—whatever containers they'd used. It had been easy for them, he thought. Dark night, nothing to repel intruders, not even a lock on the damn pumphouse door.

When he re-entered the house a couple of minutes later, Alix was no longer in the kitchen; he heard her moving around upstairs. He sat down in the living room and filled one of his pipes—the calabash that Alix said made him look like Basil Rathbone playing Sherlock Holmes. He was about to light it when she came down again.

She was wearing her robe, the wine-red velour one, and she had doused herself with Miss Dior cologne. The smell of it was cloyingly sweet in the cold room. Her face was pale, her expression one of contained anger. She might be emotional in the first minutes of a crisis, but she never let her emotions govern her for very long.

She sat opposite him. "What did they put in the well?" she asked. "Manure?"

"Yes."

"It was Mitch Novotny, I suppose."

Things had moved past the point of denial now; she had literally been struck with the truth a few minutes ago. He nodded. "Or one of his friends."

"Aren't you going to call the sheriff?"

"What good would it do? There's no evidence against him, or anyone else."

"What, then? You're not going to confront him?"

"I don't know. Probably not."

Her expression had changed; what he saw on her face now was resolve. "Jan, we've *got* to get away from here. You can see that now, can't you?"

"No," he said, "I can't. Running away won't solve anything. That's just what Novotny and the rest of them want—to drive us out. I won't let them do that."

"Why? What difference does it make?"

"It makes a big difference to me."

"There are other lighthouses—"

"Not like this one. There's not enough time."

"What do you mean, not enough time?"

"To find another one, make all the arrangements. To get my book done before you . . . go off to L.A."

"I'm not 'going off to L.A.' For heaven's sake, I can postpone things with Alison, if that's what—"

"I'm not leaving here, Alix," he said. "Not until our year's tenancy is up."

"How can you expect to stay with the well polluted, no water to bathe in?"

"There are chemicals to purify the well."

"All right, there are chemicals. But what's to stop Novotny from doing it again? And again? Or doing something else, something worse?"

"There's me to stop him."

"I don't like that kind of talk. What can you do against a man like Novotny? Against a whole village full of hostile people?"

He made no response. A thin silence built between them, like ice formed over rough water. When Alix broke it, it was as if the veneer of ice had been shattered by the weight of something heavy.

"Maybe you can stay here under these conditions," she said in a deliberate voice, "but I don't think I can. I mean that, Jan—I'm not prepared to deal with much more of this."

"Do what you have to." The words tasted bitter in his mouth, but he had no trouble saying them. Odd. He was still terrified of losing her, but the fear had been driven down deep inside him by this new threat.

"Jan," she said, and stopped, and then started again. "Jan, don't do this to us. Don't let them to do this to us. It isn't worth it. *We're* what matters, not this lighthouse, not anything else."

He was on his feet, with no conscious memory of having moved out of his chair. "I'm going to light the stove and make some coffee. We'll both feel better after we've had some coffee."

He went into the kitchen without looking back at her. There was no looking back anymore, he thought. No looking ahead, either. Soon enough there would be no *looking*, period. *Now* was what counted. The right here and the right now.

Alix

It seemed as if she spent all her time behind the wheel of this car, driving but getting nowhere, agonizing but resolving nothing. But she *had* to get away from Cape Despair this morning, if only for a little while—away from the stink of manure, away from Jan and his cold anger, his remoteness. It was behavior she'd never seen in him before, and it worried her far more than if he'd ranted and cursed and smashed things. She didn't let herself think about the implications of it. If she did, it would only unnerve her even more.

When she reached the intersection with the county road, she turned automatically toward Hilliard. It was only when the familiar, run-down buildings appeared ahead that she realized what she was doing and wondered why. There was nowhere for her to go in the village, no errand to run, no friend to visit.

But there must have been a purpose, an obscure need, buried in her subconscious: when she reached the laundromat, she turned without hesitation onto the side street just beyond it—the one that climbed the hillside to the community center and the church. The street curved up past shabby frame houses that seemed to cling tenuously to the slopes, then curved again under an arching canopy of tree branches. Just beyond the trees, on a knoll to the right, was the red-brick community center. It was shuttered and deserted, almost abandoned-looking, but a large bulletin board on its front porch was covered with notices of future events. Alix slowed the car as she passed, glancing up at the building's bell tower. Birds—some kind of smallish brown ones—came and went there; it was probably their nesting place.

Behind the center was a thick stand of pines, and above their tops she could see the white steeple of the church silhouetted against the sky. The sky itself was streaky, with patches of blue showing through the gray—the first break in the dismal weather all week. She followed the road through a sharp S-curve and up the hill to the church.

It had been her destination all along, but she felt odd as she stopped the car in front. She wasn't especially religious, hadn't attended services in years. But the minister, Harvey Olsen, had seemed approachable when she'd met him in the general store; if there was anyone in Hilliard she could talk to, wouldn't it be a man of the cloth?

The church was a traditional-style rectangular white building that reminded her of many she'd seen in New England, but it was less aesthetically pleasing than most of those because it fronted on an unpaved parking lot that was rutted and gouged in places. Behind it to the left was a small weedy graveyard; behind it to the right was a smaller building that looked as if might be a parsonage. Even the encircling pines that covered most of the hill at this elevation failed to give the church much visual appeal.

Alix got out of the station wagon and stood for a moment, breathing in the tangy scent of the pines. There was a ten-year-old Dodge parked between the church and the parsonage, which must mean that Harvey Olsen was somewhere on the premises. But where? She started toward the parsonage and then saw that one half of the double-doored entrance to the church was ajar and altered her course. She went up to the open door, pushed it all the way open, and stepped into the gloomy interior.

The church was long and narrow, with stained glass windows that were deeply shadowed by the encroaching branches of the trees outside. There were several rows of wooden pews and a rather plain altar. The floors were of hardwood, badly scarred by the feet of generations of worshippers. The enclosure felt damp and cold—an atmosphere that she guessed never left the place, even in the heat of summer. She stood just inside the door, reluctant to call out and break the heavy silence.

In the wall to the right of the altar was another door that also stood ajar. After a moment she started down the center aisle, thinking the minister might be in the sacristy at the rear. But her steps were hesitant now; she was beginning to feel uncomfortable about being there. After all, she wasn't one of the congregation, barely knew Harvey Olsen. And she was in no way accustomed to airing her troubles to strangers. Still, she told herself again, ministers were trained to listen to other people's problems. Olsen would see nothing odd in her coming to him.

She was halfway down the aisle when she heard footfalls behind her. She turned. Harvey Olsen had come in the front way and was approaching her, clad in a bright red jogging suit and the same knitted cap he'd had on the first time she'd seen him. His face was shiny with sweat and his wire-rimmed glasses were fogged. As he neared her he took the glasses off, wiped their lenses on the baggy sleeve of his suit.

"Mrs. Ryerson, isn't it?" he said. "I wondered who was here when I saw your car."

For a moment she was at a loss for words. And even more uncomfortable. She'd expected to find Harvey Olsen in vestments, and here he was in a jogging suit and all sweaty from his morning run.

As if he sensed her discomfort, Olsen patted his midriff, smiled, and said, "Have to keep the old weight down. I like pasta too much, and after forty . . ."

She nodded, answered his smile with a faint one of her own.

Olsen put his glasses back on and peered intently at her. "Did you just come to see the church? Or is there some problem?"

Something about the way he said it—not the phrasing, but the inflection—told her he knew all about what the villagers were saying about Jan. For a paranoid instant she wondered if he might even know about their trouble at the lighthouse and who was responsible for it. Mitch Novotny was probably one of his parishioners. . . .

Harvey Olsen was waiting for her to speak, his head cocked to one side like a bird's. The eyes behind his glasses held a gleam of intelligence softened by compassion. But there was something else there too, she thought, something she couldn't quite identify in the weak light.

She cleared her throat and said, "You know about the murder, of course—the young girl who was found out on the cape."

He nodded sadly. "A tragic thing."

"And I suppose you've also heard what some of the villagers are saying about who might be responsible. Lillian Hilliard, for one. Adam Reese, for another."

"Yes, I'm afraid I have." Olsen took off his knitted cap and scrubbed his fingers through pale, thinning hair. "It's disturbing, and very unfair. But it's just talk, you must remember that. The idle pursuit of idle minds."

The platitude made her impatient. "The only reason they're saying these things about my husband is the accident with Mitch Novotny's dog—"

"Yes, I know about that too."

"Well, it *was* an accident. My husband apologized to him, offered to buy him another dog, but he wouldn't listen. He wants revenge."

"Revenge?" Olsen looked more alert.

"He's been harassing us," she said. "At least, we think it's Novotny. There might be others involved, too."

"What sort of harassment, Mrs. Ryerson?"

"Someone shot at our car, did quite a bit of damage to it. There have been threatening telephone calls." She wasn't certain of this, but it was the obvious explanation for Jan's behavior with the phone this morning. "And sometime last night, our well was fouled with manure."

"Good heavens." Olsen sucked in his breath with a soft whistling sound and stood up straighter. But his eyes moved from her face to a point over her right shoulder.

She started to tell him the rest of it—Jan's headaches, her own doubts and fears—and then stopped abruptly when she realized that Harvey Olsen was no longer listening to her. He stood very still, his eyes focused on the distance. It was only when he became aware that she had stopped speaking that he blinked, seemed to shake himself out of it, and looked at her again.

"Just what is it you want from me, Mrs. Ryerson?" he said.

The question surprised her; she was still caught up in her emotions. Frowning, she said, "Understanding. Advice. A sympathetic ear."

"I can listen, but I can't give you advice. Only you can know your own conscience, your own marriage—the dynamic that operates there."

"That's the trouble—I don't. The 'dynamic,' as you call it, seems to have changed in the last year."

But Olsen didn't seem to want to listen to that, either. He sat on one of the benches, crossed one leg over the other, examined the toe of one well-worn sneaker. Finally, he said in a reflective voice, "As for the men in the village . . . you must remember that most of them are fishermen and that they are under a severe strain. You do know their situation?"

"I know the fishing has been bad, yes . . ."

"Some, such as Mitch Novotny, are living marginally," Olsen said. "Mitch owns his home and boat, but both are heavily mortgaged and he is afraid of losing them. And he has another child on the way—did you know that?"

Again she felt herself growing impatient. "What does that have to do with his harassment of my husband and me? I'm sorry he's having financial problems, but that doesn't give him or anyone else the right to victimize other people."

"Mrs. Ryerson, please try to understand—"

"I might say the same to you, Reverend Olsen."

He blinked at her in his sad way, gave her a look that was almost pleading. But it touched her not at all. She had tired of his excuses and platitudes; they made her feel foolish, and very sorry that she had come here.

"We're being terrorized," she said. "Doesn't that mean anything to you?"

"Of course it does . . ."

"But you don't want to hear about it or do anything about it. All you want to do is protect your friends and neighbors."

"That's not true."

"It is true. Take a good look at yourself, listen to yourself. You're afraid to help us because we're outsiders, because it'll make you look bad in the eyes of your parishioners, and because you're afraid what the gossip-mongers like Lillian Hilliard are saying might be true."

Olsen was silent, his expression both pained and troubled.

"Well, think about this, Reverend. Think about how you'll feel if something more serious than having our well polluted or our car riddled with bullets happens to us. Think about the consequences if one of *us* is shot instead."

"Oh, Mrs. Ryerson, I'm sure it will never come to that."

"Are you? Are you, really?"

Olsen raised his pale eyes to her. And behind the torment reflected there, she saw clearly what had been masked in them before—the true essence of the man. It was weakness augmented by fear and self-doubt; it was cowardice. The Reverend Harvey Olsen was a poor excuse for both a minister and a human being.

She stared at him for several seconds, letting him see her anger and her contempt. Then she turned abruptly and stalked out of his church.

Alix

When she came in sight of the lighthouse an hour later, she saw an old olive-colored humpbacked sedan parked just outside the gate. She didn't recognize it—but she did recognize the woman walking across the yard. It was Cassie Lang, wrapped in a heavy brown sweater and matching scarf.

Her surprise gave way to wariness as both she and Cassie neared the old sedan. Had Cassie come because she was still a friend? Or was she there for some other reason, one that confirmed she was on the side of Lillian Hilliard and the other villagers? A friendly face would be welcome, God knew . . . but even at that, her timing could have been better. It was Jan she wanted to talk to now.

After she'd left the church she'd driven aimlessly for a while, following the coast highway nearly a dozen miles south before she turned back. Her anger and disgust had gradually faded, leaving her determined not to confide in anyone else, to deal with the situation strictly on her own from now on. And even more convinced that she and Jan must leave the lighthouse as soon as possible. Subtle argument hadn't swayed him; neither had a more direct approach. But what about a direct approach in a less emotionally charged setting than Cape Despair? If she could persuade him to go someplace for dinner—anywhere but Hilliard—then maybe they could talk, really talk, and she could make him understand her position.

As she neared the gate, Cassie waved and pulled it open for her. Alix drove through, stopped the Ford near the garage, and got out. Cassie had shut the gate again and was coming toward her, smiling in a friendly way.

"Hi," Cassie said. "I was afraid I'd missed you."

"I've been out for a drive."

"Where's your husband? No one answered when I knocked on the door."

"He was working on his book when I left," Alix lied. "He gets so involved sometimes, he doesn't pay any attention to his surroundings."

"Well, I can understand that. I'm the same way."

"Yes, so am I." Alix paused. "I stopped by to see you the other day, but the gallery was closed."

"I wasn't feeling well—a touch of the flu, I guess. I spent the day in bed. Did you ring the bell at the house?"

"Yes, as a matter of fact."

"I must have been asleep; I'm a heavy sleeper. I'm sorry I missed you."

"Me, too," Alix said, and felt herself relax. So she *did* have one friend in the village after all. She'd all but written Cassie off for no good reason. She should have known better than to jump to conclusions, even in a place like Hilliard.

Cassie said, "I should have called before I drove out, but I'm feeling so much better today and I decided an outing would do me good . . . I hope you don't mind."

"No, not at all."

"I thought if you're not busy, I'd take you up on your offer of a tour of the lighthouse."

"Well . . . this isn't a good day for it, I'm afraid. Jan's working and I don't like to disturb him."

"Oh, I understand. We could walk on the beach for a while, though, couldn't we? Unless you have something you need to do?"

Alix hesitated, glancing toward the light. "I don't know . . ."

"Just for a little while? It's such a nice day."

There was something plaintive in Cassie's voice—a need for companionship that Alix understood all too well. And it *was* a nice day, at least as far as the weather was concerned: the last of the overcast had blown inland or burned off, leaving the sky cloudless, and there was very little wind. The sun transformed objects that had previously seemed drab or ugly, invested the patchy grass with a subtle green, the rocks with a rich brown, the sea with deep blues and turquoises. It was the kind of rare fall day made for a walk on the beach.

Well, why not, then? It was early yet; what difference did it make if she talked to Jan now or an hour from now? Talking to him tonight, away from Cape Despair, was the important thing.

"I guess I can spare an hour or so," she said. "Can we get down to the beach from here?"

"Oh, yes." The plaintive quality was gone; Cassie seemed almost animated now, as if spending an hour with Alix—with anyone—meant a great deal to her. "I know a way down the cliffs you probably haven't discovered. One of the women in the village told me about it. I've been there three or four times when the weather's good, to pick through the driftwood."

The route down to the beach, it turned out, was only a short distance from the lighthouse gate—no more than four hundred yards. Cassie led her on a zig-zag course among dun-colored outcrops and boulders to a series of natural—and crumbling— "steps" that scaled the cliff wall. Alix paused as the gallery owner started down, feeling a brief flash of vertigo. But when she saw that Cassie didn't seem to have any trouble keeping her balance, she took a deep breath and followed.

It took almost ten minutes to make it all the way down the series of knobs and outcrops and niches; in one steep place she had to scoot a couple of yards on the seat of her jeans. When she finally reached the beach she was a little winded. But Cassie, in spite of her recent illness, looked nearly as fresh as when they'd started out.

The beach here was narrow, no more than fifty yards wide. A third of it was strewn with driftwood, all sizes and shapes, some of the jumbled pieces driven back and up into declivities in the rocks by the force of the wind and the sea. Here and there, the stark white and gray of the wood was garnished with brownish-green seaweed. Cassie set off at an angle through the coarse, pebbly sand, Alix at her side. The sea was remarkably calm this afternoon. Further down the beach, small shorebirds—sandpipers? grebes?—ran from the breakers, then turned to chase them as they receded. Cassie made no attempt at conversation, and neither did Alix. She breathed deeply of the salt air instead, feeling it relax her even more; even the strain of her thigh muscles as she slogged through the loose sand was not unpleasant.

As they approached the waterline, the birds scattered in a great gray and brown and white cloud, screeching their disapproval of the human interlopers. Alix sat on her heels, let one of the waves break up close to her so she could test the water. It was icy enough to make her jerk back her hand.

Cassie's voice came from behind her right shoulder, startling her. "On days like this, I'm almost glad I moved here."

"Only almost?"

"Yes."

Alix stood, drying her fingers on her jeans. Then in silent accord they both turned and began to move along the wet hard-packed sand toward where the beach narrowed and finally disappeared altogether. It was windier than it had been up by the lighthouse, and Alix buttoned her jacket to the neck and thrust her hands into her pockets. Beside her Cassie seemed to be lost in thought, perhaps trying to decide if she wanted to reveal any more about her feelings for this place and for the village.

At length Cassie said, "I hated it here when I first arrived— the bleakness, the loneliness. Now it's . . . home, I guess, as much as any place can ever be for me."

"What about Eugene? That's where you used to live, isn't it?"

"Yes."

"You weren't happy there?"

"Well, it's a nice town. I had a lot of friends. Belonged to an art cooperative and had my studio there. Took courses at the university extension—cooking, French, calligraphy, whatever happened to interest me at the time. And there were concerts and plays. . . ."

"Then why did you leave?" Alix asked. "I know you mentioned you were divorced, but Eugene is a sizable town; surely you wouldn't have run into your ex-husband very often."

"It wasn't that. I *had* to leave, for my own peace of mind. Ron spoiled the town for me—all my memories as well as my enjoyment of the present. Staying there would have been more than I could bear."

"He must have really hurt you."

Cassie stopped walking and turned to face the water, standing still with her back to Alix. There was a fishing boat on the horizon, a small speck that barely moved; she seemed to be watching it. But Alix sensed she wasn't.

After a time Cassie said, "Ron is a professor at the university. Anthropology. There were women from his classes, girls really . . . a constant stream of them almost from the first year we were married. You're a faculty wife; you know how some professors are, the temptations, sex in return for a decent grade. . . ."

"Yes, I know," Alix said a little awkwardly. "I've seen it happen at Stanford."

"But not to your husband."

"No."

Thank God he'd never fallen into that trap, she thought. Not that she knew of, at least. The extension of the thought came as a mild surprise; she'd never suspected him of straying since the time she'd gone up to Boston and checked his closet for another woman's clothing. Surely she'd have known if there had been someone else, wouldn't she?

But lately, in some ways, it seemed she'd never known him at all.

". . . an old story, isn't it?" Cassie was saying bitterly. "Happens all the time."

"More often than we care to think about." But Alix's mind was still on Jan.

"I wouldn't have cared about an occasional fling," Cassie said. "I can understand temptation and weakness as well as the next person. But with Ron it was constant, one romance after another."

"He didn't tell you about them, did he?"

"Oh no. He was very discreet; he had to be, because of his position. But I knew. I always knew."

"What finally made you leave him?"

Cassie was silent for a moment. "I guess," she said then, "he went one romance too far."

She turned, hugging her sweater closely about her, and continued on toward where the beach ended in a fall of rocks. Alix fell in at her side, wondering what she would have done in such a situation. The same as Cassie, probably. Only she wouldn't have waited nearly so long. Or would she?

They walked in silence until they reached the jumble of rocks. Then, as they turned and started back, Alix said, "Well, all that's behind you—your life in Eugene, I mean. You've made a new start here, and it's to your credit that you did it on your own."

"I suppose so," Cassie said. But her smile was wry. "But is the past ever really dead? Don't the bad things come back to haunt us sometimes, in one way or another?"

Alix felt a small chill. "It doesn't have to be like that."

"Not for you, maybe. I hope it never does. I hope all that's happened here doesn't come back to haunt you."

"Why do you say that?"

Her voice was sharper than she'd intended it, and Cassie glanced at her, then glanced away. There was a pause, awkward now. Then Cassie said, "Well, one can't help but hear things in a place this small. I told you before, Lillian Hilliard's stock in trade is rumor and gossip and innuendo; she was in her glory when I went into the store this morning. *I* don't put any stock in that kind of malicious tongue-wagging, but I can't help wondering how it's affecting you and your husband.''

And suddenly Alix couldn't help wondering if that was the real reason Cassie had come out here this afternoon, or at least part of it. She didn't want to believe that; it would diminish the woman, make her less than the friend she seemed to want to be. But there was the evident fact that Cassie herself was something of a gossip, and that alone was enough to keep Alix from backing down on her resolve not to confide in anyone else in this area. A casual friend was one thing; an ally was another. And her only ally in this situation, the only person she could count on—at least until she could make Jan listen to reason—was herself.

She smiled wanly at Cassie and said, ''It's not affecting us very much at all. It's pure nonsense, of course.''

''Oh, of course. But . . . well, there *was* that incident with Mitch Novotny's dog. . . .''

''Accident, not incident,'' Alix said. ''Cassie, if you don't mind, I really don't want to talk about this.''

''Well, if that's how you feel.''

''I've just got too many things on my mind, that's all. And one of them is my current sketch for Jan's book. It's been pleasant, but I really should be getting back.''

As they began to scale the cliff, Cassie's expression was one of hurt, disappointment, and something else that might have been a mild irritation. Momentarily, Alix felt guilty for being so abrupt with her; after all, Cassie had confided in *her.* But Cassie's problems were in the past, while hers were much more immediate. And, she reminded herself, she couldn't be sure of Cassie's motives in pursuing the friendship. As she'd decided earlier, it was better to keep her personal affairs to herself.

Jan

Writing was impossible; he hadn't written anything for days now. Every time he sat down with his notes and his research material, his thoughts became disorganized, fragmented. He was capable of thinking of one perfectly good sentence, but seldom of the one that followed it in a natural progression.

Lately he'd spent most of his time either in the lightroom or up in the lantern working on the Fresnel lens. The lantern was where he'd gone after Alix left in the car. He had still been in the bathroom then, cleaning the tub and walls and floor with bottled water and disinfectants, and he'd heard the car and looked out and seen her driving away. She hadn't even told him she was leaving. But she would be back before long; she would never leave him permanently without saying good-bye.

He worked on the glass prisms and bull's-eyes with cleaner and soft cloth. *Catadioptric prisms refract and reflect; dioptric prisms and bull's-eye lens refract.* And what exactly does this mean, professor? *Thus, the lens bends and magnifies rays so as to create a single plane of brilliant light.* Very good. Two cohesive sentences in a row. Too bad he wasn't downstairs at his typewriter. But then if he were, he wouldn't be able to think of the next sentence. He didn't even try now.

It was cold up here, but he was sweating; a drop of perspiration rolled down his cheek, to the corner of his mouth. It tasted salty, like a tear.

He moved the lens slightly on its ball-bearing track. He had spent half a day greasing and adjusting the track, so as to once again allow the lens to move smoothly and easily. *Some large*

Fresnels were placed on wheels, others mounted on ball-bearing track, still others floated in beds of mercury. He turned the lens a bit more, to reach the rest of the catadioptric prisms near the bottom. He was almost done with the cleaning. Another few minutes would do it. *This type of lens utilizes a set flash-and-eclipse pattern, which is known as the "light characteristic"; the interval of its repetition is known as its "period."* Ah, yes. And what did the Fresnel lens say to the approaching ship? Not tonight, dear, I'm having my period.

The quality of light coming through the lantern windows brightened suddenly. He glanced up and saw a shaft of sunshine, saw pieces of blue scattered among the gray wisps outside. The fog was burning off, the sky becoming clear. He stood up, squinting against the glare. Out to sea, the sun reflected in quicksilver flashes off the ruffled water. Beautiful sight. Better enjoy it now, all simple things like this, while he still could.

He stood for a time, watching the light patterns and the restless advance-and-retreat of the surf. He wondered where Alix had gone. And wished she were here with him, up above the Mitch Novotnys of the world. And dreaded what she might have to say to him when she returned.

He knelt to work on the lens again. *In order to achieve maximum visibility, each lens had to be placed at a substantial height to compensate for the curvature of the earth—a minimum of one hundred feet for a First Order Fresnel, so that the light could be seen a minimum of eighteen miles at sea.* Awkward sentence. One maximum and two minimums made for a minimum of clarity and a maximum of confusion. He cleaned a lens, polished it, cleaned another and polished that. *First Order Fresnels can generate 680,000 candlepower, which allows them to be seen twenty-two miles at sea.* Much better. Simple, declarative, exact. Always remember the rules of good composition, professor.

He finished the last of the prisms, straightened, and moved back near the open trapdoor. The incoming sunlight made the prisms and bull's-eyes sparkle like jewels. Magnificent creation, the Fresnel. *The correct pronunciation is Fray-nell, accent on the last syllable.* More beautiful to his eyes than any diamond, any precious stone.

Reluctantly he stepped through the trap opening and started down the steep, creaky stairs. Nothing more to do in the lantern, and he needed to keep busy. That was the key to maintaining control, to keeping the crippling headaches at bay. Busy, busy. Busy, busy.

He entered the lightroom. The various parts of the diaphone and its air-compressor were strewn over the workbench: he had dismantled them again yesterday, for the third time. The tanks he had picked up in Portland were there too. But he wasn't ready to test the diaphone yet, not until he was absolutely certain the parts were clean and rust-free and in proper working order. It fretted him that the diaphone might not work after all these years because his skill as a pseudo-wickie was lacking. *In the days of manned lighthouses, keepers performed many maintenance and repair duties, among them winding the clockworks, refueling lamps, and trimming wicks. It was this last-named duty that led to the generic term "wickies."*

At the workbench he picked up one of the diaphone's internal parts, studied it for a moment. He was reaching for a screwdriver when the telephone rang downstairs.

The hair on his neck prickled; he felt himself stiffen. He stood listening to two more rings. Then, taking his time, he put the metal part down, wiped his hands on a rag, and went out and down the two flights to the living room. The bell was ringing for the eleventh or twelfth time when he picked up.

"Hello?"

"How'd you like your running water this morning? How'd it smell to you?"

"It smelled like shit. The same as you do, Novotny."

There was a pause, brief but satisfying. Then the muffled voice said, "Listen, you asshole, there's more we can do— plenty more. You stay in that lighthouse, you'll get hurt. Or your wife will."

"You can't threaten me," Jan said. "And you can't drive me out of here. I'll fight you, Novotny. With my bare hands if that's the way you want it."

"Try fighting with a rifle slug in the belly." There was a click and the line went dead.

Jan put the receiver down, gently. There was a line of tension across his neck and shoulders; otherwise he felt as he had before. His head didn't hurt at all, hadn't hurt in such a long time now that he could almost believe the pain and the bulging and the failing vision would never plague him again, that some sort of miraculous cure had been effected.

He started back to the stairwell. From outside, the sound of a car came to him faintly. He did a slow about-face, went into the kitchen, looked through the curtains. But it wasn't Alix. The car that had stopped out by the fence was unfamiliar—an old sedan—and so was the tall, middle-aged, dark-haired woman getting out of it. He watched the woman come resolutely through the gate and approach the watch house. Whoever she was and whatever her reason for coming here, he wanted nothing to do with her. He retreated from the window, climbed up into the tower to the lightroom.

He didn't hear her knock and he didn't hear her drive away; he heard nothing. He worked in a kind of vacuum, watching his hands manipulate the diaphone and compressor parts as if the fingers were the steel extremities of a machine, listening only to the random ebb and flow of his thoughts. He might have been one of the old-time lightkeepers—the last lightkeeper on the West Coast. *There are 450 lighthouses still operating in the continental United States; of that number, only thirty-four are manned. None of these is on the West Coast. It will not be long before all 450 U.S. lighthouses are fully automated under the long-range Lighthouse Automation and Modernization Project (LAMP), introduced by the Coast Guard in 1968.*

The last wickie. A man alone against the dark. . . .

He had finished reassembling both the diaphone and the compressor when Alix called his name from downstairs. It startled him: he hadn't heard the car (odd, when he'd heard the other woman's), nor had he heard her enter the house. She was just there, calling him in a voice that echoed and re-echoed in the brick hollow of the tower.

"I'm in the lightroom. Stay there; I'll come down."

He did not hurry this time either—especially not this time. Wiped his hands carefully, put some of his tools away first. Steeled himself on the way downstairs, because he expected this to be the beginning of the end. Expected to see her sitting on the couch, knees together, hands folded—her I-Have-Something-Very-Important-to-Say pose. Expected her to give him an ultimatum, and then, when he rejected it, to tell him good-bye.

But he was wrong—so wrong that a few minutes later, in a sudden release of tension, he burst out laughing.

She wasn't sitting on the couch; she was standing in front of the wood-burner, her hair wind-blown, her cheeks ruddy from the wind, smiling at him. And she didn't give him an ultimatum. And she didn't tell him good-bye.

All she wanted was to invite him out for dinner!

Alix

She turned the car left off Highway 1 and drove into the parking lot of a seafood restaurant called the Seaside Inn, two miles south of Bandon. "Look okay to you?" she asked Jan.

At first he didn't respond; he was slouched against the passenger door, apparently lost in thought. He'd been that way for much of the drive up the coast. She had monitored his silence, trying to gauge if he were suffering a headache or merely feeling introspective. Introspective, she'd decided. And not the brooding or depressed kind of introspection; the reflective kind. The cold, controlled anger of the morning was gone, and that was all for the good. Jan was a reasonable man, provided his mood was an equable one.

She asked the question again—"This place look okay to you?"—and this time her words penetrated. He roused himself, took note of their surroundings.

"Fine," he said. "You said you wanted fish, and judging from that sign, fish is what they have."

The sign was a pink neon fish standing upright on its tail fins, a jaunty smile on its face. It reminded Alix of the TV ads featuring Charlie Tuna—except that Charlie, vain as he was, would never have consented to wear the Afro-style toupee that was inexplicably perched on this fellow's head.

"Nice toup," Jan said, indicating the fish as he got out of the car. He seemed, at least in this moment, almost cheerful—his old self again.

Inside they found the standard seaside tourist-trap decor: gamefish trophies on the walls; suspended nets full of shells and glass bobbers; booths with cracked vinyl covering, checked plastic tablecloths, vases with imitation flowers. Jan ordered a half-carafe of the house white wine; when it came, Alix found it surprisingly good. They sipped it while considering the menu, and finally opted for buckets of steamed clams.

While they waited for the food to arrive, Alix kept up a running commentary on the other patrons—the fat tourist couple with large plates of fried seafood who had just sent the bread basket back for a third filling; the man in freshly pressed work clothes and woman in bright flowered polyester, obviously locals out for a night on the town; a pair of lovers, so intent on holding hands they didn't notice that the tip of his tie kept dunking itself in his untouched chowder.

"I don't think we were ever so in love that we forgot about our food," she said.

Jan looked up from the fork he was toying with. "What?"

"Nothing." He probably hadn't heard a word she'd said. "Just chattering."

He looked grateful that she didn't berate him for his inattentiveness—not that she ever did, much; he could be the stereotypical absentminded professor at times—and went back to fooling with his fork.

Alix lapsed into silence herself, sipping wine. She was about to refill her glass when she caught herself. Better watch that, Ryerson. You're the full-time family chauffeur now, remember?

Their waiter arrived with the clams—huge steaming buckets accompanied by a loaf of French bread. Alix hadn't eaten all day, hadn't wanted anything until now, but the smell of the clams made her ravenous. She ate with gusto, soaking up the clam broth with the bread, filling the side bowl with empty shells. Jan ate less than he usually did, but at least he didn't pick. And he smiled when she finished her own bucket and started in on his.

Over coffee he said, "Are you feeling better now?"

"Yes. I'd forgotten how much I enjoy going out."

"Me too." His lips quirked when he said it; he didn't appear to be having a very good time.

"I think it's good for us to get out. The atmosphere at the light is so . . . I don't know, charged with tension."

Jan frowned.

"What I mean is, we've been under such a strain. Novotny and his harassment. And that murder. All of it together is bound to take its toll."

"I suppose so." His voice and his expression were both noncommittal.

"That's why I've been pushing for a trip to Seattle," she said. "It really would do us good—"

"I know that. But I've told you and told you, Alix, I won't be driven out by circumstances, no matter what they are."

It was starting out as a repeat of all their previous conversations; his tone was reasonable and calm, but unyielding. She tried another tack. "What about your book?"

"What about it?"

"How much have you really accomplished on it since all of this started?"

His gaze flicked away from hers. He didn't answer.

She said, "How much did you write today, for instance?"

"Nothing. But . . ."

"But what?"

"I had other things to do." Defensively.

"Like what?"

"Housekeeping chores."

She was treading on thin ice here. Years ago, when they'd realized they would frequently be working at home, they had worked out a series of informal but rigid rules. Rule number one was: Don't criticize the other person's work habits. Don't complain if he works late, don't nag if she takes the afternoon off and sits in the sun. Because you simply don't know what difficulties a person might be experiencing at a given time, what internal pressures make it necessary for a night-long binge or a day-long breather.

Ordinarily she wouldn't have questioned what Jan had been doing all day. But this was no ordinary situation. She said. "Housekeeping chores. Jan, you came up here to write a book, not be a lightkeeper!"

He frowned at her. "Now look—"

"I'm not criticizing you," she went on hurriedly, "I'm making a comment on what this situation is doing to us. I'm having the same problem; it's all I can do to grind the beans for coffee in the morning. I can't work, I'm not sleeping well, I'm moody and depressed half the time. It's affecting us physically and psychologically and creatively. . . ." She realized her voice had risen and begun to wobble, and clamped her mouth shut to stem the flow of words. Steady, Ryerson, she thought.

Jan was still frowning, but it was a different kind of frown now—one of consternation rather than annoyance. He reached for a spoon and stirred his coffee, in spite of the fact he didn't take milk or sugar. At length he said quietly, "I didn't realize it was bothering you that much."

"I try not to show it, just as you do."

Again he was silent.

"You must feel it too—the tension, the waiting, as if something awful's about to happen. That business with the well . . . it could escalate into something much worse than that. You know it could."

"I admit the possibility, yes."

"But you don't think it will?"

"No."

"Well, I do. And you admit you feel the strain too?"

"Of course I do . . ."

"Then let's get away before—"

"Alix, I've tried to explain how important this time is to me! Why can't you understand that?"

"I do understand it. But I also understand that you're accomplishing nothing under these circumstances and neither am I. All we're doing is sitting out there at the light feeling miserable. Cape Despair . . . my God, what a perfect name for that place!"

More silence. She was about to break it when he said abruptly, "All right. I can see your point."

"Can you? Then let's *do* something about it."

His eyes took on a faint calculating gleam. From long experience Alix recognized the look with a sense of relief: he was about to plea bargain. She had finally gotten through to him, at least partway.

"I'll offer you a compromise," he said.

She waited.

"I still say there's a good chance Novotny will give up when he sees that we won't be forced out of the light. And even if he doesn't, we can take precautions to insure that he isn't successful with any more of his little tricks." She started to speak, but he held up his hand. "We can avoid the village completely from now on—shopping's better here in Bandon anyway—and we can get out more for evenings like this. This is a good restaurant; I'm sure there are others. And there are drives we can take, places we can visit. There's no reason we *have* to stay at the light all the time. As you said, we didn't come here to be lightkeepers."

"But—"

"The compromise is this: If anything else happens, anything nasty or even unpleasant, then we'll leave immediately. Go to Seattle, visit Larry Griffin for a minimum of two weeks. . . ."

It was a concession that pained him; she could see that. But there it was. And she could also see that it was a take-it-or-leave-it proposition.

She studied him for a moment in the glow from the red candle on the table. His jaw was set, his eyes firmly meeting hers. This, she knew, was one of the crucial moments in their relationship: she could recognize his need as greater than her own and thus ensure the survival of the marriage; or she could override his need with hers and continue a process of erosion that seemed to have already started.

No contest, Ryerson, she thought. She said, "Compromise accepted," and smiled and reached for his hand.

Alix

It was after nine when they returned to the lighthouse.

The fog had come in again; it moved in sullen, sinuous patterns over the headland, hiding the cliff edges and the sea beyond, obscuring the top of the tower so that it seemed to have been cut off two-thirds of the way up. It gave the cape a remote, alien aspect that made Alix shiver, even though the station wagon's heater was turned to high.

She drove through the gate and braked in front of the garage; Jan got out to unlock the doors. The mist made him look oddly insubstantial for a moment, even in the glare of the headlights. Then he came back to the car and she drove them into the darkness inside.

"Home," she said, making it sound as light as she could. But there was no conviction in the word.

He said, "You go ahead to the house. I'll lock up out here."

"I can use some coffee. How about you?"

"Fine. With a little brandy in it."

She hurried across the yard, taking out her house keys as she went, and unlocked the door and switched on the living room light. She shut the door quickly against the gray fingers of fog, but the chill of it was in the room—a dankness flavored with stale pipe tobacco and the vague lingering odor of manure. Or was she just imagining the manure smell? Jan had cleaned the bathroom, but another scouring wouldn't hurt; she'd do that first thing in the morning, while he took care of locating chemicals for the well. They'd have to go back to Bandon for that, probably. He would have gotten them today, except that it had been after merchant's hours when they'd arrived. Her fault. She shouldn't have spent so much time driving around or walking on the beach.

She set about building a fire in the old wood-burner, hoping that the damned thing wouldn't start smoking before it spread its warmth. She was still arranging wood on the grate inside when Jan came in. He said, "Here, let me do that. You make the coffee."

"With a slug of brandy, right?"

"Make it two slugs of brandy."

In the kitchen she took the drip grind from one of the canisters—decaf, or they wouldn't sleep tonight—and put it into the Mr. Coffee. But when she opened the cupboard, she found it empty of bottled water. There was none in the fridge, either. Had Jan used up the last of their supply cleaning the bathroom? No coffee for them tonight, if he had.

She went down the three steps and through the cloakroom to check the pantry. She had her hand on the latch when she thought she heard something inside, a kind of shuffling or skittering movement. A chill seemed to make the same sort of movement on her back, as if someone had drawn a bony finger downward along her spine. She listened for a moment, standing rigid, but there wasn't anything else to hear. Her imagination acting up, producing more horror fantasies about rats in that abandoned well under the pantry floor. That, and nerves.

She opened the door, reached inside for the light switch. It was way over near the shelves on the left; you'd think the people who had built the place would—

In the darkness something moved across her hand—something alive, something that chittered.

A cry froze in her throat; she jerked her hand back, banged her knuckles against the inner wall. Her dragging fingers touched the switch plate. Reflexively she flipped the toggle upward.

Scurrying things on the floor, on the shelves. A bag of sugar ripped open, spilling whiteness like granulated snow. Yellow eyes glaring, fangs bared, little clawed feet snicking against wood.

Rats!

The pantry was full of rats!

Her throat unlocked and she screamed, a shriek of revulsion and primal terror, and then recoiled backward, pulling the door shut with a crash. But one of the rats got through. She saw it, felt it slither across her boot—huge, half as big as a full-grown cat, gray fur matted and riddled with mange. She threw herself sideways, up against the wall, and the rat turned at the noise or movement to confront her. It came up on its hind paws, its mouth wide open as if in rictus, its fangs gleaming and its yellow eyes full of evil. Another cry tore out of her, strangled and mewling this time. Dimly she heard Jan yelling, felt herself flattening against the wall, clutching at it in a blind groping for escape.

But the rat didn't attack her; it wheeled and skittered the other way, into the cloakroom just as Jan appeared from the kitchen.

He saw it, shouted something, and the rat veered away from him, over to the wall where they kept their shoes and boots and galoshes. Through a kind of haze she saw it rear up again, backed against the wall just as she was—cornered rat, trapped rat, its eyes not yellow but red now in the gloom, like the eyes of a demon. Saw Jan yank his furled umbrella off a hook on the wall, the one with the heavy brass handle shaped like a falcon's head. Saw him lunge at the rat, flail at it with the brass end. Heard the thing squeal as it fought him like a drunken boxer, heard it squeal again, a different kind of sound, one of pain and rage. Saw blood, and more of Jan's wild swings, and the grimace of frenzy on his face—

She shut her eyes, twisted around toward the wall, and jammed her hands over her ears to shut out the thuds and grunts and squeals. She had no idea when the violence ended. She was still standing, face to the wall, eyes shut, hands pressed to her ears, when she sensed his nearness. And in spite of herself, she shuddered when he touched her.

He turned her, pulled her against him—not gently. "Are you all right? It didn't bite you?"

"No, no. . . ."

"It's dead. I killed it."

She had nothing to say. She buried her face against the rough cloth of his coat and held him, not so much for comfort but because she was afraid to look at him up close this way, afraid that the remnants of his savage fury would still be visible. The rage was still in his voice, in the throbbing rigidity of his body.

"More of them in the pantry," he said. "I can hear them. How many, did you see?"

"I don't know. Several . . . I don't know."

"All right. I'll get them out of there."

"How? You can't kill them all—"

"I will if I have to."

He turned her again, so that they were side by side and his arm was around her shoulders. She didn't look at what lay bloody and mangled on the floor of the cloakroom as they passed through it. Just let him guide her through the kitchen and into the living room, sit her down near the wood stove—the second time today she had let him lead her away from the scene of an outrage. *Déjà vu.* And things happened in *threes,* didn't they?

She glanced up as he started for the door. He was still carrying the furled umbrella in his left hand, and when she saw the blood on it she swallowed against the taste of bile and looked away again. "Jan, be careful. Don't let one of those things bite you."

"I won't."

The front door opened, banged shut again. She got up and went to the stove, stood close to its warmth. She was cold; it was all she could do to control her shivering.

From back in the pantry, she heard the squealing again.

She shut her ears to it, listening instead to the wind. It shifted, began its skirling in the tower and kitchen chimney, and the stove in turn began to smoke. She turned to it, fiddled with the damper. It did no good. If the wind kept up like this, the room would be full of smoke in another few minutes and she would have to open one of the windows. Otherwise—

The door popped open and Jan was there again. She straightened, turned as he shut the door against the undulating fog outside.

Oddly, it was his hands that she looked at first. He had put the umbrella down somewhere; he carried nothing in them. His face was congested, the rage still smoldering in his eyes. And the skin of his forehead and around his eyes was drawn tight, so that he was half squinting—the way it got when he was having one of his bad headaches.

He said, "I got rid of them. All of them."

"Did you kill any more?"

"No. They scattered when I opened the outside door. We'll have to put out traps. They'll come back after the food."

We won't be here when they do, she thought. Will we?

"Will you be all right alone for a while?" he asked.

"Alone? Why?"

"I'm going into Hilliard."

"After Novotny? For God's sake, Jan, no!"

"Yes. This is the last straw. I'm going to have it out with him."

"No! Call the sheriff, let him—"

"Fuck the sheriff," Jan said, and that frightened her all the more. He never used words like that—never. "There's nothing he can do. This is between Novotny and me."

"Jan, you promised you wouldn't drive anymore. You *mustn't* drive, not when you're having one of your headaches."

"I don't have a headache. Don't argue with me, Alix. I'm going."

"Then I'll go with you. I'll drive—"

"No you won't. I told you, it's between Novotny and me. You're staying here, behind locked doors."

"I can't stay here, not with those rats—"

"They're gone, they can't get back in the house. You'll be all right. Just don't answer the phone."

"Jan . . ."

But he was at the door, through it, gone into the mist.

She ran out after him, caught up near the garage. "Please don't go. *Please!*"

"Go back inside. You'll catch cold out here."

"I won't let you go—"

"You won't stop me. Go back inside."

The look he gave her froze her in place; he moved on to the

garage. Even in the foggy dark, it was unmistakable—a look of resolve and the kind of savage fury she'd seen when he was beating the rat to death. Chills rode her back and shoulders. She couldn't move even as she heard the car start, saw him back it out and the lights come on. Couldn't move as he drove out through the gate and fog swallowed the car. The last she saw of it was its taillights glowing bright red. Like the rat's eyes in the cloakroom just before it died.

Hod Barnett

Hod didn't like it. He just didn't like it.

Taking a few potshots at the Ryersons' station wagon, that was one thing. Even putting some shit down their well—no big deal. But the rats . . . that was an ugly thing, there wasn't any call for that kind of thing. Big ones, too, seven or eight of them. And half-starved. Mitch had got a couple of kids to trap them; the Stedlow place was crawling with the buggers, with old man Stedlow dead a year now and his kin just letting the house and barn go to ruin. Rats like that, who the hell knew what kind of disease they might be carrying? Suppose one of them bit Ryerson or his wife?

Not that anybody would say *he'd* had anything to do with it. It was Mitch's idea, and Adam had taken the cage full of rats out there tonight. All he'd done was tell Mitch he'd seen the Ryersons leaving town, driving off toward Highway 1 about four o'clock. He hadn't even known about the rats until after Adam got back. Mitch hadn't said anything to him while they were shooting pool in the Sea Breeze earlier.

Mitch and Adam were still in there, playing Eight Ball for

beers against a couple of fellows from the cannery. Cracking jokes, laughing it up, Adam hippety-hopping around like he had a stick up his ass and he was trying to shake it loose. It got on Hod's nerves; that was why he'd up and left a couple of minutes ago. It was like something had happened to the two of them, changed them. Mitch especially. Sure, Ryerson had run Red down and then threatened to have Mitch arrested on account of his car getting shot up. But that wasn't cause to go putting a bunch of filthy rats in the lighthouse, right there in the pantry with all their food—Jesus!—and maybe giving Ryerson or his wife some kind of disease. It just wasn't right.

Sitting there on the front seat of his old Rambler, Hod thought maybe he ought to go out to the lighthouse, do some-thing about those rats before it was too late. But hell, it was after ten now; chances were the Ryersons had come back long ago and it was already too late. And even if it wasn't, what if he went out there and tried to do something, and they came back and caught him? They'd think he was the one who *brought* the goddamn rats, not that he was trying to get rid of them. Be-sides, what could he do? He wasn't about to go up against seven or eight half-starved rats loose in a little pantry, maybe get bit-ten himself. He hated rats. He didn't want anything to do with the buggers.

Didn't want anything to do with Mitch's campaign against the Ryersons, either. Didn't want to know anything else Mitch and Adam decided on doing, not before and not after. Tomorrow he'd tell them that, too, straight out. If anybody's ass ended up in a sling, it wasn't going to be Hod Barnett's.

He started the Nash and drove on up the hill. When he walked into the trailer Della was sitting in the kitchen, smoking like a chimney and reading one of those silly damn romance novels she got from old lady Bidwell. *Passion's Tempest*. Jesus Christ. But he knew better than to say anything to her about it.

She'd only start in again about how they didn't have a TV set anymore and she had to have *some* pleasure in her life, didn't she?—all that crap he'd heard a hundred times before.

She said, "Well, where've you been?" but not as if she cared much.

"Where do you think?"

"Over at the Sea Breeze running up your bar tab, like usual."

"Don't start in. I had three beers, all on Mitch."

"Where'd he get money to throw away on you?"

"I said don't start in. Boys asleep?"

"They're in bed."

"Mandy?"

"She's not here."

"Where the hell is she, this late?"

"Out. She wouldn't say where she was going."

"I told her not to go running around after dark, after what happened to that hitchhiker last week. Damn it, I *told* her."

"She wouldn't listen to me, either."

"You know where she is, don't you? Off with that long-haired punk from Bandon again, that's where. Spreading her legs for him in the backseat of his jalopy."

Della glared at him. "I don't like that kind of talk. You know I don't."

"Think she hasn't been going down for him? Think she's still a sweet little virgin?"

"You've got an ugly mouth, Hod Barnett."

"No uglier than hers. Can't tell me she hasn't been acting funny lately, like she's hiding something. You know what I think?"

"I don't care what you think."

"I think she got herself knocked up," Hod said, "that's what I think."

190

"You'd like that, wouldn't you."

"Why the hell should I like it?"

"Then she'd have to get married and move out and you'd have one less mouth to feed."

"Ahhh . . ."

Hod went over to the refrigerator. He felt like eating something, but there wasn't anything to eat. Not even a slice of bread or some milk left. No use saying anything about *that* to Della, either; no damn use saying anything anymore.

He slammed the refrigerator door, and when he turned around she had her nose buried in the romance book again. What did she get out of reading that crap? Did she think some Prince Charming was going to come along and take her off somewhere, a bag like her? She hadn't been bad looking twenty years ago, when he'd met her down in Oklahoma after his Army discharge at Fort Sill. But now look at her. Letting herself go the way she had . . . he could barely stand to put his hands on her, even in the dark. Sometimes he wondered why he'd married her in the first place.

In the living room, he kicked Jason's busted-up Mr. T doll off his chair—damn kid, always leaving his toys lying around—and sat down. The Coos Bay paper was on the floor next to the chair where Della had thrown it. All wrinkled and torn, as usual—she kept right on doing that to the paper even though she knew it drove him crazy. He picked it up and got it straightened out and glanced through it.

Another story about the young college girl they'd found on the cape last week. (Why wouldn't Mandy listen to what she was told? What was the *matter* with that kid?) Still nothing new about who'd strangled her; they didn't even have a suspect. Mitch thought it might be Ryerson, but Hod didn't believe that for a minute. If Ryerson had done it, the state troopers would've arrested him by now, wouldn't they? Sure they would have.

They weren't stupid. Mitch was hipped on the subject of Ryerson. Just plain hipped on driving him out of the lighthouse, out of Oregon and back to California where he belonged. He'd probably do it, too, sooner or later, one way or another. If those rats didn't work, he'd come up with something else—something even worse, maybe, something Hod didn't even want to think about.

No sir, he didn't like it. He didn't like it one damn bit.

Alix

The sound of the telephone cut through the silence, making her jump.

Almost as soon as she'd come inside, minutes ago, the wind had stilled and the lighthouse had become eerily quiet. The phone bell was like a dissonant cry in the silence. She stared at the instrument, listened to it ring again, then moved over to it. Jan's parting words echoed in her mind: *Don't answer the phone.* But it was an admonition she couldn't heed. She was not about to cut herself off from the outside world—not now, not after what had happened here tonight. She caught up the receiver and said hello.

She half expected the call to be another anonymous one. But the voice that said, "Mrs. Ryerson?" was young, female, and familiar. It was also high-pitched, frightened-sounding.

"Yes? Who's this?"

"Mandy Barnett. Listen, I need to talk to you, I need your help. Can you come get me? Right away?"

"Mandy, what on earth—"

"Please, Mrs. Ryerson, please!"

"I . . . I don't have the car."

"What?"

"My husband took it a little while ago. He's on his way into the village—"

"Oh my *God!*"

The cry scraped at Alix's already-raw nerve ends. "What is it? What's the matter?"

"I can't talk now, there's no time. I'll come out there on my bike. I don't know what else to *do*."

"Mandy, where are you—?"

But the girl broke the connection—abruptly and noisily, as if she had banged the receiver against something before getting it into the cradle.

Alix gripped the receiver for a moment before lowering it. The call *could* have been some sort of trick, something Mandy had been put up to by her father or Mitch Novotny to lure her away from the lighthouse so they could commit further atrocities. No, that didn't make any sense, not so soon after the rats in the pantry. And the terror in the girl's voice . . . she was sure that had been real. But why call me if she's in trouble? Alix thought. A relative stranger who'd been hostile to her in the past? That didn't make sense either. . . .

She looked at her watch. Almost eleven. Jan had been gone less than fifteen minutes. Not enough time to get all the way into Hilliard. Not enough time for whatever trouble Mandy was in to involve him. Then what—?

The telephone rang again, the sudden clamor making her jump just as it had the first time. She snatched up the receiver. "Yes? Hello?"

"Mrs. Ryerson?" This time the voice was male, deep and muffled.

"Yes?"

"You looked inside your pantry yet?"

She went rigid, hearing not only the words but the undercurrent of malice.

"Better look if you haven't," the voice said. "We left you a little present—"

Quickly she replaced the receiver, taking care not to slam it down. Wasn't that what the phone company always advised you? Don't respond in any way. Just hang up quietly. But that was advice for dealing with obscene callers; this was something else entirely.

In the space of time it took to dial a number, the phone bell shrilled again. Alix backed away toward the stove. The ringing went on and on—eleven, twelve, thirteen, fourteen. The sound filled the room, seemed to penetrate deeply into her skull. She put her hands to her ears to shut it out . . . and the ringing stopped. The silence that followed it seemed to vibrate with after-echoes.

She waited, thinking that if he called again she would unclip the cord from the base unit; she couldn't stand any more of that piercing summons. But he didn't call again. And after three or four minutes of silence, she went to sit on the couch—stiffly at first, poised, listening, and then with a gradual easing of tension.

A brandy was what she needed now. But the only bottle they had was an unopened fifth in the pantry, and she couldn't go in there, even if Jan had made sure all the rats were gone. Couldn't go through the cloakroom with the one rat's blood spattered on the wall. Not now, and maybe not ever again.

Time passed. The wind picked up again, beating at the windows, playing its games in the chimney so that smoke backed up thinly into the room and stung her eyes. She remained alert, listening for movement, for sounds under the wind. When she next looked at her watch, it was five minutes before midnight. Jan had been gone nearly an hour. And it had been almost that long since Mandy's call.

Jan was in Hilliard by now. Had he found Novotny? And if he had, what then? More heated words? A fight?

She stirred restlessly, got up to check the stove. The fire needed refueling, but there was no more wood in here and she didn't want to go outside to the shed. Besides, if she built the fire up again, the wind would only blow more smoke into the room. She went back to the couch and drew the afghan over her, wishing there was something she could do besides just sitting and waiting.

But what *could* she do? Call the sheriff? Jan wouldn't want that; and there was nothing the sheriff could do either, no evidence that Novotny had been responsible for the rats. Call Cassie? She had a car; she could drive out here, the two of them could drive into the village . . . no. By that time, whatever was happening between Jan and Novotny would be finished. And Mandy was coming, and in some kind of trouble. And she couldn't involve Cassie without taking the woman into her confidence, explaining everything that had happened so far.

She closed her eyes, willed herself to relax, to remain calm. But images of the whole harrowing day played against the inside of her lids: Jan's face when he'd come back upstairs this morning, after the phone call . . . the filthy brown water streaming from the showerhead . . . Harvey Olsen's weak, tormented eyes . . . Jan, insubstantial in the fog when he'd gone to open the garage on their return from dinner . . . Jan, his face contorted with rage as he raised the brass-handled umbrella against the rat . . . Jan, with that same look on his face just before he left in the car. . . .

She grabbed one of the sofa cushions, pulled it over, and propped it under her head like a pillow. It had been such a long day, one spent riding an emotional roller-coaster: passion . . . worry . . . revulsion . . . anger . . . purposefulness . . . frustration . . . hope . . . and then the horror, the very real horror.

She was tired, bone-tired. And at some point, despite her

anxiety, she slipped into a fitful sleep. Her dreams, when they came, were reprises of her memories of the day, but surreal, detailed yet at the same time vague: Jan in a desperate struggle with Mitch Novotny . . . Jan lying broken and bloodied like the rat . . . Novotny and some of the other villagers driving on the cape road, coming for her. . . .

And then the scenes repeated, only this time Jan was winning his battle with Novotny . . . Jan was standing over the man's broken body, his face a grimace of rage and triumph . . . Jan was the driver of the car coming along the cape road, and he wasn't alone. On the seat beside him was Mandy Barnett. . . .

Alix jerked awake and sat up, looking wildly around the room, fighting off the vestiges of her nightmares. She was damp and sticky with sweat; her hair clung to her forehead in greasy strands; her mouth was dry and tasted sour. The room was cold, the fire in the stove long since gone out. And milky gray light had begun to seep around the edges of the window blinds.

Morning.

Morning!

She came off the couch in convulsive moments, blinking, staring at her watch. Close to seven. She groped her way to the front door, jerked it open, looked out. The garage doors were still open, the interior empty; there was no sign of the station wagon. Jan hadn't come home. Dear God, where was he? And Mandy . . . she hadn't come either. Why? What had happened during those dark hours while she'd slept and dreamed?

She felt a sudden, overpowering sense of urgency. She couldn't stay here any longer, couldn't take another minute of not knowing. Walking the more than three miles into the village would take too long. Whether she liked it or not, she would have to put herself in Cassie Lang's hands—call her, ask her to drive out, and then start walking to meet her.

Quickly, Alix went to the telephone table, looked up Cassie's number in the slim county directory, dialed it. It rang eight, nine, ten times. No answer. She let it ring ten more; still no answer. *Damn!* She checked the number again, redialed. Still no response. Cassie must be one of those people who didn't like to be awakened by the phone, who unplugged it before going to bed. Either that, or she'd gone out on some early-morning errand.

Frantic now, Alix tried to think of someone else to call. But no one else in Hilliard would be likely to help her. And the sheriff . . . no, she couldn't call the sheriff. It was either walk to the village or stay here, and she couldn't stay here.

Her pea jacket was on a peg next to the door; she put it on, hastily checked her pocket for the keys, and went out. The early-morning air was warmer than she'd expected, and very damp from the fog. The odor of the sea was strong, salt-laden. There was no sound anywhere except for the muffled crash of the surf against the rocks below the cliffs.

The gate stood open as Jan had left it last night. Instinctively, she tugged it shut behind her; the moisture that saturated the rough whitewashed boards made her shiver. For a moment she stood looking south along the curve of the shoreline, saw the surf roiling over the beach where she'd walked with Cassie— slate-gray water topped with white foam. Ahead of her the terrain was partially obscured by the low-hanging mist. She stifled another shiver, set off at a fast walk along the road.

On either side of her the mist was pervasive, half obliterating the shapes of scrub vegetation and rocks. It seemed to mute all sound: the waking rustles of birds in the gorse and Oregon grape, the slap of her tennis shoes on the uneven surface of the roadbed. She kept her eyes cast downward, concentrating on where she was walking, trying not to think of what might await her in Hilliard.

After a mile or so she came on the long stretch where those

strange porcupine-like clumps of tule grass grew; the mist made them look more than ever like herds of some alien animal lying in wait. Then she was into the thick copse of fir trees, and the darkness in there made her hurry, so that she was almost running by the time she emerged.

Past the open fields where sheep huddled together for warmth. Past another stand of trees. And then she was alongside the gully where the body of the strangled hitchhiker had been found . . . she recognized it with a rippling *frisson* and quickened her pace again.

How far to the county road now? Less than a mile, she was certain of that. But she was tiring rapidly, and to keep herself going she played a childlike game with herself: *See that cluster of cypress ahead? When you get past that, you'll be able to see the intersection.* And when she reached the cypress, and the county road was still nowhere in sight: *See that sharp curve up there? The junction is just past it. . . .*

She was well beyond the curve, passing through another section of sheep graze, when something caught her eye: metal glinting in the weeds in a hollow to the left of the road.

The metal was silvery, dull in the muted light. Although the grass was high, in the hollow, she could see traces of another color—a bright, electric blue.

She stopped abruptly, peering down there. What looked to be tire marks gouged the grassy verge, and a section of the fence between the road and the hollow had been knocked down, flattened, as if by something heavy—a car, perhaps. Alix frowned, biting her lip. Then, hesitantly, she moved toward the fence, closer to what lay in the high grass of the hollow. Close enough to identify it.

A bicycle.

Mandy Barnett's bicycle?

Its front tire was flat, and the handlebars were bent at an odd angle; the spokes of the rear wheel were mangled. And the bike didn't look as if it had lain there for long—it wasn't rusted, and the bright blue paint was relatively new. Bright blue paint that matched the poncho and headband Mandy habitually wore.

Alix felt a sharpening of both tension and fear. An accident? Was that why Mandy hadn't shown up at the lighthouse last night? But who would be driving on the cape road late at night, who else but—

No.

Maybe the girl was still here somewhere. Unconscious, or too weak or badly hurt to move, to call for help. Alix stood listening. All she heard was the wind, the distant bleat of a sheep.

"Mandy? Mandy?"

There was no answer.

She stepped over the broken-down section of fence, went down into the hollow. The bicycle was all that lay in the high grass there. She moved out on the other side, around a clump of spiky gorse bushes—calling as she went, focusing hard on her surroundings to keep from focusing on her thoughts.

She had gone fifty yards or so from the hollow, toward a grouping of scrub pine, when she saw something else blue in among the trees. She stopped, peering that way. Couldn't see it now. Her eyes were gritty and in the mist everything seemed to blur together. Struggling to maintain her footing on the uneven ground, she hurried toward the pines . . . and saw the blue again . . . and hurried even more.

The trees grew in a tight little circle, as if, like the sheep, they were huddling for protection from the elements. Their branches were heavy, low-hanging, and sticky with sap. Alix pushed against them, bent forward at the waist. And there, on a little patch of needled ground, she found Mandy.

The girl was lying motionless, face down, her blue-and-white poncho grass-stained and torn. The headband was gone; her red curls were spread in a tangled fan across her shoulders. One of her legs was drawn up, bent at the knee, and both arms were outflung.

Fearfully Alix knelt, touched the girl's shoulder. "Mandy?" There was no response. No sign that Mandy was even breathing.

She grasped one of the thin wrists, felt for a pulse, didn't find one. Unheedful of warnings about moving accident victims, she took hold of Mandy's shoulder and turned the girl onto her back.

"Oh dear God!"

Mandy's face was a purplish-black hue, the tip of her tongue visible between her lips. Her head was twisted at an odd angle. Across her cheeks and neck were bloodless scratches. And her eyes . . . her eyes were wide open, bulging, blood-suffused, grotesquely sightless.

Alix recoiled, fought down a surge of nausea. Scrambled to her feet and batted her way free of the pines and began to run back toward the road. Even in her state of shock, she knew she would never forget those dead staring eyes.

Strangled . . . just like the hitchhiker . . . run down with a car while riding her bike, chased or carried or dragged over here and strangled. . . .

And Jan took the station wagon . . . and Jan didn't come home last night. . . .

Part Three

Mid-October

Mad or sane, it does not matter, for the end is the same in either case. I fear now that the light-house will shatter and fall. I am already shattered, and must fall with it.

—EDGAR ALLAN POE
AND ROBERT BLOCH,
"The Light-House"

Jan

He couldn't remember.

Last night was a blur, its images as gray and formless as the fog piled up dirtily outside the station wagon's windshield. He couldn't even remember waking up; he was just sitting here behind the wheel, shivering from the cold, staring out at the fog, with a sour taste in his mouth like that of sleep and hangover.

Where was he? He didn't even know that. The fog obscured his surroundings, except for glimpses now and then of rocks, stunted trees, a flat stretch of stony ground. Some distance away surf made a faint hissing sound, like voices whispering angrily in the mist.

Another blackout.

His head hurt; he couldn't think straight. But it wasn't the bulging, only vestiges of it—a dull pounding as steady and rhythmic as the sea hammering at the unseen shore. He lifted his hands, pressed the palms against his temples; but he was shaking so badly, they set up a vibration in his head that intensified rather than eased the pain.

He pulled his hands down, tucked them into his armpits to warm them, and leaned forward with his forehead against the wheel. After a time the worst of the shaking stopped—and he thought of his watch, the time, what was the time? 8:33, he saw when he looked. 8:33 in the morning. Out here all night, he thought.

Out *where* all night?

Impulsively, he opened the door and got out of the car. Moved away from it, away from the sound of the ocean. The grayness parted, broke up into wisps and streaks, ugly, cold, like strips of something diseased sloughing off in the wind. He was on a rocky lookout, he realized; a short access road connected it with a deserted two-lane highway. What highway? Highway 1? The county road that branched off it and led to Hilliard? He couldn't tell; none of the terrain was familiar.

He went back to the car, stumbling a little on the uneven surface, his teeth clenched against the pain in his head. The station wagon, he saw then, was nosed up against a dirt retaining wall at the outer edge of the lookout. Beyond the wall was a steep slope, gouged by the elements into deep fissures, and then the sea hammering, hammering, hammering against a jumble of rocks fifty feet below.

If that retaining wall wasn't there I might have driven right over the edge. Better if I had. Better for me, better for Alix—

Alix.

And some of last night came back, with a force that drove him sideways against the car. The rats in the pantry, the rat he'd killed . . . the wild rage . . . the need to do something, fight back, confront Novotny . . . ignoring Alix's pleas and driving off in the car like a madman . . . the road, the dark all around him . . . and the sudden bulging . . .

That was all. There was nothing beyond that—a void, an abyss. Where had he gone? What had he done?

Was Alix all right?

Alone at the lighthouse, out there alone all night.

"God!" He said the word aloud, in a voice that seemed to crack in his ears like glass breaking. He dragged the car door open, got back under the wheel, fumbled at the ignition. The keys were still there. But the engine was cold; it whirred, whirred, whirred again before it finally caught. He backed the car, got it turned around, drove along the access road to the two-lane highway. Which way should he go?

Left. Try left.

The fog was so thick at first that his visibility was no more than a few hundred feet in any direction. A pickup trick came hurtling out of it like some kind of phantom, made him swerve in sudden panic, and then disappeared again into the grayness. But then, after a mile or so, the road seemed to angle away from the sea and the mist grew thinner, patchier, letting him see forested hills and sheep graze. Going the right way, he thought. Toward Hilliard, not away from it.

Another mile, and more of the fog burned off. He passed the sheep ranch; in the distance, then, he had a vague glimpse of the bay, the buildings of the village. The cape road would be coming up pretty soon; he began looking for the big sign that marked it.

But it wasn't the sign that caught his attention first, that made him brake so suddenly the station wagon skidded on the damp pavement. It was the telephone booth in the little rest area on this side of the cape road; it was the woman standing next to it, alone, bundled in a familiar blue coat, a familiar scarf and cap.

Alix.

He veered across the road, into the rest area. But he pointed the car away from where she stood, some distance to one side: he was suddenly afraid of losing control, of hitting her. He jammed on the emergency brake, got out, ran toward her. And then stopped, because she had run a few steps and then stopped herself. She stood rigidly, arms down at her sides, her face . . . the expression on her face . . .

"Jan, for God's sake, where have you been?"

He shook his head; he couldn't seem to find words. He put a hand out to touch her, but she moved away abruptly—not as if she were rejecting him; as if something had drawn her away.

It was the car. She half ran to it, around to the front, and bent and looked at the grille, the bumper. Thinks maybe I hit something else last night, he thought dully. Then he thought, much more sharply: Did I? He went there himself, looked himself— looked for dents, scrapes, broken headlights, broken signal lights. Looked for blood.

Nothing. There was nothing to see.

Alix faced him again, and some of the rigidity had left her; but the look on her face and in her eyes was still the same. Fear, and something else, something darker, primitive. She put both hands on his arms, as if re-establishing contact between them.

"Where were you all night?"

He found words this time, forced them out of the rusty cavern of his throat. "Down the road a few miles. A lookout . . . I spent the night there."

"Another bad headache?"

"Yes. Alix, why are you *here?* How did you—?"

"I walked. I was worried about you."

"This morning?"

"Yes. Jan, listen to me—"

"Nothing else happened at the light?"

"Not there, no. On the cape road, a mile or so from here."

Something began to crawl inside him—a thin worm of dread. "What do you mean? What happened?"

"There's been another murder. Mandy Barnett. Somebody ran her and her bicycle off the road last night and then strangled her."

He couldn't comprehend it at first; refused to comprehend it. All he said was, "No."

"It's true, I found the body. I've already called the state police."

He shook his head. "No," he said again.

"Now you listen to me," she said. She gripped his arms more tightly; he could feel the bite of her nails through his coat. "I want you to go out to the lighthouse. Right now, before the authorities come, before anybody sees you here."

"And leave you alone? Why?"

"The way you look, that's why. The way you're acting. I don't want them to see you like this."

It was seeping into him now, the full awareness of what she had told him and what she was getting at. A sudden chill wracked him. "You don't think that I—?"

"I don't think anything." She said it urgently, in a tone of voice he had never heard her use before. She kept looking out toward the empty highway, her head cocked to one side, listening. "I don't want *them* to think anything either. I don't want them to see you like this and I don't want them to know you weren't home last night."

"You mean . . . lie to them?"

"That's just what I mean. I'll say you were at the lighthouse all night and you say the same thing. You were with me the whole time. Now go, hurry!"

She was pushing him toward the car as she spoke. He wanted to resist and yet he didn't, he couldn't. He opened the door, bent his body in under the wheel.

"Wash your face and change your clothes when you get there," she said. "Try to get a grip on yourself."

"I'm all right now. Alix, I didn't, I couldn't . . ."

"I know. Just go, go!"

She slammed the door, and he started the engine and drove away from her, out onto the still-deserted highway. In the rearview mirror he watched her grow smaller, less distinct in the mist; it was as if pieces of her were being consumed by it, so that only diminishing fragments—part of her face, one blue-coated arm, the lower halves of her legs—remained. And then they, too, were gone, and he was turning past the sign that said CAP DES PERES LIGHTHOUSE, 3 MILES, CLOSED TO THE PUBLIC, jouncing along the rutted cape road, alone again in the darkening gray.

I didn't, I couldn't . . .

Could I? he thought.
Did I?

Alix

She watched Jan closely as they talked with the state homicide detective, Frank Sinclair. He was sitting in the single chair near the woodstove, his head backlit by the side window. The comparative darkness of the room accentuated the paleness of the skin around his beard, made his cheekbones seem more prominent. His face was immobile as Sinclair posed his questions; only his eyes gave any hint of his inner upheaval.

She wanted to believe that Sinclair saw Jan's agitation as nothing more than the normal reaction of a man who has been awakened from a supposedly sound sleep to the unsettling news of another murder. Jan was adept at hiding his true feelings behind his professorial facade—from others, at least. What she saw in his eyes were emotions much more complex than simple shock. And one of them was fear.

"Mrs. Ryerson?"

She blinked at Sinclair, realizing she'd lost the thread of his questioning. He was a chubby man dressed in a gray tweed jacket and gray slacks; his mustache was the only distinctive feature in an otherwise bland face, and that only because it grew more fully on the right side than on the left. He seemed sensitive to the defect, because periodically he stroked the sparser side—as if it were a defenseless animal in need of comforting. To the casual observer, his appearance might have been deceptively reassuring, but her artist's eye picked out the determined ridges of muscle around his mouth, the sharp intelligence concealed beneath the bland exterior and thick dark-rimmed glasses. When he'd questioned them after the murder of the hitchhiker, she had recognized and been made wary by those qualities. After close to an hour with him this morning, she had come to regard him as a man who would be a dangerous adversary.

She cleared her throat and said, "I'm sorry, I'm afraid I didn't hear what you said."

His mouth twitched reprovingly; he patted the left side of his mustache as if it were responsible for the twitch and he wanted to calm it. "I said that I'd like to go over the chronology of events another time, to make sure I have everything straight."

"All right."

Sinclair looked down at the notepad he'd been writing on. "Now, Mrs. Ryerson, you say you couldn't sleep, so you got up early and went for a walk?"

"Yes, that's right."

"Was there any particular reason for your sleeplessness?"

"No. I was just . . . restless. Things on my mind."

Sinclair cocked his head interrogatively.

"The book my husband and I are working on," she said.

"Ah, yes. A history of North American lighthouses, isn't it?"

"Yes. He's writing it and I'm illustrating it."

Sinclair nodded. "What time did you leave on your walk?"

"Close to seven."

"And your husband was asleep at the time?"

"He was, yes."

"Mr. Ryerson," Sinclair said to Jan, "were you aware your wife had gone out?"

"No. I'm a very sound sleeper."

"And you were still asleep when she came back and told you what she'd found?"

209

"Yes."

Again Sinclair consulted his notepad, allowing the silence to build. Jan was also looking at it, as if trying to read what the detective had written there. Then his gaze flicked up and over to Alix. There was a vague glassy quality to them, she thought, as if they were filmed with a thin layer of ice. But Sinclair wouldn't have noted that. Or had he?

The questioning continued. Why had Alix walked so far this morning? Because she'd wanted to exercise. What had made her notice Mandy's bicycle? Why had she gone as far as that circle of pines looking for the girl? On and on, some of the questions asked more than once, in subtly different guises. Then he shifted gears and asked again about the trouble they'd been having here at the light. Alix had explained it once, holding nothing back; it would have been foolish not to, and it diverted suspicion away from Jan, perhaps to where it actually belonged.

"Mr. Ryerson," Sinclair asked, "why didn't you call us when these things started happening—the polluted well, the rats in the pantry?"

"What could you have done without proof of who was responsible? What can you do now?"

"Talk to Mr. Novotny, for one thing. Surely you could see the value in at least filing a report."

"I suppose so."

"I think we might have done that today," Alix said quickly. "Even if this terrible new thing hadn't happened."

"Mandy Barnett's murder, you mean?"

"My finding her body. Yes."

"But that *is* why you told me about the incidents?"

"Well, we didn't want to hold anything back," she said, "anything that might be important. Mandy's death could be related to what Mitch Novotny has been doing to us, couldn't it?"

"In what way?"

"I don't know. But her father is a friend of Novoţny's. It's possible he was involved in those malicious acts against us."

Sinclair made a note but said nothing.

Alix went on. "And the girl *was* on her way to see me last night. She said on the phone she needed to talk to me. I don't see what else she could have wanted to talk about except the harassment; there was no other connection between us."

"You think she wanted to tell you who was responsible? Or something else?"

"I just don't know."

Sinclair stroked his lopsided mustache. "You can be sure we'll look into that possibility, Mrs. Ryerson. Among others. Meanwhile, I think it would be a good idea if you and your husband filed a report on the incidents as soon as possible."

"Yes. Whatever you say."

"Mr. Ryerson? Do you agree?"

Jan nodded. "Yes, all right."

More questions. On and on, until the sound of his voice began to grate on Alix's nerves. She continued to watch Jan closely, to see if he was starting to weaken under the constant barrage of questions. But he seemed the same as he had at the beginning, with his fear still masked beneath his calm exterior, just as Sinclair's bulldog tenacity was masked beneath *his* calm exterior.

It was another half hour before Sinclair finally seemed satisfied. He rose then, thanked them for their cooperation, and issued the standard warning not to leave the area without first notifying his office. His departure left them in an echoing silence that Alix broke by saying, "Thank God that's over!"

"Is it?" Jan said. He gave her a bleak look. "I'd guess it's just starting."

He was right, of course. There would be other interrogations, other questions. Sinclair was no fool; he could sense that something was wrong here. But that was not her immediate worry. Jan was.

She refused to believe he was a murderer; if she even admitted the possibility, after the horrifying, elemental experience of finding Mandy's body, she would be risking her sanity. And it wasn't just blind faith in his innocence, either. There was physical evidence: she'd examined the front of the car at the rest area, found no scrapes or dents, no streaks of electric blue, as there would have been if he were the one who'd run Mandy down on her bicycle. No, the man she knew, loved, lived with was the same decent, harmless man he'd always been. It was something else, something profound, that had made him afraid, made him need her so much. Something to do with those headaches. She would find out what it was, and they would deal with it together.

But not here. She couldn't reach him here; he couldn't seem to talk to her. They had to get away from Cape Despair first. If she knew nothing else, she knew that that was imperative for both their sakes.

She was about to speak, to put her thoughts into words, when Jan raised his head—he had been staring at his hands—and looked at her. His eyes seemed to have lost their thin film, as if it had melted under some sudden heat—the heat of decision, of resolve.

He said, "Alix, I think you should leave here. Right away."

It was almost an echo of her thoughts, and the last thing she had expected him to say. "Do you mean that?"

"Of course I mean it. Go to Bandon, take a motel room for a day or two."

"Both of us?"

"No. Just you."

She stared at him. "What about you?"

"I'll stay here."

"Jan, I don't understand. . . ."

"We need some time apart. I need it . . . some time alone."

"But *why?*"

"I can't explain now." He got to his feet, came over to stand in front of her. His eyes were almost pleading, now. "Please don't argue with me, or ask me any more questions. Just pack a bag and leave. In a day or two . . . then you'll understand. I promise you that."

Would she understand? She didn't now; she felt again that they were on the brink of losing each other, of becoming strangers. The bond between them was so fragile. If she left him at this crisis point, it might snap.

And what would he do out here alone? What if he had another bad headache? Or what if Novotny came back, retaliated further? She wanted to ask him, demand reassurances, but she couldn't. He'd said, "Please don't argue with me, or ask me any more questions." It would be a breach of faith, another strain on the bond, if she ignored that plea. Might make the crisis even worse.

His eyes were still pleading with her, filled with his need. She felt a sudden wrench of pain. Jan had seldom needed her at all, and now his need had become a negative one. Nonetheless, it was one she couldn't ignore.

"All right," she said. "All right, I'll go."

Hod Barnett

Adam kept saying, "Poor Mandy. Jesus, that poor little girl."

Mitch kept saying, "It was Ryerson. Nothing like this ever happened around here until that goddamn psycho showed up. It was Ryerson, I tell you."

Hod didn't know what to say, what to think. He felt numb.

He felt as if somebody had scooped a big piece out of him somewhere inside. The place where it had been didn't hurt yet. It would pretty soon, he knew that, but right now it didn't. It was just numb, like the left side of his face had been numb that time he'd had the impacted wisdom tooth and the dentist in Bandon had shot him full of novocaine.

Della wasn't numb, though; better for her if she was. She'd screamed when they told her, and then collapsed, and Mitch's wife and his mother-in-law had come over and calmed her down and put her to bed. They'd got a doctor to come from Bandon and give her something, a shot of something—Mitch said don't worry, he'd pay for it—and now she was resting in their trailer, with Marie Novotny and her mother right there to keep anybody from bothering her. They were taking care of Tad and Jason, too. The boys didn't understand what it was all about, they were too young, but they knew something bad had happened to their sister and they'd both been bawling their heads off when Hod had left with Mitch and Adam.

And now here he was, sitting in Mitch's living room—just the three of them, no more troopers, no more sheriff's men, no more questions, and for the time being no more neighbors standing around gawking. Just him and his two best friends, drinking beer he couldn't taste, listening to words that didn't mean anything to him because of that big numb place inside that wouldn't let him feel anything.

"Poor Mandy," Adam was saying, "that poor little girl."

"Troopers better arrest Ryerson damned quick, that's all I got to say," Mitch said. "Before anything else happens."

"Mad dog like that," Adam said, "he ought to be shot. No trial, none of that crap where a smart shyster can get him off. Just take him out and shoot him."

"Shoot him or lock him up," Mitch said, "just so he can't hurt no other young girls."

"Jesus, poor Mandy. That poor kid."

"He's a psycho, that's what he is. Gets his kicks killing people, animals—just *killing* them."

"Son of a bitch ought to be shot dead."

"Hod," Mitch said, "you okay?"

"Yeah," Hod said, "I'm okay."

"Another beer? Something to eat?"

"No, not right now."

Mitch put an arm around him, the way he had two or three times today. "You sure you're okay? You want to lay down or something?"

"No," Hod said, "I don't want to lay down."

"Maybe be alone for a while? Go back to your place?"

"No. I don't want to be alone."

"Stay here with us, then, that what you want to do?"

"Yeah."

"Sure you can. Stay as long as you want."

"We know how you feel," Adam said. "Don't we, Mitch?"

"Sure we do. We know just how you feel."

Mandy's dead, Hod thought, my daughter's dead. And he still couldn't *feel* anything.

Alix

She replaced the telephone receiver in its cradle and sat on the edge of the hard double bed, staring at the bland motel wallpaper. It was—what else?—a seashell pattern, dozens of turquoise cowries alternating with pink conches against a tan background that was probably supposed to be sand. When you looked at it for more than a few seconds it all merged into a muddy swirl, as if waves had engulfed the vinyl-coated beach.

Her first act after setting her overnight bag down on the luggage rack had been to call Jan and give him the name and phone number of the motel. He had been pleasant, had sounded glad to hear she'd arrived safely, and yet she sensed that underneath the superficial normalcy he was withdrawn, brooding. Yes, everything was all right, he'd said. Yes, he would be talking to her again soon; in the meantime she wasn't to worry about him.

She was worried.

Why did he need to be apart from her for a day or two, alone at the light? Did he have some romantic notion of defending it against Mitch Novotny, some dangerous plan that he didn't want to risk involving her in? Or was it just that he wanted time to work out whatever was plaguing him, perhaps to make up his mind to confess it to her? She fervently hoped that was the answer. It was the one thing, more than any other right now, that would reinforce the fragile bond between them.

She sighed and fumbled in her purse for Frank Sinclair's card. The next order of business was to inform his office of her whereabouts. The card was a no-frills white with black lettering, and it bore an address in Coos Bay. She debated driving up there instead of calling—getting out of this room, which was already beginning to make her feel claustrophobic. But a curious lethargy seemed to have taken hold of her, and the debate lasted only a few seconds before she again picked up the telephone receiver, punched the button for an outside line, and dialed.

Sinclair was in his office, and she was able to give him her message personally. There was a pause—he was probably noting down the address and number—and then he said, "I think you were wise to leave Cap Des Peres, Mrs. Ryerson. And since you're fairly close by, I'll be expecting you and your husband to come in soon and file a report on those incidents you mentioned.''

"Would tomorrow be all right?"

"Yes, fine."

"Is it . . . all right if I come alone? Or do you need both of us to sign the report?"

"Isn't your husband there with you?"

"No. He . . . decided to stay at the lighthouse alone for a day or two. He seems to feel it shouldn't be left unattended."

"I see." She could picture Sinclair stroking the straggly side of his mustache.

When he didn't go on, she took a breath and said, "Mr. Sinclair, I'm concerned for my husband's safety. Have you talked to Mitch Novotny yet?"

"I have. He denies any harassment of you and your husband."

"Of course he does. But what if he tries something else?"

"I don't think that's likely. I suggested to him that it would be a very unwise thing for anyone to do."

"I hope you're right. Is there any chance . . . well, that he's the one who killed Mandy Barnett and the other girl?"

"We have no reason to think so. Do you, Mrs. Ryerson?"

"No. It's just that . . . well, he'd been at the light earlier, to put the rats in the pantry. What if he came back—to do something else, or to see what our reaction had been? Or what if he was the reason Mandy was so afraid . . . because he'd tried to attack her or something?"

"Anything is possible at this stage of our investigation," Sinclair said mildly. "However, Mr. Novotny has a very strong alibi for the approximate time of Mandy Barnett's murder: he was home with his wife, children, and mother-in-law. They all swear to that fact. Also, he doesn't own a dark-green automobile."

"Dark-green?"

"There were green paint scrapings on the bicycle. Whoever ran Mandy Barnett down did so in a green vehicle headed toward the lighthouse, not away from it."

"How do you know that?"

"Physical evidence—tire marks, for one thing."

Sinclair's news relieved her in one way. Their station wagon was brown—the final piece of evidence, if she really needed it, to prove that Jan hadn't been responsible for Mandy's death.

And then she thought of the first time she'd seen Mandy: smoking grass on the headland with a young man several years older, her "connection for dope." The car they'd been leaning against had been green.

She said as much to Sinclair. And he said, "Yes, we know. His name is Mike Wilson and we've already questioned him. His car is the wrong green, and undamaged, and he also has an alibi for the approximate time of the girl's death."

"Oh," she said, and paused, and then said, "May I ask you one more question? A . . . favor, actually."

"What sort of favor?"

"Can you give my husband some sort of protection while he's staying alone at the lighthouse?"

Sinclair hesitated. When he spoke, his tone was softened, almost apologetic. "No, Mrs. Ryerson, I'm sorry I can't."

She'd expected as much, but still she said, "Why not? It would only be for a couple of days. I think he'll make up his mind to leave by then."

"My office is working on two homicide investigations," Sinclair said patiently, "as well as a number of other cases. We're understaffed. I can't spare anyone without at least some evidence that your husband's life is in danger. And I can't request a patrol officer for the job for the same reason."

"You're saying my fears are groundless?"

"Not exactly. I'll do this for you: I'll have one more talk with Novotny, just to strengthen the suggestion I made to him. That's all I can do."

"Thank you."

"You could try the sheriff's department," Sinclair said, "but I'm afraid they'll tell you the same thing I have. The only way to insure your husband's safety is to convince him to leave Cap Des Peres."

And she couldn't seem to do that, she thought as she ended the conversation. At least not yet. Nor was she convinced, despite Sinclair's reassurances, that Jan was in no danger from Mitch Novotny.

She considered calling her father. Matthew Kingsley would know what to do in a situation like this. He had connections everywhere, including Oregon; he could bring pressure to bear on the state police. After all, he'd always told her that when you don't receive satisfaction at one level, you should go higher with your demands—to the top, if necessary.

The idea of picking up the phone and calling the familiar number in Palo Alto was a tempting one. But it was also a thoroughly bad one, she decided. For one thing, Jan would never forgive her for bringing her father into what he considered a personal problem; such an action would probably provide the severing blow to the thread that bound their marriage. And what if Matthew behaved with his characteristic bluster, chartered a plane, and showed up here demanding action? That would not only enrage and alienate Jan, but would further strain matters in Hilliard.

No, it was better for both her and Jan if they weathered this particular crisis alone. Jan had claimed he would be all right, had wanted her to trust him. And trust him she would, even if it involved a terrible risk.

Mitch Novotny

Mitch was surprised when he saw the state police car come up the hill, park next to Hod's old Rambler, and the plainclothes homicide detective, Sinclair, get out of it. What the hell was he doing here, half an hour before Mandy's funeral? Unless he had some news about Ryerson . . . maybe that was it. Maybe he'd come to tell Hod and Della that the law'd finally quit diddling around after two days and arrested the psycho.

Mitch had been helping Marie unload food from the trunk of their car—potato salad, cold cuts, deviled eggs—for the funeral supper. He handed her the last covered dish as Sinclair approached. "You manage that all right, hon?"

"I can manage." She seemed to want to hang around, to see what Sinclair wanted, but he shooed her away. She waddled when she walked now, like a damn duck. Still a couple of months before she was due, and already she was big as a house.

Sinclair stopped and took off his hat. Behind those thick glasses of his, his eyes flicked over Mitch, over Hod's trailer, over the handful of villagers who'd already showed up to pay their respects to the bereaved. He looked a little uncomfortable, as if he hadn't realized they were getting ready to have the funeral.

Mitch said, "Hod's inside getting dressed, if you're looking for him."

"Actually, I came to see you, Mr. Novotny."

"About what?"

"Jan Ryerson and his wife."

"What about them? You finally arrest Ryerson?"

"No." Sinclair ran a finger over one side of his mustache. "We have no cause to arrest him, I told you that before."

"No cause. Christ. Just let him keep running around loose, murdering young girls, is that it?"

"There's no evidence Mr. Ryerson murdered anyone," Sinclair said. "This is the United States of America, Mr. Novotny. A man is innocent until proven guilty. That goes for Jan Ryerson, and it also goes for you."

"What the hell is that supposed to mean?"

"You know what it means."

Mitch felt himself getting hot inside his Sunday suit; little trickles of sweat had started to ooze down his sides. "That why you're here? That crap again? How many times I have to tell you I didn't have nothing to do with what's been happening out at the lighthouse?"

"Mr. Ryerson thinks you did."

"I don't give a damn what he thinks," Mitch said. He was really hot now; it was all he could do to keep himself from shaking. "He make some other complaint against me? That why you're here, hassling me right before poor Mandy's funeral?"

"I didn't know the funeral was today; if I had I would have waited until tomorrow to talk to you again."

"Yeah, sure you would. You didn't answer me about Ryerson. He make another complaint?"

"No. There's been no complaint."

"Then why're you here? Tell me again to stay away from the Ryersons?"

"Do I need to tell you that, Mr. Novotny?"

"No," Mitch said, and then he remembered something and all at once he *knew* what this was all about. This time he did start to shake. He could feel the blood all hot and pounding in his head. "Now I got it," he said. "His wife's old man is a politician, right? She went crying to papa and he made some calls and now you're here.''

"That's not it at all—''

"Sure it is. That's why you haven't put Ryerson in jail where he belongs. Man's got the right connections, he can get away with anything in this lousy country.''

Sinclair was mad, too, now. His chubby face was pinched and his eyes looked dark and swollen behind his thick glasses. But he had himself under control just the same. He said, ''Nobody gets away with any crime if I can help it. Not murder, not malicious harassment either. Just remember that, Mr. Novotny.''

He turned on his heel, walked back to his car. You fucking Gestapo, Mitch thought, and he wanted to shout the words aloud; but he didn't do it. He just stood there shaking, glaring, as Sinclair got back into his car and made a U-turn and drove on down the hill out of sight.

"Christ, Mitch, what was that all about?''

Adam Reese had come up beside him, with Seth Bonner at his heels; they'd been over by the trailer getting an eyeful. Mitch couldn't talk for a minute, he was so worked up. When he finally started to calm down he told them what it had all been about.

"It ain't right,'' Adam said. You could see it festering on him, too, making him fidget from one foot to the other. "It just ain't right.''

"Somebody's got to do something,'' Bonner said. "He's crazy, that Ryerson. I told you all along, didn't I? Didn't I?''

"Cops,'' Adam said, and spat on the ground. "What the hell good are they?''

"No good, that's what. No damn good at all.''

Mitch was barely listening to them. His head hurt now; he wished he had a drink, and not just a Henry's either. You can

222

only take so much, he was thinking. Goddamn it, a man can only take so much!

Jan

He was on his way across the yard to the pumphouse to see what he could do about purifying the well when the loneliness overcame him.

It was cold—a raw misty afternoon, with the wind blade-edged and cutting against his bare skin. He wasn't thinking about anything at first. Just walking slowly, hunched over against the pull of the wind. And then the random thought came that the only people he'd talked to since Alix left two days ago were the man at the supply house in Coos Bay who'd taken his telephone order for the chemicals, and the truck driver who'd delivered them this morning. That thought gave birth to another: He'd expected the homicide inspector, Sinclair, to come back with more questions, but Sinclair hadn't come. Why? It must be because he really did believe in the innocence of Jan Ryerson, believed that a man like Jan Ryerson could never, never hurt two young girls no matter what sort of state he was in. Alix believed it, didn't she? And Jan Ryerson did too.

I couldn't, I didn't . . .

Could I? Did I?

No, I couldn't.

No, I didn't.

And then he thought: I'm going to be blind pretty soon. And the loneliness struck him—a wave of it sudden and fierce, making him feel almost agoraphobic. All at once the sky and the sea seemed immense, the sense of desolation greater than he'd ever imagined it, the voices of the wheeling gulls like shrieks of despair. Cape Despair. A place of lost hopes and hollow desires. The edge of nowhere. One short step from the abyss, the consuming darkness.

He turned, feeling dizzy, and went back to the house, sat down in the living room. His head ached, but it was not another of the bulging headaches—he hadn't had another of those. But he'd had more frequent spells of failing vision, distortion of the form and size of objects, a narrowing of his visual field. Happening fast now. How much time did he have left?

Fear gnawed at him, but it was a different kind of fear than the one he'd been living with the past two days, even the past few months. Not fear of the unknown—fear of the alone. This lighthouse, the stand he'd made against Mitch Novotny and the other people of Hilliard . . . none of that meant anything, really, not even as a symbol. Staying here like this was not only foolish, it was meaningless. Polishing the lenses, rebuilding the diaphone, painting the catwalk, trying to do something about the well, all the frantic activity of the past couple of days . . . meaningless.

The room, the entire lighthouse, felt strange to him now—a vast echoing chamber of loneliness. Why had he sent Alix away? Why had he thought he needed some time alone? Being alone was the thing that frightened him most, the thing that had kept him from confiding in her. The ordeal of telling her the truth, facing the consequences, couldn't be any greater than the ordeal of the past two days, the past two weeks.

You can't put it off any longer, he thought, and he was standing beside the phone, reaching down for the receiver, when he realized that he didn't *want* to put it off; that no matter what Alix's response, the truth was something he could no longer deal with alone.

Alíx

The afternoon was thick with fog—not the unleavened gray mist that often hung over the coastline, but an opaque white curtain that shifted and billowed before a strong Pacific wind. The offshore rocks were shrouded, as were the hills to the east. The broken lines centering Highway 1 seemed to leap up suddenly, giving little or no warning of curves, and the edges of the pavement bled off into nothingness. When she came to the first exit for Hilliard she turned automatically, even though the route would take her through the village; it was shorter than continuing down the highway and then doubling back on the county road, and she was eager to get to the lighthouse, to see Jan and hear what it was he had to say to her.

The trailer park on its little hill to her left as she entered Hilliard was a blurred scattering of lonely ill-assorted shapes. It made her feel cold in spite of the warmth inside the station wagon. She thought of how depressing life must be inside one of those boxes, with only the thin walls as protection against the elements. And then, with a twinge of pain, she thought of the Barnetts, Della and Hod and their other children, alone with their loss; and of Mandy, who would never return to even that poor shelter.

The cannery loomed on her right, pinpoints of light shining along the clumsy line of its roof. Then the road curved, and she was on the main street. The fluorescent interior of the marine supply glowed through the fog, making the windows look like giant TV screens. The green neon sign of the Seafood Grotto was muted and hazed. The street was empty of pedestrians, and most of the buildings had a closed-up, deserted look.

Just past the general store, however, a line of cars was moving slowly, some of their taillights flashing left-turn signals onto the sidestreet that climbed the hillside toward the church. Alix put her foot on the brake to keep from overtaking them. The lead car made the turn across the road, its headlamps probing the mist and quickly becoming dissipated in whiteness. It was a large boxy vehicle, black with ornate chrome trim; shirred white curtains masked the windows of its elongated rear compartment.

It was a hearse. She'd come up behind Mandy Barnett's funeral cortege.

Other cars followed the hearse, their headlights making the same slow arc: a ten-year-old Cadillac sedan, presumably belonging to the undertaker and containing the bereaved family; a beat-up Volkswagen van; an equally battered pickup truck; three old cars of nondescript make. It was a poor showing, undoubtedly a poor funeral—as poor as the brief life of Mandy Barnett. Again Alix felt a wrench of pity for the girl, and blinked at the wetness that came to her eyes.

She remembered the day Mandy had come to the light with her "business proposition," the way she'd spoken of Hilliard: "I *hate* it! It's ugly and cold, and everybody's poor." And the way she'd spoken of California: "Nobody goes to Hollywood and gets rich and famous anymore; that's a lot of shit. But I figure I could get by down there, and at least it's sunny and warm." Mandy hadn't had much in life; hadn't wanted all that much, either. And this bleak good-bye was to be all she ever got.

Alix wondered if Mandy had even owned a decent dress to be buried in. Probably not. Perhaps they had laid her out in her bright blue-and-white poncho. In a way, she hoped so: it and the matching beaded headband seemed to have been the girl's favorite outfit.

Once more she pictured Mandy—that day in the laundromat, angry at her mother and stamping her foot, her red curls bouncing and the beaded ends of the headband clicking together. And then—unbidden and unwelcome—came the image of the girl's body lying broken on the pine-needled ground, her blood-flecked eyes hideously staring. . . .

She shuddered, trying to banish the ugly vision. For a moment, as the last car ahead made the turn and began climbing the hill, she contemplated following and paying her last respects. But she knew it would be a self-indulgent gesture, perhaps even a dangerous one; the Barnetts and their friends would be certain to resent her presence—an outsider, the wife of the man some of them were saying was Mandy's murderer. No, there was no place for her at the cemetery beside the run-down little village church.

She watched the taillights as they wound up the road, disappearing into the wall of mist. Then she drove on to Cape Despair, the lighthouse, and Jan.

Hod Barnett

The funeral was a blur: Della crying, the boys crying, Reverend Olsen up on his pulpit saying Mandy was a good girl and God in His mercy had already welcomed her into His Kingdom for all eternity (What mercy? Hod remembered thinking. What kind of mercy is this?), then all of them leaving the church, entering the fog-wrapped graveyard, and the pallbearers—Mitch and Adam and Barney Nevers and Les Cummins and Seth Bonner and Mike Carstairs—lowering her coffin into the hole in the ground, clods of earth falling on it, "ashes to ashes and dust to dust," and Della on her knees wailing, "My baby, my baby!"

and him just standing there because he couldn't do anything else, couldn't even cry.

The ride home and the funeral supper was a blur too. All the people telling him how sorry they were, Lillian Hilliard saying, "If you need anything, Hod, you just let me know, your credit's good with me from now on," as if he gave a damn about groceries at a time like this, and Della all of a sudden red-faced and smiling, acting like they were having a party, running around with plates of food and saying, "Have something more to eat, won't you have something more to eat?" He couldn't stand it after a while, too many people and too much noise, and he went out and walked around, he didn't even remember where, and then he was back at the trailer and Mitch put a drink in his hand—whiskey and some ice—and he drank it, didn't taste it, drank it like it was water, and Mitch gave him another one, and he drank that, and pretty soon he knew he was drunk but he didn't feel drunk. Somebody tried to get him to go back inside, eat something, but he couldn't make himself do it. Then Adam said, "Let's go up to my trailer, I got another bottle up there," and he went. Anything to get away from all those people, all that noise.

Mitch and Seth Bonner went, too. And they sat around and drank more whiskey. And then he cried. It came over him all at once, like something breaking, spilling over inside him. He put his head down on the table and cried and cried for his dead daughter until there weren't any more tears in him. Then he sat up and wiped his face, and he was all right. For the first time in three days he could feel again. For the first time since they'd walked into Adam's trailer he could pay attention to what was being said, take part in the conversation.

Mitch poured him another drink. The bottle was almost empty.

Alix

The interior of the watch house was cold and drafty, despite the fire in the woodstove. Outside the wind gusted and whistled, and gray fingers of fog trailed past the windows. She sat on the couch clutching a snifter of brandy. Jan was on the chair across from her, peering down into his glass and swirling the liquor around its convex sides. He looked tired, a little haggard, a little drained—the same way she felt.

She had waited a long time for this conversation, and she knew she should now be patient, should allow him to find his words and tell it in his own way. But instead she was filled with a prickly irritation; every flick of his wrist as he sloshed the brandy nettled her; every moment that he didn't speak set her nerves on edge. There was something familiar about the scene—something nostalgic yet vaguely unpleasant that she couldn't place and which nagged at her and increased her annoyance.

She was about to take a sip of brandy, hoping it would steady her, when the wind gusted strongly, baffling around the tower, and then increased to a maniacal shriek. She sat up straighter, a *frisson* rippling along her spine.

The sound brought it all back to her: that night in Boston, in Jan's old apartment in the condemned building on Beacon Hill. The night he'd told her about the murder in Madison during his college years. With the memory came a strong sense of *déjà vu*. It was as if they were reenacting that scene in Boston. The cold, the wind, the brandy, even their positions relative to each other, not touching, formal . . . it was all the same.

Convulsively she raised her glass and took a long swallow. As if it were a signal, Jan stirred and looked at her and then said, "Alix, this isn't easy for me." He paused, rolling the brandy snifter between his palms. This, too, called up an image of a younger Jan making a similar gesture before he confessed to the loneliness and emotional poverty of his life. "I'd better start at the beginning," he went on. "With the headaches I've been having."

The headaches. His health. It was what she'd expected, and something she could cope with.

"When I told you Dave Sanderson didn't know what caused them, it was only a half-truth. They—the doctors; I've seen several specialists—they *do* know what is causing them. It's a degenerative disease that affects the optic nerve. Both optic nerves, in my case."

The word "degenerative" seemed to hang in the air between them. She felt a coldness spreading outward to her limbs.

"What they don't know," Jan said, "is exactly what causes the disease. Some kind of virus, maybe; they're just not sure because it's rare." He drew a deep breath. His fingertips, pressed tight around the snifter, were white. "They also don't know how to treat it, to stop or even slow down the degeneration. They've had some success with drugs, cortisone and some others, but . . . a few patients respond, most don't. If they don't, the disease progresses and . . . eventually they lose their sight."

Numb now, she sat very still, waiting.

"The drugs haven't worked on me, Alix. The pain and other symptoms are getting worse. There's nothing they can do. In a year or two, I'll be blind."

Blind!

That word, too, hung in the air between them. And echoed inside her head. She couldn't speak, couldn't think clearly.

Then, as she began to feel the impact of what he'd said, it was as if a fine mesh screen had been drawn down between them. She could see him hazily, hear him, but she seemed cut off from him by a gray veil.

Her silence seemed to encourage him. He went on more confidently, using terms like "uveal disease" and "image distortion" and "systemic chorioditis." She heard it all, but somehow it did not quite register. It was like reading a medical text in which all the unfamiliar terms merely form a pattern on the page—something incomprehensible, arcane.

Jan went on and on, relating medical facts in a too-cool, too-rational tone. Finally, when she'd heard enough, she set her glass down and pushed her hands toward him to stem the meaningless, strange-sounding words and phrases.

"Please stop."

He stopped. And after a moment, when the screen between them seemed to dissolve and her own vision cleared, she lowered her hands.

"Why didn't you tell me this before?" she said.

"I couldn't. I just . . . couldn't."

Let that go for the moment, she thought. "All right. I'm glad you finally have." Now *her* words were too-cool, too-rational. "The details are too much for me to take in right now. I'll have to talk with . . . one of your specialists before I fully understand."

"Yes," he said, "I guess you should."

"The headaches . . . they've been getting worse, haven't they?"

"Much worse."

"And the other symptoms—what are they?"

He licked dry-looking lips. Behind the panes of his glasses, she saw the fear come into his eyes again.

"Jan, what are they?"

"Nothing the doctors told me to expect," he said. "I had no warning. They . . . they're blackouts."

"Blackouts?"

"I didn't have the first one until we came here." Then the words came out in a rush. "Periods of time—hours—when apparently I'm conscious and moving about, doing things, but afterwards I can't remember what they are. The night I hit Novotny's dog . . . I had one then. And the night coming back from Portland. And the night Mandy Barnett was . . . the night she died. Alix, I don't know how or why I ended up out on that lookout; I just don't know what I did the whole time I was gone."

The unspoken lay heavy on his mind, if not on hers. He had had blackouts three times, and on each occasion someone—or something—had died. First the dog, and finally Mandy Barnett. And part of his fear was that he might be responsible for the deaths of those two girls as well. She could see that fear, feel it, almost smell it.

The empty snifter slipped out of Jan's hand, bounced on the rag rug and then onto the floor, and lay there rolling slightly back and forth. He didn't seem to notice. But Alix watched it as if it were an object of fascination.

"Ah Christ, Alix," he said in a choked voice, "don't you see? I don't know what I do when I have those spells, what I might be capable of. I can't believe I could hurt anyone, and yet . . . Novotny's dog . . . I just don't *know*."

She wanted to go to him, comfort him, but she felt frozen, suspended in a time warp between the present and that long-ago night in Boston. Then, as he'd revealed the emptiness and sadness of his life, his pain had been genuine and deep; but this pain cut to the core of him, a hundred times more acute. All this time, since he'd first learned of his disease, he had been living a hellish existence: alone when he should not have been alone, shouldering a torment—a series of torments—that he should have shared with her.

She could do nothing to change the past, or alleviate his fear of his imminent blindness; but she could relieve him of the other part of his terror. She said, "The dog was an accident. And you didn't hurt anyone else; you couldn't have."

"Are you so sure of that?"

"Yes. I *know* you, I know you're not capable of—"

"You're my wife. Naturally you feel that way."

Had she been so absolutely sure of him all along? If she hadn't, she must never admit it even to herself. She said, "There's more than that. Actual physical evidence. The detective, Sinclair, told me Mandy was killed by someone driving a dark-green car or truck; you couldn't possibly have run her off the road. And whoever strangled Mandy must have strangled that other girl, too. You had nothing to do with either one."

He sat motionless for a moment. Then he took off his glasses, scrubbed at his eyes as if to wipe away some of the fear. And at last, seeing him do that, she was able to go to him—to kneel down to him, pull his head into the protective curve of her shoulder.

"The dog—" he began.

"An *accident*."

"But the blackouts—"

"Whatever you do during them, you're not dangerous to anyone except when you're behind the wheel of a car. The doctors will find out why they're happening, how to control them. They've got to."

He was silent for a moment. Then he raised his head, but not to look at her; his gaze fixed on a point over her left shoulder. "No matter what the doctors find out about the blackouts, I'm going to be blind. Do you realize what that will mean? If you're still with me, I'll become a burden to you. A sick, dependent, *blind* husband.''

Now the reason for his silence about his illness was becoming clear. He'd been afraid she would leave him! But how could he have been so unsure of her? And needlessly so; leaving him had never crossed her mind, even when she had doubted his sanity.

She said, ''You can't really believe that matters so much to me.''

He continued to look away, not answering.

She reached up, put her hand against his bearded cheek, moved his head until he was looking into her eyes. ''Why would you even think that it makes a difference? That I'd leave you?''

''Because . . . dammit!'' He took her wrist, removed her hand. ''Because people have been leaving me all my life. Why not you, too?''

Anger flared up; she struggled to control it. After a moment she said, ''I'm not just 'people.' I'm your wife and I love you. I'd have to have a far better reason than blindness to make me go away from you.''

His face, squeezed tight by tension, relaxed slightly. ''I admit,'' he said, and stopped and then started again, ''I admit I was probably being irrational. But I just couldn't bring myself to tell you, to put it to the test. I was terrified of losing you.''

She'd been aware that in a marriage of many years' duration, the partners tended to conceptualize their spouses—not necessarily as they were, but as extensions of their own selves. Somehow, though, she had never applied this common psychological phenomenon to her own marriage, and yet that seemed to be exactly what she and Jan had both been doing. Years of comfortable routines and patterns had evidently robbed them of real communication, and each had transferred his own fears and failings to the other. Jan had translated his fear of loved ones leaving him to actual potential desertion on her part. And she, because she sometimes doubted her own worth as an adult woman, had imbued him with a similar lack of worth, doubted him as she doubted herself.

The irony was that these mutual doubts had surfaced with the first major crisis they'd had to face in years. At a time when they should have drawn closer, the doubts had threatened instead to pull them apart.

Now that she understood what had gone wrong, she would be able to verbalize it to Jan. But not now, it wasn't the time. What he had to have now, to shore up his sagging defenses, was simple reassurance.

She reached up and drew his head back against her shoulder—a trifle less gently than before, because she was angry with both of them. "I'm not going anywhere," she said. "I'll stay with you no matter what happens. We'll get through this together, the same way we've gotten through everything else. Do you believe that?"

The resistance went out of him; she could feel it. He said, "Yes," and leaned against her, and she thought: It's going to be all right.

After a time, holding him, she glanced at the window and saw that darkness had fallen. She said, "Jan, I can't spend another night in this place and neither can you. You know that too now, don't you?"

"I know," he said. He straightened, disentangled himself from her arms. There was a sadness on his face, and she could feel his sense of loss: he had really loved this lighthouse, before all that had happened to spoil it for him. And yet at the same time he seemed relieved at the prospect of purposeful activity. He got to his feet, saying, "Did you keep your motel room in Bandon?"

"Yes."

"Then we'll pack our things and stay there tonight. And if Sinclair says we can leave the area, we'll start back home tomorrow."

"Once we leave, we won't come back. Are you sure you're ready to accept that?"

"As ready as I'll ever be," he said.

Quickly, now that they were in agreement, they set to work. Alix packed the supplies and equipment in her studio, then started on the kitchen. Upstairs she could hear Jan clearing out his study, then moving about the bedroom packing their clothes. As she worked, she felt energized, buoyed by relief. Tomorrow they would be free of this desolate point of land, of the depressing village and the hostile people who lived there. And the day after that they would be home, in the comfortable, familiar surroundings of Palo Alto—

And next year, or the year after that, Jan will be blind.

She paused in the act of loading pots and pans into a carton, looked up, and saw her reflection in the darkened pane of the kitchen window. She moved closer, studying her face. There were lines between her brows that she hadn't noticed before. Her lips pulled downward, bracketed by strained parentheses.

Maybe he *won't* lose his sight, she thought. Maybe there's still hope. He said the doctors don't know much about his disease; it's possible they'll find a cure. But even if they don't . . . it's not the end of the world. It just isn't.

She already had a good livelihood, and it would be an even better one after she joined Alison in the new firm. If it became necessary, she could support the household. But that probably *wouldn't* be necessary; Jan had tenure, and the university would be accommodating about shifting his teaching load as his health problems demanded. Blind professors were not unheard of; many published and lectured at the same pace as their sighted colleagues. Knowing Jan—his determination, his dedication—

she wouldn't be surprised if he wrote other books on light-houses after he finished *Guardians of the Night*.

No, it wouldn't be the end of the world for either of them. If only he'd had more faith in her, he'd long ago have come to the same conclusion.

She heard Jan descend the staircase and set down their suit-cases in the living room. When he went back upstairs, she made a trip out to the station wagon and laid her drawing board flat in the rear so things could be piled on top of it. The night had turned cold and the mist had thickened. The wind was icy, the smell of the sea extra sharp.

Jan was standing next to the couch when she came back in-side. Several of his shirts had fallen off their hangers and he clutched them by their limp sleeves, a helpless, serio-comic ex-pression on his face. For the first time in days Alix smiled as she went to his aid.

"Damned things," he said.

"Don't worry about them—they'll only get wrinkled in the car. When we get home I'll take everything to the cleaners."

They set about untangling the garments. It seemed an impos-sible task; the hangers kept slipping to the floor, the shirts slith-ering after them. Finally, Jan went into the kitchen to get a plastic garbage bag. They'd dump the shirts into it, carry them home that way.

He held the bag and she picked up the clothing. But as she started to stuff them into the bag, he tensed and his head cocked in a listening pose. "What was that?"

"I didn't hear anything."

"Sounded like somebody moving around outside."

She listened. "It must have been the wind."

"Maybe." Frowning, he let the bag fall and started for the door.

Outside and not far away, there was a sudden echoing report—one she'd heard before, one she recognized as a rifle shot. It froze Jan halfway to the door. Froze her with one hand at her mouth.

And before the echoes of it died away, male voices rose in an excited clamor out there. Close, very close. In the front yard.

"Ryerson!" one of them shouted. "Come out of there, Ryerson, or we'll come in and get you!"

Adam Reese

Adam yelled it again. "Come out of there, Ryerson, or we'll come in and get you!" Then he threw the Springfield up and squeezed off another round. Put that sucker right into the lighthouse wall, right under the nightlight—saw the splinters fly, saw the hole it made, heard the echoes rolling off into the foggy night like some kind of sweet thunder.

Pretty soon lights went out inside. Place was dark now, except for the nightlight and one window up on the second floor.

He felt like jumping up and down; hell, he *was* jumping up and down, he couldn't stand still. He couldn't remember the last time he'd been this excited. Goddamn, this was something. Goddamn, they should of come out here a long time ago.

Old Seth kept whooping and cackling like he was about to lay an egg. "Shoot out one of the windows, Adam! Shoot out one of the windows!" But Mitch and Hod, they weren't into it yet. He could understand about Hod—poor bugger was still all tore up about Mandy, and so damn drunk he was wandering back and forth like he didn't even know where he was. Well, they were all drunk—all except Adam. He hadn't drunk as much whiskey as the others. He didn't need no Dutch courage to prime *his* pump. No, sir. He'd been ready for this for a long time.

It was Mitch he couldn't figure. Mitch had been ready for a long time, too, hadn't he? His idea they come out here tonight and get Ryerson, make him confess, make a citizen's arrest and haul him in to Coos Bay and dump him in that cop Sinclair's lap. But now that they were here, into it, he wasn't saying much, was just hanging back kind of nervous, watching. It wasn't that he was shitfaced, no, he wasn't much worse off than Adam was. It was like he was having second thoughts or something, like he figured maybe they'd bit off more than they could chew.

But they hadn't bit off anything yet. Not yet.

"Bust one of the windows, Adam!" Bonner yelled.

He threw the Springfield up to his shoulder, sighted at the kitchen window, fired. Glass shattered, sprayed; the curtain inside flapped, blew out in the wind. Bonner let out another whoop and danced a little jig. Mitch stood there staring, fidgeting.

"Come on out, Ryerson!" Adam yelled.

"He's not coming out," Mitch said. His face was wet with mist; he wiped it off on the back of his hand. "He'll never come out, not with his wife in there with him."

"Then we'll go in and drag him out."

"That's it," Bonner said. He clapped his hands like a kid. "Drag him out, make him confess. How do we do it, Mitch? How do we go in and get him?"

Mitch didn't say nothing. He was staring again, wiping his face, fidgeting.

Why, hell, Adam thought suddenly, he's *scared*. He couldn't figure it at first. He'd always looked up to Mitch, always figured him to be tough and strong, the leader type. But now . . . well, you had to believe your eyes. Mitch was scared, backing-down scared—there was no question about it. And Bonner's crazy, he thought, and Hod's drunk and that leaves just me, don't it?

He squeezed off another shot, blew out an upstairs window this time. Bonner whooped. Mitch stared and fidgeted.

I'm in charge now, Adam thought. Yes, sir, I'm the real leader here. Give the orders, do things any way I want. Any way *I* want. Bust in there, drag Ryerson out, make him confess . . . even kill him if I want. Shoot him down like a dog if I want. And her? What about her? Nobody's said anything about her, but she's as bad as he is, helping him, protecting him, and all the time with her nose in the air like her shit don't stink— what about her? Do anything I want to *her*, too, when the time comes.

Do what I should of done to that bitch up in Lake Oswego. Put this baby's muzzle up against her head, let her feel cold steel against her head, make her beg a little . . . any damn thing I want!

Jan

He heard the second bullet whine and smash into the outside wall before he heard the shot boom. Riding the echoes of the shot was Alix's voice: "What's happening, what's going on?" Her face was white, the folds of the red shirt she clutched like splashes of blood against her breasts.

Jan grasped her hard by the shoulders, pushed her down to her knees. "Stay down!" He dropped down beside her, crawled quickly to the front door, raised up to throw the bolt lock. Then he swung back toward the window in the side wall. He was more angry than anything else at this moment, but the anger was muted by an almost detached calm. The emotional scene with Alix earlier had left him drained, incapable for the time being of fear or any other strong feeling.

Outside the voices were loud, excited, the words indistinguishable now. Jan reached for the lamp cord, yanked it out of the socket in the side wall, yanked the room into darkness. Under its protective cover, he pushed himself up into a standing crouch. Behind him he could hear Alix's breathing coming fast and ragged: she was on her knees alongside the couch.

He groped his way across the room. Alix heard him moving and said, "Where are you going?" Her voice shook but she sounded in control.

"Kitchen window. See who's out there."

He made his way into the kitchen. Light filtering through the window made a diffused wedge across the sink and the linoleum floor. He ducked under the sill of the window, came up on the far side, and leaned up over the drainboard to look past one corner of the curtain.

The sixty yards or so between the house and the parked station wagon were illuminated by the nightlight. Details close to the building—clumps of grass, the gravel of the path—stood out in sharp relief. Farther back, where the four men moved around in a ragged group, the shadows were longer and details were blurry, so that the figures had a kind of surreal, two-dimensional look.

Novotny was one of them. And Hod Barnett. And . . . Bonner? Yes, Seth Bonner, jumping around, letting out war whoops—drunk. All of them lynch-mob drunk. The fourth man was half-turned away from the window, but after a moment he shouted something and pivoted, and Jan recognized the village handyman, Adam Reese. There was a long-barreled rifle in Reese's hands, cradled across his chest military-fashion. Light gleamed off its metal surfaces. It was the only weapon Jan could see, but that didn't mean the rest of them weren't armed with handguns.

Then Reese swung the weapon up, aimed it at the house, aimed it straight at the kitchen window as if he knew Jan was there watching. Jan was already falling away, throwing his hands up over his head, when Reese fired. Glass burst above him and the bullet slashed through, screeched and thudded into the metal door of the refrigerator. Shards rained down, one of the sharp edges opening a stinging cut on the back of his left hand.

In the living room Alix was shrieking, "Jan! *Jan!*"

"I'm all right, stay there. Get on the phone—call the sheriff. Hurry!"

His glasses were askew; he pushed them back into place and scuttled away from the sink, cutting knees and palms on the broken glass, ignoring the pain. The pantry door . . . was it locked? He couldn't remember. Locked doors wouldn't keep them out, not for long, but just a few minutes might mean everything to Alix and him. On his feet again, he stumbled over the big carton of pots and pans and dishes she'd left on the floor, almost fell, regained his footing again.

One of the upstairs windows burst, the breaking-glass sounds lost in another echoing report from Adam Reese's rifle.

Jan's mouth was full of thick brassy-tasting saliva as he stumbled down the steps into the cloakroom. He got the pantry door open, groped his way across to the outside door, grasped the knob. Locked. But the fact brought only a small, fleeting relief. He pivoted away from the door, staggered back into the kitchen.

"Jan!"

In a crouch he moved over into the doorway, saw the shape of Alix come out of the darkness, felt her hands clutch at his arms.

"What is it? What happened?"

"The phone . . . it doesn't work. It's dead, Jan, the line is dead!"

Alix

"What are we going to do?"

The sound of her own voice frightened her even more than she already was: it trembled, wobbled, verged on a slow-building scream. Her chest was constricted, felt as though it might burst. Fear pounded a frantic rhythm in the hollow of her throat.

"Don't panic, for God's sake."

"They must have cut the telephone wires. . . ."

"If we panic, it's all over. You know that as well as I do. Stay calm."

She took several deep breaths with her mouth open wide; the last thing she needed now was to start hyperventilating. Outside she could hear shouts, whoops, lunatic laughter; she shut her ears against the sounds. And some of the constriction left her chest, the rising terror checked and then began to abate. The wild moment was over. She had her control back again.

"I'm okay," she said, and her voice no longer trembled on the edge of a shriek. "Better now. How many of them are there?"

"Four. Novotny, Barnett, Reese, and Seth Bonner. All of them drunk."

"Have they all got guns?"

"Reese has a rifle; he's the one who's been shooting. I couldn't tell about the others."

Reese . . . that evil, smirking little man. She suppressed a shiver, heard herself say, "We've got to protect ourselves."

"With what?"

"Knives. Butcher knives."

243

"Knives won't be much good against four armed men."

"They might not all be armed. Jan, we've got to have some kind of weapons. . . ."

"Okay. You're right."

He put his arm around her, turned her into the kitchen, bent her low under the sill of the window. Most of the glass had been ripped out of it by the rifle bullet, she saw; only a few shards, like broken snaggleteeth, remained in the frame. Fog blew in through the opening in gray wisps. Fog, and the icy wind, and the loud drunken voices of the four men out there.

"Did you pack the knives?" Jan said against her ear.

"Yes. In the carton with the pots and pans."

They found the carton, squatted beside it, began to rummage inside. Alix found the elongated newspaper-wrapped bundle that contained the butcher and carving knives. She pulled it from the carton, started to unwrap it.

Outside, Reese's rifle cracked again. Almost instantaneously there was a violent whooshing explosion—a thunderous roar that seemed to rock the house. And a mushrooming flash of light and flame turned the night beyond the broken window as bright as noon.

Mitch Novotny

Adam had blown up the Ryersons' station wagon. Drawn a bead on it with that 30.06 of his, put a bullet in the gas tank, and blown it sky-high.

They'd all backed off when they saw what he was going to do, Mitch dragging Hod by one arm. But the heat of the explosion had seared him anyway, driven him farther back; he could still feel it hot and pulsing against his face, still hear the thudding echo of the blast. The fireball had rolled up fifty feet or more, boiling through the fog, staining it bright orange, bright red at the edges like blood. The fire was still burning hot; in the center of it, the car was nothing but a black cinder shape. The flames hadn't reached any of the buildings yet, but the garage and the pumphouse were close by, and the wind was already swirling sparks like pinwheels through the darkness and the mist. The outbuildings could torch off any minute. The lighthouse too . . . with Ryerson and his wife in there.

Adam and Bonner were watching the car burn, Adam hopping from one foot to the other, Bonner letting out whoops like a goddamn Indian. Bonner was tetched in the head, they should never have brought him along, but Adam . . . it was like he'd gone crazy, too. All the shooting he'd done, blowing up the car like that, and now he was laughing, head thrown back and the laughter bubbling out of him like this was *fun*, like it was a party or something.

Christ, Mitch thought, it wasn't supposed to be like this. Come out here, get Ryerson, force him to talk, take him to Coos Bay—do what the fucking sheriff and state troopers wouldn't do. But this . . . all this . . . this wasn't the way it was supposed to be.

His head hurt; he felt woozy, sick to his stomach. Shouldn't have drunk all that whiskey. Shouldn't have come out here at all. But it seemed like the right thing to do . . . nobody else was doing anything, were they? Poor Mandy lying dead in her coffin . . . what Ryerson had done to the other girl . . . and Red, too . . . it *was* the thing to do, goddamn it. Ryerson was an animal, a mad dog. They had every right to be here, doing this. Every right. . . .

"Ryerson! We're coming in, Ryerson! You can't hide, you can't get away!"

It was Adam doing the yelling, just like before. Why? What was the sense in that? Don't talk about it, just do it.

"Don't talk about it, Adam," he called over the thrumming beat of the fire, "let's just do it."

"Damn right we're gonna do it."

"Bust down the door," Bonner yelled. "That's it, that's what we'll do, ain't it, Adam? Bust down the door."

"The door or one of the windows. Mitch, run back to the van, get that big six-cell of mine. They ain't got guns but maybe they got something else, knives or something. We don't want him coming out of the dark at us."

Mitch hesitated. "Let Seth get it."

"No, you got steadier hands. Hurry it up, Mitch, come on."

Who're you to give me orders? Mitch thought. But he didn't say it, didn't argue. The hell with arguing, just get it over with. He turned, ran back to where Adam's van was parked outside the lighthouse gate. He found the six-cell flashlight in the rear. Thought about looking for the bottle—he needed another drink, bad—and remembered they'd finished it on the way out here. He slammed the rear door, viciously, and ran back uphill with the flashlight.

Hod was down on one knee, puking into the grass. Mitch veered over to him, squatted, put his hand on Hod's shoulder. "Hod? You all right, buddy?"

"Sick," Hod muttered. "Jesus, what's going on?"

"I don't know," Mitch said. And he realized that he didn't, not anymore. He didn't know what the hell was going on.

"Mitch! Bring that six-cell!"

He didn't want to leave Hod, didn't want to break into the lighthouse after Ryerson, didn't want to do any of this anymore. But he had to. He couldn't stop himself now, it was too late. *Just get it over with.* He straightened, moved ahead to where Adam and Bonner were waiting, firelight dancing over their faces, making them look odd and unreal. Like strangers, men he'd never seen before.

The wind had kicked up, was blowing sparks in swirls and showers like some kind of crazy Fourth of July show. One corner of the garage was already starting to burn.

Jan

They were in the kitchen, backed up against the wall next to the cloakroom, Alix clinging to his arm. Through the broken window, he could see the four men moving around, backlit by the flames of the burning station wagon. The pulsing glow of the fire made the fog look like luminescent smoke, made it seem as if the very fabric of the night were burning.

"Jan, we can't just stay here—waiting."

Fear in her voice, tension, but no panic. She was good in a crisis, always had been. She wouldn't come apart. And him? What about him?

His fingers moved spasmodically around the blade of the butcher knife. He wanted to let go of it; it felt alien in his hand, no longer a tool, not even a weapon—more a symbol of menace that crackled as loudly as the fire out there. "We can't fight them," he said grimly. "Four against two. And they've got guns."

"We could go up in the tower . . . the lantern. That trapdoor is made of solid oak."

"I've been thinking the same thing. But not you, just me. You've got to get out of here before it's too late."

"Get out? There's no way. . . ."

"Yes there is."

"How?"

"By hiding down here while I make them think we've both gone up into the tower. They'll chase me, and when they do you get out through the pantry, run for help."

"Jan, I can't leave you here alone—"

"You've got to!" The urgency in his voice made it shrill. "Look at them out there. Listen to them. They're drunk, half crazy—capable of anything. Rape, and worse."

He felt her shudder. "Where can I hide that they wouldn't find me? One of them might look around down here. . . ."

He told her where. Felt her shudder again.

"No," she said, "I can't."

"You can and you will. It's our only chance."

"Can't we both hide?"

"No. They'd search, and if they searched long enough they'd find us."

"I still say we can both go up into the lantern. Someone will see the fire, someone will come. . . ."

"Not likely, not with the fog, not all the way in Hilliard. Besides, they blew up the car. What's to stop them from setting fire to the lighthouse?"

They were coming toward the house now, three of them in a tight little group, Reese with his rifle and Bonner with an ax handle he'd found somewhere and Novotny with a heavy-duty flashlight. They passed out of his line of vision—and then there was a sudden, savage banging on the front door. One of them began yelling obscenities. The door was solid-core, it might not yield, but then all they had to do was break out the glass in one of the windows and come in that way. If they weren't drunk they'd have thought of that already.

He swung Alix around to face him, kissed her hard on the mouth, pushed her away from him. "Hurry! Before it's too late!"

"Oh God, Jan, I love you. . . ."

"I love you too. Hurry!"

Hod Barnett

Bad dream. That was what it was, the worst kind of bad dream.

He kept backing away from the lighthouse, the fire, Mitch and Adam and Seth Bonner over at the door, pounding on the door, yelling and whooping. He was sick, confused. All that whiskey he'd drunk . . . the shooting . . . the explosion . . . His head was spinning, it wouldn't stop spinning.

He had to puke again. Went to one knee, emptied his stomach. It didn't help; he felt worse when he was done, weak and shaky. And they were still pounding, still yelling over there— Mitch and Adam and Bonner, his friends. What were they doing? It didn't make sense what they were doing.

He killed Mandy, Hod.

We got to go after him, Hod.

No, it was crazy. Crazy. He shouldn't be here, why was he here? Mandy in her grave a few hours, and here he was hog drunk, sick, the Ryersons' car all blown up and burning, garage burning, night full of fire and noise and crazy images . . . he couldn't stand it anymore, he had to shut it out, it was all just a bad dream.

He lurched away from the fence, stumbled out through the gate, ran until he got to Adam's van. Yanked open the door, threw himself across the seat inside. Lay on his belly with his hands over his ears to shut out the noise, his eyes squeezed tight to shut out all the swirling images.

Bad dream, whiskey dream. Sleep it off, wake up and find

out none of it happened, Mandy was still alive, everything was like it had always been, nothing had happened, *none of it had happened!*

Bad, bad dream . . .

Alix

The trapdoor banged shut above her and the darkness in the abandoned well was total.

She clung to the corroded iron rungs on the wall, her heart pounding wildly. She was afraid of losing her grip, of falling; afraid of what might be hidden below. Her arm brushed against the rough concrete and something slimy smeared off on it. Gooseflesh rippled; she gasped, sucking in dank, evil-smelling air that seemed to catch in her throat. She gasped again; her chest heaved but still she felt she was suffocating.

Then, from somewhere above, she heard a muffled crashing and splintering noise, male voices yelling in bloated triumph. They were inside the house. . . .

A hiccoughing sob came out of her, echoing in the black cavern. *Don't make noise! They'll hear you!*

Footsteps. Shouts.

"Ryerson, you cocksucker, where are you?"

"You can't hide. We'll find you!"

Her palms were wet, slipping on the rungs. Her right hand lost its grip, and she clutched frantically at the rung below; the violent motion dislodged her feet, pulled her other hand loose, and she fell with a stifled cry. Sharp objects tore into her buttocks, her back. She lay trembling, feeling claustrophobic, trying to breathe.

Something heavy fell somewhere inside the house. Footsteps drummed on the floor above. The shouting voices overlapped to form a continuous lusting bellow. Then one set of footsteps seemed to be coming this way, toward the pantry. She'd closed the door; now she heard it open, followed by a faint snapping sound. The light switch? She looked up and saw lines of light, the faint outline of the trapdoor.

The carpet! She hadn't put the carpet back!

She'd pulled the square of it up in a panic, tearing her finger-nails, ripping it from around the tacks that held it down. Grabbed the metal ring on the floor and yanked the trapdoor open. And then stood there, looking down into the fetid cavern, her flesh crawling, unable to move. She'd had to fight off panic to make herself climb into the well, had done it in a single scrambling motion that took her down the rungs and brought the door down so quickly it had almost banged her head. It had never even occurred to her to replace the carpet. . . .

She got up on her haunches, ignoring the pain in her buttocks and back. The knife—what had happened to the knife? She'd had it when she entered the pantry. Had she set it down when she ripped up the carpet? Dropped it climbing into the well? All she knew was she didn't have it now.

In a frenzy she felt around her feet, then to either side. Her fingers encountered rocks, pieces of glass and metal. Recoiled from something damp and spongy. Didn't find the knife. Didn't find anything that could serve as a weapon—

Hard footsteps in the room above.

Oh God, they've seen the trapdoor!

And a voice shouted distantly, "I hear 'em! They're up in the tower!"

"Adam! Come on!"

Overhead the footfalls turned abruptly, started away. In the dim light from the low-wattage bulb, whoever it was *hadn't* seen the square of carpet or the iron ring. She was still safe.

She let out a sobbing sigh, moved over to the wall, and found the rungs and started to climb them. Twice before she reached the door she had to stop and dry first one hand and then the other on her pants legs. She listened. The footfalls were gone; all the sounds she could hear were muffled by distance. She pushed at the door. It was heavy and resisted; she heaved at it, almost losing her balance. It rose a few inches, then fell back.

What if I'm trapped in here?

She heaved again, her breath coming in ragged gasps. This time the door moved about a foot. She jammed her arm into the space just before the heavy wood fell back again. Pain shot through her elbow; she almost bit through her lip stifling a cry.

The trapped arm braced her. She moved onto the top rungs so that her hunched shoulders were wedged against the door. Then she shoved upward with the strength of her whole body—and the door lifted, fell backwards against its hinge stops.

She scrambled through the opening onto the pantry floor. Knelt there for a moment, listening. They were all in the living room, shouting, beating on the tower door. And in the next instant she was up and running to the outside door, dragging it open, stumbling over the jamb, almost falling headlong as she plunged out into the fog-shrouded night.

Jan

When he locked the downstairs door behind him and pounded up the tower stairs, he had no clear idea of what he was going to do. But by the time he reached the second-floor landing he did have an idea—a dangerous one, a last resort to be undertaken only if the situation became desperate enough. But even if he didn't implement it, preparing for it was better than just sitting up in the lantern, waiting for Alix to bring help, waiting for God knew what to happen.

He ran into the cluttered bedroom, through it to the bathroom. Packing box on the floor, half full of sundries and items from the medicine cabinet. He rummaged inside, found the bag of cotton balls Alix kept in there. Back in the bedroom, he began pulling the pillows and blankets and comforters off the bed, wadding them under his arm. All the while he could hear them down below—inside the house now, yelling, running around, hammering on the locked tower door.

Please, God, don't let them find Alix.

He ran out onto the landing, trailing bedding, almost tripping on it. He made as much noise as he could running up the stairs and through the open trap, releasing the catch and letting the door slam shut. He knelt to throw the locking bolt, then straightened and pounded up the rest of the way.

Inside the lantern he dropped the cotton and the bedding, went to the glass side that overlooked the grounds. The station wagon was still burning, though with less intensity now, but the garage had caught fire, a blaze that was spreading rapidly under the lash of the wind. Sparks danced and swirled in the mist. If the wind turned gusty, blew sparks and burning embers this way . . .

His head had begun to hurt—not badly yet, thank God. He pressed his thumbs hard against the upper ridges of his eye sockets, then stood staring down toward the pantry door in the side wall. Get out, he thought, come on, *get out!*

And the door popped open and Alix stumbled into view, looked around, started to run.

He watched tensely, but when she reached the gate and nobody else appeared, he felt the first stirrings of relief. And something else, too—a realization that he was no longer afraid.

So much fear had been stored up inside him the past few months, irrational and unnecessary, growing, festering, coloring his judgment, controlling his thoughts and actions; but now it had been purged, bled out of him by a simple act of confession, a simple acceptance of what should have been self-evident all along. How could he have thought he couldn't depend on her?

He leaned against the glass, watching her until she was fifty yards along the road, running into the gray wall of fog—running away but not from him. When he could no longer see her he turned toward the stairs, his hands clenched at his sides. He was ready now.

For the first time since he'd learned of his coming blindness he was ready to fight.

Adam Reese

When Adam came back into the front room the lights were blazing—Mitch or Bonner had found out what was wrong and got them working again—and the two of them were over at a closed door in the inner wall. Mitch was rattling the knob. Bonner was standing there yelling.

"They're up in the tower, Adam! They went up in the tower and locked this door behind 'em!"

"Break it down, then."

"Solid-core like the front one," Mitch said. "We'll need something heavy."

"Couch over there. We'll use it for a battering ram."

They picked up the couch, Adam and Bonner on one side, Mitch on the other, and brought it over and started slamming the end of it against the door. It creaked, groaned, bowed in a little. But it wouldn't give—bastard wouldn't *give*.

Adam felt wild inside, kind of lightheaded with the need to get up there, get his hands on Ryerson and the woman. Do anything he wanted with them, both of them, if he could just get *up* there. "Harder!" he yelled at the other two. "Slam it in there! Slam it in there!"

It took them six more tries, working in a frenzy now, before the wood began to splinter, the lock began to bust loose from the frame. Two more slams and the fucker finally burst inward. Bonner let out one of his whoops. They dropped the couch, shoved it back out of the way, and Adam fought past the other two, got through the doorway first and pounded up the stairs with the Springfield pointed up ahead of him like a hard-on.

"Ryerson! We're coming, Ryerson!"

On the second floor he poked open one door, another. Both rooms were empty. Bonner was on the landing now; he'd taken the six-cell from Mitch and was aiming its beam up the rest of the stairs.

"Bet they went all the way up, Adam. Into the lantern. That's what I'd do if I was them."

"There a way to lock themselves up there?"

"Trapdoor. It's a heavy bugger."

"You and Mitch go up and look. I'll make sure they ain't hiding around here."

Bonner nodded, grinning, and he and Mitch ran on up into the tower. The light was on in one of the rooms—bedroom where they slept, looked like—and Adam turned in there, heading for the bathroom on the far side. But he stopped before he got there. Came up short next to the window.

Somebody was moving out there, down past his van, down on the road—running like hell along the road.

The woman, Mrs. Ryerson.

He could see her plain as day in the fireglow from the burning car, the burning garage. Hair flying, legs pumping, trying to get away. Trying to get help.

Adam spun away from the window, his lips pulled flat against his teeth, and ran out onto the landing. Up in the tower Bonner yelled, "Adam? I was right, they're up there! I can hear 'em—and the trapdoor's locked tight!"

"Find a way to bust it in," Adam yelled back. But he didn't go up there, and he didn't hesitate: he ran downstairs instead, across the front room, outside.

Ryerson could wait. Let the others have Ryerson. It was the woman he wanted.

Alix

She ran along the cape road, her tennis shoes slapping against its bumpy surface. The chill air tore at the membranes of her mouth and nose, seemed to pierce her lungs. The pain in her back where she'd hurt it falling in the well was nothing compared to the searing that had started up in her left side.

A deep rut threw her stride off. She stumbled, went to one knee, felt the rocks scrape through her jeans. Got up, kept running. Her breath came in loud gasps; her lungs ached; blood pounded in her head in counterpoint to the wild beating of her heart. She couldn't have run more than half a mile, and already she was winded.

She drew her flailing hands in toward her upper body, the way she'd seen runners do. Help was a long way off; she had to conserve energy, eliminate unnecessary motion. She was in good condition from her aerobics at home. It was just a matter of pacing herself.

Her feet took up a ragged rhythm. Gradually her breathing came under control. The road cut through a stand of trees, and when she got in among them she couldn't see anything; she slowed to a walk, bent over, peering at the ground to keep from stepping into a pothole, spraining an ankle or worse.

When she came out of the trees, fog blew around her like snow. She could see the road surfaces better here, and once more she started to run. Surprisingly, her fear had subsided. Or maybe she was just becoming numb—

Sound behind her, a deep-throated rumbling.

Motor sound.

Car coming from the lighthouse.

She twisted her upper body, trying to see back along the road without slackening her pace. No headlights were visible, but the trees screened her vision. The growl of the car engine was louder now, coming fast.

Fear rekindled inside her, flared high. One or more of them must have seen her escape, were coming after her. In a matter of seconds the car would be clear of the trees. . . .

She veered sharply to her left, plunged off the road, all but flung herself over a wooden fence. Fell, got up. And ran headlong across the open field beyond.

Mitch Novotny

Bonner kept yelling, "Son of a bitch! Son of a bitch!" and beating on the trapdoor with that ax handle he'd found. He sounded wild, out of his head. Like Adam. Like all of them.

Adam . . . why wasn't he here? Disappeared all of a sudden, ran downstairs a while ago and never came back. Where was he?

"Son of a bitch!"

"Shut up, Seth, will you shut up! Quit beating on that door!"

Bonner stopped his hammering. From up in the tower, then, Mitch could hear noises—scraping sounds, as if something heavy were being dragged across the floor; hard footfalls on the stairs.

"Listen to that," Bonner said. "They're up to something. We got to get up there, Mitch."

"How? That trap's made of solid oak."

"Get a tool, crowbar or something. Might be able to wedge a bar up in there and snap the lock."

"We haven't got a crowbar. . . ."

"One in Adam's van," Bonner said. He was so excited, spit came spraying out with every word. "I seen it, Mitch. I'll run down and get it."

Adam's van. Adam. Where the hell *was* he?

"No," Mitch said, "I'll go. You stay here."

Up in the tower, there was a loud thumping. Then a sliding, dragging, slithering sound—something heavy and loose being hauled up the stairs.

"No telling what them damn people are up to. We got to get up there, Mitch!"

Mitch turned his body in the cramped space, started down the stairs. He was almost to the bottom when Bonner yelled, "Son of a bitch!" again and beat another tattoo on the trap with that fucking ax handle.

Alix

She ran through the night in a haze of terror.

Staggering, stumbling, losing her balance and falling sometimes because the terrain was rough and there was no light of any kind except for the bloody glow of the flames that stained the fog-streaked sky far behind her. The muscles in her legs were knotted so tightly that each new step brought a slash of pain. Her breath came in ragged, explosive pants; the thunder of blood in her ears obliterated the moaning cry of the wind. She could no longer feel the cold through the bulky sweater she wore, was no longer aware of the numbness in her face and hands. She felt only the terror, was aware only of the need to run and keep on running.

He was still behind her. Somewhere close behind her.

On foot now, just as she was; he had left the car some time ago, back when she had started across the long sloping meadow. There had been nowhere else for her to go then, no place to conceal herself: the meadow was barren, treeless. She'd looked back, seen the car skid to a stop, and he'd gotten out and raced toward her. He had almost caught her then. Almost caught her another time, too, when she'd had to climb one of the fences and a leg of her Levi's had got hung up on a rail splinter.

If he caught her, she was sure he would kill her.

She had no idea how long she had been running. Or how far she'd come. Or how far she still had left to go. She had lost all sense of time and place. Everything was unreal, nightmarish, distorted shapes looming around her, ahead of her—all of the night twisted and grotesque and charged with menace.

She looked over her shoulder again as she ran. She couldn't see him now; there were trees behind her, tall bushes. Above the trees, the flames licked higher, shone brighter against the dark fabric of the night.

Trees ahead of her, too, a wide grove of them. She tried to make herself run faster, to get into their thick clotted shadow; something caught at her foot, pitched her forward onto her hands and knees. She barely felt the impact, felt instead a wrenching fear that she might have turned her ankle, hurt herself so that she couldn't run anymore. Then she was up and moving again, as if nothing had happened to interrupt her flight—and then there was a longer period of blankness, of lost time, and the next thing she knew she was in among the trees, dodging around their trunks and through a ground cover of ferns and high grass. Branches seemed to reach for her, to pluck at her clothing and her bare skin like dry, bony hands. She almost blundered into a half-hidden deadfall; veered away in time and stumbled on.

Her foot came down on a brittle fallen limb, and it made a cracking sound as loud as a pistol shot. A thought swam out of the numbness in her mind: Hide! He'll catch you once you're out in the open again. Hide!

But there was no place safe enough, nowhere that he couldn't find her. The trees grew wide apart here, and the ground cover was not dense enough for her to burrow under or behind any of it. He would hear her. She could hear him, back there somewhere—or believed she could, even above the voice of the wind and the rasp of her breathing and the stuttering beat of her heart.

Something snagged her foot again. She almost fell, caught her balance against the bole of a tree. Sweat streamed down into her eyes; she wiped it away, trying to peer ahead. And there was more lost time, and all at once she was clear of the woods and ahead of her lay another meadow, barren, with the cliffs far off on one side and the road winding emptily on the other. Everything out there lay open, naked—no cover of any kind in any direction.

She had no choice. She plunged ahead without even slowing.

It was a long time, or what she perceived as a long time, before she looked back. And he was there, just as she had known he would be, relentless and implacable, coming after her like one of the evil creatures in a Grimm's fairy tale.

She felt herself staggering erratically, slowing down. Her

wind and her strength seemed to be giving out at the same time.
I can't run much farther, she thought, and tasted the terror, and
kept running.

Out of the fear and a sudden overwhelming surge of hope-
lessness, another thought came to her: How can this be happening? How did it all come to this?

Dear God, Jan, how did it all come to this? . . .

Jan

At first he thought the air hose wouldn't be long enough. But
then he got it uncoiled and all the way up into the lantern, and
he found that it *was* long enough, by at least a couple of feet.
He paused to wipe the sweat from his forehead, and to listen to
the shouting and banging below the trap. It seemed to be just
one voice now—Seth Bonner's. Were the others still down
there with him? Or were they up to something else?

I'm going to have to go through with it, he thought.

He moved sideways to the glass wall, looked out. Two-thirds
of the garage was burning now, but so far the wind hadn't
spread it any farther. He scanned the area for some sign of the
other men; but his headache was worsening and now his vision
had started to kick in and out of focus, especially when he tried
to look at anything in the distance. If they were out there, where
were they? *Up to something, damn it.* The thought freshened his
sense of urgency, drove him away from the glass and down the
stairs again to the lightroom.

He had anchored the diaphone in the doorway, using the barrel of fire sand to wedge it against the jamb with its flanged
mouth pointing downward. He'd loosely connected the air line;

now he tightened the connection. Straightening again, he stepped over the diaphone and lifted the heavy bulk of the compressor. Struggled with it up the stairs into the lantern.

When he set the compressor down he found himself looking at the Fresnel lens. And he felt twinges of both pain and reluctance. The vibration, even using the smallest possible volume of air, would be tremendous—enough to shatter every prism and bull's-eye in the lens. Shatter all the glass in the lantern walls, too. And the noise, trapped in the confines of the tower . . . it might burst *his* eardrums as well as those of the men below. He had the cotton and the pillows and bedclothes for protection, but there was no guarantee he wouldn't be deafened, or hurt by flying glass or in some other way. And what if all four weren't inside the lighthouse when he was ready?

Too dangerous, he thought grimly. Too problematical. Keep waiting . . . do it only if the situation becomes critical.

But suppose I don't know it's critical until too late?

Goddamn them, what are they up to?

And he thought again: Sooner or later I'm going to have to go through with it.

Mitch Novotny

Adam's van was gone.

Mitch saw that as soon as he came out of the lighthouse, into the cold of the wind and the smoky heat of the fires. It made him angry and scared and sick to his stomach, all at the same time. Adam had run out on them, that was plain. But why? He'd been the one who'd shimmied up the pole to cut the telephone wires; he'd been doing all the shooting, giving most of the orders. And then all of a sudden he'd just up and quit on them. It didn't make sense.

Mitch's head was throbbing, and the oily smell of the smoke wasn't helping it any; he couldn't think straight. He looked over his shoulder at the lighthouse. One thing he knew—he wasn't going back in there. Crazy Bonner yelling, pounding with his ax handle . . . he couldn't take any more of it, the hell with Bonner, the hell with Ryerson. It was all crazy, none of it made any sense. And now Adam was gone . . . the hell with him too. And Hod, where was Hod? Gone with Adam?

I got to get out of here myself, he thought.

And all of a sudden the wind was like a hand shoving him, prodding him into a fast walk, a trot, a run—away from the lighthouse, through the gate, onto the road. He ran past the spot where Adam's van had been, the wind pushing him into a stagger, and when he regained his balance he saw the dark shape in the grass, somebody lying there in the grass. He slowed, fighting the wind and his fear, and veered over there. He still had the six-cell flashlight in his hand, he realized then; he switched it on, shined it down.

It was Hod. Lying in the grass like a bundle of something that had been thrown away. At first, Mitch thought he was dead. But he wasn't dead—just dead-drunk, passed out. He moaned when Mitch pulled him up by one arm, slapped his face.

"Hod, you hear me? Hod?"

No answer, just another groan.

"Come on, Hod, wake up, get on your feet. We got to get out of here!"

Hod just lay there, groaning, his eyes shut tight and his head rolling on his neck like it was busted. There was puke all over the front of him.

"Hod! I can't carry you, goddamn it!"

Mitch slapped him again. Again. Again. It didn't do any

good. Hod wasn't going to wake up, wouldn't be able to walk if he did. He didn't even know who he was.

Can't just leave him here like this, Mitch thought. He's my friend, been my friend a lot of years. Can't leave him like Adam left me, that fucking Adam. . . .

But the wind was pushing at him again, harder now, and the next thing it had him on his feet, it had him rushing down the road. Wouldn't let him stop, wouldn't let him look back, wouldn't even let him think anymore.

Run, Mitch! it kept shrieking in his ears. Run, run, *run!*

Alix

She scrambled into the ditch beside the cape road, some fifty yards from its junction with the county road. Knelt there in the tall wet grass to catch her breath. When she could breathe without gasping she crawled back up to where she could look around. The county road, hazed in fog, was deserted in both directions: no help there. But nothing moved, either, back the way she'd come. She must have lost him. Where or when or how she wasn't sure. One minute he'd been behind her as she'd fled, skirting high clumps of gorse; the next he'd been gone. But the realization brought no release of tension. He could reappear again any second—closer than he'd been before, close enough to use that rifle he was carrying.

She was sure it was Adam Reese who was after her. Back at the light, the handyman had been the one with the rifle; and twice during her flight she'd seen it cradled across her pursuer's chest. He moved, too, in Reese's peculiar, hopping gait. She would have been less terrified if it had been Novotny or one of the others. There was something evil about the little man. If he caught her . . .

But he wasn't going to. He mustn't.

Several hundred yards to the south was the rest area and telephone booth. But the booth was out in the open, and even if she managed to complete an emergency call, she didn't want to risk hiding there in the dark woods to wait for the authorities. Much better, much safer was Cassie Lang's. It was the closest house, not more than a fifth of a mile from where she was. The ditch extended to within thirty yards or so of the junction, then angled to the north to roughly parallel the county road into Hilliard. If she heard or saw a car, she could jump out and hail it . . . no, there was no telling who might be behind the wheel, it could be one of Novotny or Reese's friends . . . better to just go on to Cassie's, call the sheriff and the state police from there.

She moved along the ditch, in a crouch where the banks were high, on her hands and knees where they were low. There was standing water in its bottom, but her numbed limbs barely registered the cold. Now and then she caught for balance at the sparse vegetation that grew there; nettles and sawgrass cut into her hands. She barely felt that, either.

From time to time she stopped, held herself still and listened. It was very quiet, eerily so. She couldn't take reassurance from the silence; Reese could be anywhere close by. Finally, after what seemed an interminable time, she judged she had gone far enough and crawled up the east bank and risked another look around.

Cassie's house was still two hundred yards away, tall and dark, forbidding in its garlands of fog. The gallery and garage squatted nearby, also devoid of light. The branches of the cypress windbreak between the house and garage cast twisted shadows across the driveway.

The best place to leave the ditch and make her run for the

house, she decided, would be at the edge of the gallery parking area. She slid back down to the bottom of the ditch and continued her walk-and-crawl through the damp vegetation. The next time she checked her position, she found she was only a few yards from where she wanted to be.

She studied the layout of the three buildings carefully. In one short sprint she could be out of sight in the shadows alongside the gallery. And from there it was only thirty yards or so to Cassie's front porch.

She moved ahead a short ways. Listened again, but heard nothing. And scrambled up the side of the ditch, ran in a crouch to the edge of the parking area, then across that seemingly endless open space to the gallery. In its shelter, she leaned against the wall, panting, listening again.

The wind in the trees, nothing more.

She eased along the wall, peered around the corner toward the house. All the windows were dark. Was Cassie asleep this early? Or out somewhere for the evening? God, if she wasn't home . . .

No use speculating. She looked back the way she'd come, out across the headland. Nothing moved there or anywhere else, except for trees or bushes under the bluster of the wind. Still, the coppery taste of fear remained sharp in her mouth. She studied the wide expanse of lawn again, stared intently at the front of the house and the cypress windbreak beyond. Then, taking a breath, she ran across the empty space and into the concealing shrubbery along the front porch.

The leaves of the thick bushes were wet. They dripped moisture on her as she slipped through them to the steps, half crawled onto the porch, and leaned up to press the doorbell. Chimes rang inside the house. She waited tensely, casting furtive looks over her shoulder.

No response.

She tried the bell again. Again. The echo was hollow, as if
the house were empty not only of people but of furniture. Cassie
must be out. God, now what?

She tried the doorknob. Locked. And the door itself was solid
oak, hung on heavy iron hinges. She glanced to the left, where
a big curtained window overlooked the porch. She could smash
it, climb inside, use the phone—

No. The sound of shattering glass was loud and would carry a
good distance. Besides, it would take time to remove enough
glass to get inside without badly cutting herself. And she had no
idea where Cassie kept her phone, how the house was laid out;
she would have to turn on a light to find out. And if the shattering glass didn't alert Reese, the light probably would.

Do *something!* she told herself. You can't keep crouching
here on the porch. Go out on the road, run for the next house?
No. The nearest house was another fifth of a mile away and she
would be exposed out on the road, with no place to hide. Where
then?

The garage? she thought. Was it possible there was a telephone in Cassie's garage? Not likely; but some people kept
phones in garages. Or spare keys to the house. Or maybe she'd
gone out with somebody else and her car was there. . . .

Alix hurried down the steps, ran to the cypress windbreak.
Beyond, the sagging roofline of the garage stood outlined
against the gray-black sky. The garage had big double doors,
but they were exposed, and even if they were unlocked they
might make noise when she tried to open them. But on one side
. . . was that a regular door? Yes; and it hung partway open.

She dashed from the shelter of the trees, not chancing another
look around. Ran through the narrow opening of the door and
stumbled, catching for balance at the frame. It was unrelievedly
black inside the garage, and the air was musty—redolent of dry
rot, motor oil, and something organic like fertilizer. She stood

with her hand against the splintery frame, waiting for her eyes to adjust to the deeper black. And when they did, she made out the humpbacked shape of Cassie's old car.

She rushed toward it, bumping against what felt like a pile of cordwood, dislodging one of the pieces so that it clattered dully on the floor—a sound that wouldn't carry much beyond the confines of the garage. When she yanked open the driver's door, the dome light came on. That allowed her to see that the ignition was empty. But she'd expected that; what she had to look for was one of those little magnetic spare-key boxes that people kept under dashes or inside tire wells or behind bumpers.

She crawled in behind the wheel, bent forward to search beneath the dash. As she did so, something on the floor caught her eye—a flash of bright color against the worn rubber floor mat. Then the color registered as electric-blue, and she stared at the object, identified it as a long piece of leather tipped with beads.

Her skin prickled with sudden cold. She reached down, felt under the seat, unhooked the leather from where it was jammed on the height-adjustment lever. Held it up to the pale dome light.

An Indian headband.

Mandy Barnett's headband, missing from the wildly disheveled red curls when she had found the girl's body.

She felt her lips part, form the word "Oh," but heard no sound. She raised her eyes, stared out at the hood of the car. She couldn't tell the color in the gloom, but she remembered it was an olive color. Dark-green. And Sinclair had told her it was a dark-green car that had run Mandy and her bicycle off the road. . . .

The silence in the garage seemed to hum around her. She could hear her own breath coming in short, swift intakes. Her hand, clutching the headband, grew moist.

There was no way the headband could have come to be there

unless it had been carried in by Mandy's murderer. Carried unwittingly, no doubt, caught in a pocket or a trouser cuff or on some other article of clothing. And it had lain unnoticed for days—until now.

"Cassie?" she said aloud. "Dear Lord, *Cassie?*"

And yet the evidence in her hand seemed irrefutable—one nightmare piled on top of another.

It was Cassie Lang who had strangled Mandy Barnett.

Adam Reese

He saw her crossing from the trees alongside the Lang woman's house to the garage nearby.

The sight of her moving silhouette brought him up short, flattened his lips against his teeth. He was back in the trees maybe a hundred yards away, just about to come out of them, frustrated as hell because it seemed she'd got clean away after he'd chased her all that distance from the lighthouse—on foot, in the van once he'd pulled Hod out of it, on foot again, seeing her, losing her in the trees and fog, seeing her, losing her. . . . Christ! Scared, too, by then, because what if she got to a phone or woke somebody up and told them?

But now . . . now he'd seen her again, knew right where she was: inside that garage, went right inside that garage. Hadn't roused nobody at the house; it was still dark. Nobody home. Nobody around anywhere. Went into the garage to hide, maybe. Or look for a weapon or the Lang woman's car. Well, she wouldn't find nothing in there, least of all a place to hide. All she'd find, pretty soon, was him.

He left the woods, moving slow, watching the side door,

thinking about what he was going to do when he got in there with her, feeling the excitement build again down low in his belly. Oh, he wanted her bad, real bad. And the queer thing was, he knew the Springfield did too, like it was telling him so, like it was something alive and hungry in his hands.

Jan

He was ready—the air hose connected to both the diaphone and the compressor, the cotton in one hand, the pillows and blankets in the other. All that remained was to swaddle and insulate himself against the noise and vibration, lie on the floor, reach out a hand to open the air valve on the compressor. He was ready.

And he couldn't do it. No matter what happened here, he couldn't do it. Not because of what it might do to him; because of what it would surely do to the light, the Fresnel lens.

A hell of a thing to be worrying about at a time like this, and yet the thought of destroying all those carefully cut and polished prisms and bull's-eyes had been like a canker all along, paining him, filling him with revulsion. It would be like willfully destroying a rare painting or sculpture, something old and beautiful and virtually irreplaceable. In a fundamental way it would reduce him to the level of those animals down below. Fighting them, hurting them, wasn't worth the price of the Fresnel, and it wasn't worth the price of his own humanity. There had to be another way.

He threw the bedding down, turned to the window glass again. The pain behind his eyes was worsening, not to the critical point yet but not far from it either. He pressed his forehead against the chilled glass, squinting, blinking, trying to bring the grounds and the terrain beyond into focus.

Somebody was running on the road.

Not toward the lighthouse; away from it. A man. One of the invaders? He couldn't tell, couldn't see clearly enough. Running . . . why?

His vision cleared completely for a few seconds, the way it did at intervals, and he realized the van was gone. Reese's van, the one they'd all come in. It had been parked out there beyond the fence; he'd seen it earlier. Now it was gone.

And the man was running . . . running away, was that it? One drunken vigilante giving up his act of terrorism?

Or was he running *after* something, someone?

Alix, he thought.

He peered harder through the glass. Couldn't see anything in the distance; the clarity was gone as suddenly as it had come and the distance was just a blur. The running man had become part of the blur: gone.

Jan struggled to think logically. Alix had been gone at least half an hour, more like an hour; the running man *couldn't* be chasing her, not after all this time. But the van . . . how long had it been gone? He didn't know, couldn't remember the last time he'd seen it.

Maybe they're not up to something, he thought. Maybe the running man is running because he's running away.

The words chased themselves around inside his mind like a nonsense jingle. But they weren't nonsense; they were a statement of fact. He wouldn't let himself believe otherwise. The running man is running because he's running away.

And somebody else drove the van away.

And there had only been four of them to begin with.

How many are still here?

He pushed away from the glass, went to the edge of the stairs. Bonner was still shouting obscenities below the trap, still pounding on it—but not so loudly or so often now, as if he were winding down. Jan listened. Bonner's was the only voice, had been for some time. Hadn't it? Yes, he was sure it had.

Just Bonner left, then? Or was somebody with him, somebody who didn't make noise?

If it's Bonner alone, he thought, I can handle him. There's a way . . . there's a way. Have to do it quickly, though, before the pain and my vision get any worse. No time to waste—make a decision!

It's just Bonner, he thought, and started quietly down the stairs.

Alix

Her mouth was dry now. When she tried to swallow her throat spasmed and she felt as if she were choking.

Why? she thought. What earthly reason would Cassie have had to kill Mandy Barnett? Or that other girl, that hitchhiker . . . she *must* have been responsible for that murder, too, because of the similarities of the crimes—

Never mind that now. Jan, think of Jan. You've got to get help for him.

Hastily, she felt under the dash for a spare-key case, found none, and tried the glove compartment. Nothing there, either. She backed out of the car, started to shut the door.

Something made a sound behind her—a shuffling movement.

She whirled, saw someone move in through the shadows from the open side door. Her pulse accelerated; a cry rose still-born in her throat.

It's Reese, he's found me!

But it wasn't Adam Reese. The figure stepped to one side just as Alix threw the door shut to cut off the dome light, and before she could move away from the car, find a place to hide, a single naked ceiling bulb burst into light. And she was facing the tall wiry figure of Cassie Lang.

The gallery owner stood flat-footed, wrapped in a dark bathrobe, a look of surprise and dismay on her face. In her right hand she was holding a long-barreled pistol. "Alix! What on earth . . ."

Then, as Alix flattened back against the cold metal of the car, Cassie saw the beaded headband that was still clutched in her hand. The surprise vanished and a different look, one of grim despair, replaced it. She raised the pistol, pointed it at Alix, bringing her left hand up to steady the weapon.

"So you know," she said.

Alix licked at papery lips, tried to speak. But no sound came out.

Cassie stared at her along the barrel of the gun. Her stance was that of someone familiar with handguns, the "good shot" she'd once claimed to be—feet apart, weight evenly balanced, hands and arms and weapon steady. But her eyes . . . they were like windows in a house where neither lights nor fire burned. No one lived there anymore. No one to appeal to for mercy.

But Alix wouldn't beg for her life, not even if begging would save her. She'd fight, she'd use the only weapon she had now: words. She swallowed, made herself speak, willed her voice to be steady as she did so. "You don't want to shoot me, Cassie. We're friends . . . I thought we were friends."

No response, not even a headshake.

"You must have had a good reason for . . . for what you did. I'm your friend, I can help you—"

"No one can help me anymore." Flat voice, emotionless. "I have no friends."

"Not among the villagers, no. I know how those people are, they despise me too just because I'm an outsider—"

"Outsider. Yes, that's right, that's what I am."

Keep her talking, Alix thought, try to get her to put the gun down. Or distract her, try to take it away from her.

Cassie said, "You're afraid."

"Of course I'm afraid. You're pointing that gun at me. You're the second person who's done that tonight."

"Second person?"

"The other one is Adam Reese. He's outside somewhere, not far from here, and he has a rifle. That's why I came in here, Cassie. I was afraid he'd shoot me."

Cassie was frowning. "Do you expect me to believe that?"

"It's the truth! He and Mitch Notovny and Hod Barnett and Seth Bonner showed up at the lighthouse tonight, crazy drunk. Reese shot out the windows, blew up our car, broke in—"

"I don't believe you."

"Why would I lie? They tried to kill us, Cassie, I swear it to you. I got out, ran for help, but my husband's still trapped out there. I've got to call the state police. Won't you let me do that?"

"No!"

The gun wavered, and for a sickening instant Alix thought Cassie would fire. Then the woman's head jerked slightly to one side, as if she might have heard something outside. She listened for only a moment, but when she again gave her full attention to Alix, the critical moment had passed.

"I don't believe you," she repeated. "You think you can put me off my guard. Why would those men do things like that?"

"They've been harassing us for a week, trying to force us to leave the lighthouse—all sorts of ugly tricks. Now . . . I think they believe it was my husband who killed Mandy."

Cassie was silent.

Alix said softly, "Why, Cassie? Why did you do it?"

"Why? She wanted too much, that's why. The first time she came here and said she knew about Miranda, I gave her the five hundred dollars she asked for. She said she'd go away, but she didn't. She came back for more."

Miranda, Alix thought. According to the newspaper stories, that had been the name of the murdered hitchhiker—Miranda Collins. Then she remembered another fact from the news stories: Miranda had been a student at the University of Oregon. The university located in Eugene, Cassie's former home. The university where her former husband had taught.

"Mandy knew you'd killed Miranda," Alix said. "That's it, isn't it? That's why she tried to blackmail you."

"She saw me put Miranda's body out on the cape that night. God knows why *she* was out there. Wild little thing. She should have known better."

Yes, Alix thought, she *should* have known better. But Mandy had wanted so desperately to get out of Hilliard, and her attempt to extort money from Alix—the information she'd wanted to sell must have been nothing more than things she'd overheard Novotny and her father and the others plotting to do against the outsiders at the lighthouse. How foolish she'd been. And how dearly she'd paid for her foolishness.

Alix said, "How much more did Mandy want?"

"A thousand dollars. I don't have that much money. I told her that when she came here the other night, while I was working late at the gallery. But she didn't believe me, oh no. She pranced around in there, saying I must have money, look at all the expensive artwork for sale, and then she started batting the windchimes, tossing one of the big driftwood birds in the air, and she dropped the bird and it broke one of my nice chambered nautiluses. I couldn't let her get away with that. I took her by the throat, I slapped her, I told her I'd kill *her* if she didn't leave me alone. It scared her. She pulled away and went running out of the shop."

It must have been immediately afterward that the girl had called the lighthouse, probably from the phone booth at the rest area down the road. By then she'd realized she had mixed herself up in something she couldn't handle. She'd been afraid to talk to her parents about what she'd done; she couldn't call the police because it would have meant confessing to blackmail. So in her panic she'd called the one person she thought might help her, might perhaps give her the extra money she felt she needed to leave Hilliard—the woman who hadn't turned her in for attempted extortion, Alix Ryerson.

"You didn't go after her right away?"

"I didn't go after her at all," Cassie said. "No, I just wanted to get out for a while, go for a drive, try to think. But there she was, pedaling along the cape road; I could see the reflector lights on her bicycle. Even then I didn't follow her, not for a while. Then I thought, why not go out there and talk to her, try to reason with her again about the extra thousand dollars. So I did. I didn't intend to hurt her. It just happened, that's all, like it did with Miranda."

The woman's expression was distracted now, her gaze jumpy. But the pistol was still steady in her two hands. Alix desperately wondered how far she could push her. And yet she had to keep trying, had to find some way to either make her surrender the weapon or try to take it away from her. Jan's life as well as her own might depend on it.

"Did Miranda want money too?" she asked. "Is that why you killed her?"

The question seemed to surprise Cassie. "Money? Oh, I suppose it would have come to that. What she *claimed* she wanted when she showed up here was advice. Advice, help, succor, sympathy. She wanted to keep the baby, she wanted Ron to pay child support. She thought I might be able to give her some . . . what did she call it? Insight. Some insight into how to get him to acknowledge her—that was the word she used, *acknowledge* her and the baby.''

Now Alix remembered two more seemingly unrelated facts. Miranda Collins had been four months pregnant when she died. And Cassie's ex-husband, the anthropology professor who had a weakness for coeds, was named Ron.

''She'd been sleeping with Ron for two years, the little bitch,'' Cassie said. ''All very secret, of course, because he was such a *fine, upstanding* faculty member. Very secret from everybody except me. The wife always knows.''

''But why did she come to *you?''*

''Who knows? I don't understand these young people; their morals aren't like ours. Maybe she thought that since I was another woman Ron had treated badly, I'd understand her plight and we'd form a united front against him. But how could I do that, after what she'd done to me? *She* was the one who put an end to my marriage; *she* was the one who'd conceived the child I could never have with Ron.''

Cassie was breathing raggedly now. Alix clenched her fists, watching the woman's jumpy, frightening eyes. Cassie wasn't going to relinquish that pistol without a fight, that was clear now; and in her worked-up state, she might decide to pull the trigger at any moment. If Alix hoped to survive, she would have to make some kind of move against her and would have to do it very soon. Maybe she could drop down, throw herself at Cassie's feet . . . but not from where she stood now, there was too much distance between them. Move away from the car, then, one slow step at a time. And keep Cassie talking while she did it. . . .

''But you didn't mean to kill Miranda,'' she said, and eased one foot out in front of her. ''Isn't that what you said?''

"Oh no. It just happened. I don't even remember doing it. Funny, though—afterward, the next day, I knew Ron would realize I'd done it, even though he didn't know she'd come down here to see me. Because of where her body was found, so close to here. I should have taken her a long way from Hilliard, a long, long way, but I was so scared that night, I just wanted to get rid of her. But Ron never said a thing to the police. I kept waiting for him to call and accuse me and he didn't do that, either."

Alix had moved one full step away from the car and was about to take another. But when Cassie paused, she stood very still. She would need at least two more steps before she was close enough to hurl herself at the woman's feet—

"Well, now I know the reason," Cassie said. "I should have known it right from the first. He couldn't risk his affair being found out. Oh, I can picture him mouthing platitudes to his colleagues: 'How could such a terrible thing happen to such a lovely girl?' He didn't care about Miranda any more than he cared about any of the others. Or me. But he should have cared about that baby. He—"

Cassie broke off again, and again cocked her head to listen. Alix heard nothing except the wind in the trees outside . . . and then she *did*, she heard movement at the open door to Cassie's right. And she saw someone come in, a shadow at first, then the shape of a man—

Adam Reese, holding his rifle at an angle in front of him, his clothing damp and disheveled and his eyes bright, hot, flashing a fragmented blue-and-white as they sought Alix, found her, pinned her. His lips were pulled back in a feral grimace, spittle flecking them at the corners. Then he saw Cassie and stopped moving; a look of amazement crossed his features, as if he hadn't heard them talking from outside, as if he'd expected to find Alix there alone. His body dipped into a crouch and he started to swing the rifle's muzzle toward Cassie.

But Cassie was quicker. She pivoted in an absurdly graceful motion, like a ballerina doll in a music box, and the pistol bucked in her hand. The sound of the shot was deafening in the confined space. Reese jerked, lost his unfired rifle, staggered with his hands coming up to his chest. Cassie fired a second bullet into him, and Alix heard but didn't see him fall.

She had already moved by then. She was down on her stomach slithering frantically under the car.

Jan

At the doorway to the lightroom he rolled the barrel of fire sand out of the way, then unhooked the air hose and pulled the diaphone over until it was balanced on the edge of the sill. He went back up to the lantern, unhooked the hose from the compressor, hefted the unit in his arms, and brought it back down to the lightroom, where he set it in the doorway next to the diaphone.

The noise he made doing this seemed to have refueled Bonner's rage: the obscenities and the pounding increased to another fever pitch. Bonner was still ranting when Jan descended to the trap, but stopped while he was still two risers above it. Jan came to a standstill, breathing through his mouth, listening, as Bonner must have been on the other side. He pushed up his glasses, rubbed at his stinging eyes, squeezed them shut against the gathering pain.

God, he thought, let me get through the next few minutes. Just these next few minutes.

"Ryerson! What you doing up there, you murdering son of a bitch!"

And the pounding started again, savage, rhythmic—one driving thud against the bottom of the trap every two or three seconds.

Quickly, Jan moved down the remaining steps, bent, and threw the locking bolt free of its ring, timing it so that the sound the bolt made releasing was lost in the hollow thud of wood on wood. He was turning, starting back up to the lightroom, when the next blow came. This time the door rose an inch or so in its frame, fell back with an audible bumping sound. There were no more blows—just a heavy silence that lasted five seconds, ten, while Bonner's slow wits took in the fact that the trap was now unlocked. If he thought that his pounding had somehow broken the lock, if he didn't suspect a trap above the trap . . .

The door lifted again, slowly—one inch, two. Jan tensed. And then Bonner shoved up fast and hard, threw the trap back against its hinge stops. His head and shoulders appeared in the opening, eyes wide and wild and gleaming in the weak light.

With his foot Jan shoved the diaphone off the sill, sent it plunging downward. It hit one of the steps with a ringing metallic clatter, bounced straight at Bonner, who threw his arms up in front of his face and started to cry out. The diaphone struck him on one forearm and the side of his head, knocked him backward out of sight. His cry changed into a strangled shriek that was lost, cut off, in the echoing, thumping noise of the heavy instrument and Bonner's body tumbling down the stairs. When the sounds finally stopped, the silence that filled the tower seemed riddled with ghostly echoes just beyond the range of hearing.

Jan was out on the stairs by then, peering downward, trying to bring the gloom at the bottom of the stairs into focus. He was ready to dislodge the compressor, send that hurtling downward, too, if necessary—but it wasn't necessary. Bonner lay twisted below, unmoving, the diaphone canted across his legs so that only his upper body and his feet were visible.

The sudden release of tension made Jan's own legs feel weak, rubbery, as he descended. Bonner's weapon, an ax handle, lay on one of the steps partway down; Jan bent to claim it before he went the rest of the way. When he got to where Bonner lay, the silence that had built around him was thick, no longer echoing, broken only by the faint thrumming duet of the wind and the fire outside.

He bent to look more closely at Bonner, afraid that he'd killed the man; the last thing he needed right now was a death on his conscience, even the death of a tormentor. But Bonner wasn't dead. There was a bloody gash on the side of his head where the diaphone had struck him, and one of his legs was bent at an angle that could only mean a bone had shattered; but his mouth was open and he was breathing in ragged, painful gasps.

Jan swallowed against the taste of bile, stepped over him and out into the wreckage of the living room. Holding the ax handle cocked at his shoulder, he looked into Alix's studio, then hurried through the kitchen, cloakroom, pantry. All of them were empty. He went through the pantry door, around to the front yard. Stood for a moment to let the icy breath of the wind clear his head, dry the sweat on his body.

The station wagon was a blackened hulk inside a dying ring of fire. Beyond it, the garage was sheeted by flame, burning hot and smoky from the paint and oil and chemicals stored inside. If the wind had been strong, gusty, there would have been a danger of the fire spreading to the lighthouse. But it had died down, changed direction—capricious wind. What sparks and embers blew free were being carried away to the southwest, out to sea.

In the fireglow he could see that the grounds were as deserted as the house. Outside the fence, the road—as much of it as his narrowing vision could make out—also appeared to be empty. Nobody here now, just Bonner and him. Just *him*.

But he couldn't stay here, couldn't just wait, because he couldn't be absolutely sure Alix had made it safely to a telephone. He'd been right about Bonner—but what if he'd been wrong about the others?

He began to run.

It was a hard run at first, but he couldn't keep up the pace. He was out of shape, and exhausted from the tension and exertion of the past two hours, and his head ached, throbbed with every step. He was worried that the fresh exertion would bring on the bulging, or worse, one of the blackout periods. Or that he would drop from sheer fatigue.

He slowed to a trot, then to a fast walk, and when he had his wind back he began to trot again. The night was black around him, streaked with fog. Anything more than a few feet away appeared to him as smears and blobs. He kept swiping at his eyes, poking and pinching at them in a vain effort to widen his field of vision.

He had gone a mile or so—he had no real sense of distance, nor of passing time—when he came around a bend in the road and one of the larger blobs ahead of him materialized into Reese's van. He came to an abrupt halt when he recognized it, then warily moved closer. It was angled off on the side of the road, lightless, the driver's door yawning open.

Abandoned here, he thought. Why?

He went around to the driver's door, leaned inside. Empty. The ignition lock was empty, too; whoever had been driving it—Reese?—had taken the key. Frustrated, feeling a new surge of anxiety, he backed out and stood indecisively for a moment, knuckling his eyes, staring ahead into the blurry darkness.

Alix, he thought then.

And once more he began to run.

Alix

She lay flat on her stomach, her cheek pressed against the cold concrete. The floor under the car was slick with motor oil; the smell of it made her want to retch. She closed her throat against a surge of bile, remained perfectly still.

She could see Cassie's bare feet and the hem of her robe several yards from the car; she could also see the crumpled body of Adam Reese, the splotch of blood on the front of his jacket. Cassie hadn't turned, hadn't moved since she'd shot Reese—as if the act had momentarily paralyzed her. It was another few seconds before the feet moved, turned once again toward the car with such suddenness that the robe puffed out to expose thick ankles. There was a quick intake of breath, and then—

"Alix? Where are you?"

Alix held her breath.

Cassie's voice rose querulously. "Where did you go?"

After a moment the feet moved out of Alix's line of vision, back toward the front of the car, shuffling like those of an old woman. She turned her head then, peered out the other side. There was a line of cardboard cartons some four feet away, with a space large enough for her to wriggle through between two of them. She was too confined here under the car; if Cassie realized where she was, there would be no way to defend herself, no way to escape a bullet. Behind those boxes, she would still be protected, yet have more freedom of movement.

But what if she made sounds and Cassie heard them? With that overhead light on, she would make a perfect target, even with the car between them—

The side door slammed resoundingly. When the echo died, the silence was once again acute.

Alix lay motionless, taking in small amounts of air through her mouth. Her chest ached, blood pounded in her temples. She realized she was still clutching Mandy's headband; her fingers pressed the beads as if she might be about to say a rosary.

You've got to move sooner or later. Do it now, while she's still over by the door.

She made herself move in the direction of the cardboard cartons. She was almost to the rear wheel when she saw an old bathroom plunger lying behind it. It was good-sized, with a wooden handle two feet long. Not much of a weapon, but better than nothing.

Inching along, she stretched her arm out until her fingers could just touch the handle. Then she lay still again, listening. Heard nothing except the heavy silence. But once she came out from under the car, exposed herself in the light . . . that damned ceiling bulb hung right over the car. . . .

Smash it, she thought then. It hangs down low, you can reach it with the plunger . . . and in the dark you've got a much better chance . . . smash it!

She crawled forward, took a firm grip on the wooden handle; her head was out from under the car now. Behind her, on the other side of the car, Cassie moved and then called, "Alix?" again. The sound of her name drove her the rest of the way out from under, up onto her knees.

Cassie heard her, shouted something unintelligible just as Alix located the bulb, and lunged up at it swinging her club.

But her first swing missed high, hitting the cord instead and setting the light swaying and dancing crazily; light swirled, weird shadows climbed the walls and then fell back again. Cassie fired a shot, but in her haste her aim was off-line: the bullet cut a furrow across the top of the car to Alix's left with a sound like fingernails dragging down a blackboard.

Wildly, Alix swung again at the swaying light. She lost her grip on the plunger as she did so, but in flying out of her hand it struck its target. The bulb shattered; the garage was plunged into darkness.

Another shout from Cassie, but no more shots. Alix dropped to her hands and knees again, crawled behind the row of cardboard cartons. When she'd gone as far as she could she got up in a crouch and extended her hands into the darkness around her, searching for another weapon. At first they encountered only empty space, then she felt a lumpy plastic shape, probably a large sack of potting soil or fertilizer. Her touch stirred up what was inside and a faint but pungent filtering of dust tickled her nostrils. She put a hand up in a vain effort to stop a sudden sneeze.

The sneeze came out as a little choking noise, loud in the electric stillness that filled the garage.

Cassie said, "I hear you, Alix. You can't get away, not even in the dark." She began moving, coming toward the car.

When she got to it, would she think to open one of the doors for the dome light? Alix squeezed the plastic sack, seeking more shelter. When she tried to straighten, her head banged into solid wood. Wincing with pain, she raised a hand and felt the rough underside of a shelf. Probably a potting shelf, like many old garages had.

Cassie said, "I hear you!" Her tone was horribly gay, like that of a wicked child playing hide-and-seek.

Alix was disoriented now, but she guessed she had moved at an angle toward the rear corner. The potting shelf must be built into the right angle formed by the walls. If she went the other way . . .

"I've got you now," Cassie said. "You can't see where you're going in the dark."

Neither can you.

As if Cassie had read her mind, she said, "I know where things are in here. I can get around without light; you can't."

Then maybe she *wouldn't* put on the dome light. And that would be to Alix's benefit. Cassie knew the garage, yes, knew the whereabouts of everything that was in it; but moving around a familiar place in light or even half-light was entirely different than trying to find your way when you couldn't see at all.

Alix could hear her now, no longer making an effort to be quiet as she felt her way around the hood of the car at the back wall. Alix moved too, away along the side wall toward the front, keeping on the balls of her feet, knees bent, hands touching the exposed studding for balance. Ahead she could make out the faint outline of the big double doors, a lighter gray-black against the clotted darkness within.

Were the doors locked? Even if they weren't, they might be difficult to open and get through quickly. Still, they were the closest means of escape: she would have to try them.

Behind her, Cassie was still moving. It sounded as if she was now feeling her way along the side of the car, on the other side of the line of boxes.

If she sees or hears me at the doors, Alix thought, will she try shooting in the dark? She might; or she might *want* me to get outside, where the light is better. How many bullets does a gun like hers hold? Six? Don't most pistols hold six? Two on Adam Reese (God!), another intended for me. That leaves three, if the gun was fully loaded to begin with. Three too many. . . .

She continued to make her way blindly toward the faint outline of the doors, her hands picking up prickly little splinters from the rough studding. Somewhere, she realized then, she had lost Mandy's headband. Why she should even think of that she didn't know. Abruptly, the studding ended and she touched something that felt like pegboard. She paused, listening to Cassie's movements and trying to gauge the distance to the double doors. Not more than ten feet.

It sounded as if Cassie had reached the rear of the car. Her breathing was more ragged now, almost asthmatic. Alix suspected she wouldn't be able to hear small sounds; she shifted her weight, moved forward, testing. Cassie remained where she was.

Alix felt the wall again. It was definitely pegboard, the kind of material people use to hang things on. Tools, garden tools. Maybe—

"You can't hide from me, Alix. You can't! You'll just make me kill you and I don't want to do that."

The hell you don't, Alix thought.

She inched along, her fingers touching the tines of a bamboo rake. No weapon, that.

"I didn't want to kill Adam, either. He made me. They all made me. I never wanted to kill *anyone*." The words trembled with pathos and self-pity.

Go ahead, Alix thought, keep on maundering. Keep on listening to the sound of your own voice so you won't hear what I'm doing.

She kept moving, groping along the pegboard. A broom hung there, and a mop. A row of smaller tools—pliers, screwdrivers. She took the largest of the screwdrivers, tucked it into the back pocket of her jeans. Hardly adequate, but at least it was something sharp.

Behind her Cassie had begun to whine. "I didn't want any of this to happen! I just wanted to be left alone!"

Alix's fingers touched something more sharply pointed than the screwdriver—hedge clippers, heavy iron with solid wood handles. She felt for the hook, timing her movements to Cassie's now-loud rantings. Took the clippers, slid them upward and out—

The metal hook slipped from the pegboard, fell to the concrete floor with a ringing metallic noise. Alix caught her breath. Lowered the clippers, brought them up in front of her.

Cassie had stopped speaking and was coming her way quickly. But she misjudged the distance and crashed into the pegboard a couple of feet away. Tools rattled, something else clattered to the floor. Cassie gave a dismayed cry; Alix felt the woman's arms flail, lashing out at the air around her.

Gripping the hedge clippers by their handles, she reeled backward, her feet slipping on an oil slick. In the next instant she slammed into the double doors. Over by the wall, Cassie was grunting and thrashing about. Alix turned, threw her weight against the doors, felt them buckle outward but not come open. She heard someone else grunting and realized it was herself.

She lunged at the doors again, and again they bowed but held. Through the foot-wide crack that appeared between them, she could see moving wisps of fog—a glimpse of freedom.

Now Cassie was on her feet. Coming toward her. She tried to dodge, but the woman collided with her; Alix felt the gun in her hand, smashed at her wrist, but didn't have enough leverage to dislodge the weapon. Cassie had no leverage, either, when she tried to use the pistol as a club. Instead, she managed to loop an arm around Alix's neck, began squeezing.

Alix's breath came shorter; the pressure caused blackness to swirl behind her eyes. She dropped the clippers, clawed at Cassie's arm. The gallery owner's grip was steel-hard. Alix's legs broke at the knees and she sagged against Cassie, and they fell together against the doors.

Weakened by the previous battering, whatever had held the doors together now broke with a snapping sound and they flew apart. Cassie's arm pulled free of Alix's neck as they both toppled onto the gravel outside. Alix rolled away, pawing at her throat, gasping. When she came up she saw Cassie trying to scramble to her knees; the woman seemed dazed, but the gun was still clutched in her hand.

The raw edge of panic cut at Alix again. She tried to get to her feet—and saw the hedge clippers lying in the doorway. Without thinking, she crawled to them on hands and knees, snatched them up. At the same time she gained her feet and turned, Cassie pushed onto her knees, lifted the pistol, and took wobbly aim at Alix's body.

Alix lunged forward with the clippers upraised. Brought them slashing down in a desperate chop at Cassie's head just as the gallery owner pulled the trigger.

Jan

He didn't remember running the two miles from the abandoned van to the junction, or turning off the cape road onto the county road. But the county road was where he was now, heading toward the village, his legs cramped, his breath coming in little wheezing pants, a band of pain across the bridge of his nose. Another blackout . . .

He couldn't see very well, and at first he thought it was the too-familiar distortion of his vision; but then he realized it was only that his glasses were coated with mist. He took them off, squinting into the darkness ahead. Where was Alix? Where were the authorities? Why hadn't he met *someone* in all this time?

Ahead of him, he realized then, were the gallery and house that belonged to Alix's artist friend, Cassie Lang. Alix's friend . . . that must have been where she had gone for help. The house was ablaze with light—and as he drew closer, he saw someone on the porch, standing there as if waiting, looking his way. A woman . . . Cassie Lang?

Alix.

It was *Alix!*

The last of the tension went out of him with such suddenness that he stumbled, almost fell. Some of the pressure behind his eyes seemed to abate as well, so that all at once he was thinking and seeing with an intense clarity. He found his voice, shouted her name, but she had recognized him too and she was already coming down off the porch, running toward him—the last running either of them would have to do on this long, bad night.

Epilogue

Alix waited by the rented van while Jan brought their suitcases from the lighthouse, then went back for the last of the boxes. The day was clear, with only a few high-piled clouds; the wind blew sharp and cold. The headland was bathed in the pale yellow light of late fall; by comparison the burnt-out hulk of the station wagon and blackened remains of the garage looked grotesque—reminders of evil.

But they were not the only ones. Everywhere were signs of the assault of two nights before: smokestains curled up the round whitewashed tower, seemed to be clutching it like the fingers of a dirty hand; the broken windows were like dead eye sockets; the bullet- and club-scarred front of the house was like a face pocked by some disease.

There were reminders in the village, too, she thought—more subtle but nevertheless present. When they'd passed through on their way from Bandon to pick up their belongings, Hilliard's streets had been deserted. Behind the walls of the stores and houses, life might go on; but for most of the residents it would be forever altered by the knowledge of what four of their own had become, and of the price those four had paid for their mischief. Adam Reese: dead. Seth Bonner: in a Coos Bay hospital in serious condition with a broken leg, broken ribs, internal injuries. Mitch Novotny and Hod Barnett: home with their families, but only because the Ryersons had declined to press charges against them; free physically, but not in spirit, forced to live the rest of their lives with the memory of what they had done—and what they had almost done—on a night when they had unleashed the animal that lurks beneath the civilized surface of man.

That was the primary reason, Alix supposed, that she and Jan felt no lingering hostility, no grudge toward them or the village itself: none had escaped punishment, and the sentences the survivors would serve would be long ones. All they felt now was pity—for Hod Barnett, who had lost his daughter; for Barnett and Novotny, who had lost a semblance of their humanity; for the little dying town of Hilliard that had lost its self-respect. Pity, and a deep, ineradicable sorrow.

She was glad that she and Jan had been in agreement on not pressing charges; the last thing she would have wanted was to return to the area for a trial. Her fondest hope was never to see Hilliard or Cape Despair again.

There would be no need for them to attend or testify at Cassie Lang's trial, either. Cassie had confessed, as fully and compulsively to the authorities as she had tried to do to Alix in the garage. Intellectually, Alix knew she should feel some sort of sympathy for the woman; Cassie had been ill-equipped to handle her own passions or the pressures of an unkind world, just as Mitch Novotny and Hod Barnett had been unable to. But her only feeling when she thought of the woman she had once considered her friend was one of revulsion—and an occasional sparking of the terror she had experienced in the confines of that dark garage.

Jan returned with two boxes balanced one on top of the other. "That's the last of it," he said. "You want to check around inside, see if we've forgotten anything?"

She was about to say yes, but a vague sense of unease, a tightening in her throat kept the word back. She said instead, "If we've left anything, it's probably not important."

He nodded in understanding. "I'll lock up then."

She turned her back on the lighthouse, climbed in behind the wheel of the van. Tonight they would drive as far as Crescent City, and tomorrow they'd be home. And the day after that, Jan would check into the medical center for further tests to determine the cause of his blackouts. It was her opinion—and Jan's, too, now—that they were not organic in origin, but rather a by-product of his eye disease brought on by intense stress; if that was the case, it seemed reasonable to assume they wouldn't recur if precautions were taken to avoid stressful situations.

Once the tests were finished, they would make plans for the future, for the alterations in the patterns of their existence that would become necessary if Jan did in fact lose his sight. But it was possible for them to do that now, to start over from a whole new basis and with a unified strength. Months ago she wouldn't have thought so, wouldn't have thought herself—or Jan—capable of such courage. But when you have survived an ordeal so much worse than any you could have imagined, no crisis seems quite so awesome or insurmountable anymore.

Jan slid into the passenger seat and shut the door. His wan smile held the same relief she had started to feel. For him the light was no longer a sanctuary, a place he refused to be driven out of; like its name, it had become a symbol of his despair, a place that had finally been driven out of him.

She drove them out of the yard and along the pot-holed road, not once glancing up at the rearview mirror. But then, after they'd gone about a mile and reached the rise from which she had first seen the lighthouse, she slowed on impulse, pulled over, and stopped. Looked back.

The headland lay barren and lonely, looking much, she thought, as it had when the pair of Basque sheepherders had first come to it more than a century ago. Beyond its scalloped reaches the harsh waves beat against the cliffs as they had when ships foundered there and Cap Des Peres became known as

Cape Despair. And above it all was the ancient light, a severe white column piercing the sky.

From here she could see none of the smoke damage, nor the broken windows, nor the scarred walls. It looked as it had on that first day: a thing of beauty, guardian of the night, comfort and hope to the lost and the frightened.

For perhaps a minute she and Jan looked at it in silence. Then she released the brake and drove on, her eyes on the road, her mind on the future—neither lost nor afraid.

FINE MYSTERY AND SUSPENSE
TITLES FROM CARROLL & GRAF

☐ Allingham, Margery/NO LOVE LOST	$3.95
☐ Allingham, Margery/MR. CAMPION'S QUARRY	$3.95
☐ Allingham, Margery/MR. CAMPION'S FARTHING	$3.95
☐ Allingham, Margery/THE WHITE COTTAGE MYSTERY	$3.50
☐ Ambler, Eric/BACKGROUND TO DANGER	$3.95
☐ Ambler, Eric/CAUSE FOR ALARM	$3.95
☐ Ambler, Eric/A COFFIN FOR DIMITRIOS	$3.95
☐ Ambler, Eric/EPITAPH FOR A SPY	$3.95
☐ Ambler, Eric/STATE OF SIEGE	$3.95
☐ Ambler, Eric/JOURNEY INTO FEAR	$3.95
☐ Ball, John/THE KIWI TARGET	$3.95
☐ Bentley, E.C./TRENT'S OWN CASE	$3.95
☐ Blake, Nicholas/A TANGLED WEB	$3.50
☐ Brand, Christianna/DEATH IN HIGH HEELS	$3.95
☐ Brand, Christianna/FOG OF DOUBT	$3.50
☐ Brand, Christianna/GREEN FOR DANGER	$3.95
☐ Brand, Christianna/TOUR DE FORCE	$3.95
☐ Brown, Fredric/THE LENIENT BEAST	$3.50
☐ Brown, Fredric/MURDER CAN BE FUN	$3.95
☐ Brown, Fredric/THE SCREAMING MIMI	$3.50
☐ Buchan, John/JOHN MACNAB	$3.95
☐ Buchan, John/WITCH WOOD	$3.95
☐ Burnett, W.R./LITTLE CAESAR	$3.50
☐ Butler, Gerald/KISS THE BLOOD OFF MY HANDS	$3.95
☐ Carr, John Dickson/CAPTAIN CUT-THROAT	$3.95
☐ Carr, John Dickson/DARK OF THE MOON	$3.50
☐ Carr, John Dickson/DEMONIACS	$3.95
☐ Carr, John Dickson/THE GHOSTS' HIGH NOON	$3.95
☐ Carr, John Dickson/NINE WRONG ANSWERS	$3.50
☐ Carr, John Dickson/PAPA LA-BAS	$3.95
☐ Carr, John Dickson/THE WITCH OF THE LOW TIDE	$3.95
☐ Chesterton, G. K./THE MAN WHO KNEW TOO MUCH	$3.95
☐ Chesterton, G. K./THE MAN WHO WAS THURSDAY	$3.50
☐ Crofts, Freeman Wills/THE CASK	$3.95
☐ Coles, Manning/NO ENTRY	$3.50
☐ Collins, Michael/WALK A BLACK WIND	$3.95
☐ Dickson, Carter/THE CURSE OF THE BRONZE LAMP	$3.50
☐ Disch, Thomas M & Sladek, John/BLACK ALICE	$3.95
☐ Eberhart, Mignon/MESSAGE FROM HONG KONG	$3.50

☐ Fennelly, Tony/THE CLOSET HANGING $3.50
☐ Freeling, Nicolas/LOVE IN AMSTERDAM $3.95
☐ Gilbert, Michael/ANYTHING FOR A QUIET LIFE $3.95
☐ Gilbert, Michael/THE DOORS OPEN $3.95
☐ Gilbert, Michael/THE 92nd TIGER $3.95
☐ Gilbert, Michael/OVERDRIVE $3.95
☐ Graham, Winston/MARNIE $3.95
☐ Griffiths, John/THE GOOD SPY $4.50
☐ Hughes, Dorothy B./THE FALLEN SPARROW $3.50
☐ Hughes, Dorothy B./IN A LONELY PLACE $3.50
☐ Hughes, Dorothy B./RIDE THE PINK HORSE $3.95
☐ Hornung, E. W./THE AMATEUR CRACKSMAN $3.95
☐ Kitchin, C. H. B./DEATH OF HIS UNCLE $3.95
☐ Kitchin, C. H. B./DEATH OF MY AUNT $3.50
☐ MacDonald, John D./TWO $2.50
☐ Mason, A.E.W./AT THE VILLA ROSE $3.50
☐ Mason, A.E.W./THE HOUSE OF THE ARROW $3.50
☐ McShane, Mark/SEANCE ON A WET AFTERNOON $3.95
☐ Pentecost, Hugh/THE CANNIBAL WHO OVERATE $3.95
☐ Priestley, J.B./SALT IS LEAVING $3.95
☐ Queen, Ellery/THE FINISHING STROKE $3.95
☐ Rogers, Joel T./THE RED RIGHT HAND $3.50
☐ 'Sapper'/BULLDOG DRUMMOND $3.50
☐ Stevens, Shane/BY REASON OF INSANITY $5.95
☐ Symons, Julian/BOGUE'S FORTUNE $3.95
☐ Symons, Julian/THE BROKEN PENNY $3.95
☐ Wainwright, John/ALL ON A SUMMER'S DAY $3.50
☐ Wallace, Edgar/THE FOUR JUST MEN $2.95
☐ Waugh, Hillary/A DEATH IN A TOWN $3.95
☐ Waugh, Hillary/LAST SEEN WEARING $3.95
☐ Waugh, Hillary/SLEEP LONG, MY LOVE $3.95
☐ Westlake, Donald E./THE MERCENARIES $3.95
☐ Willeford, Charles/THE WOMAN CHASER $3.95

Available from fine bookstores everywhere or use this coupon for ordering.

Carroll & Graf Publishers, Inc., 260 Fifth Avenue, N.Y., N.Y. 10001

Please send me the books I have checked above. I am enclosing $_____
(please add $1.25 per title to cover postage and handling.) Send check
or money order—no cash or C.O.D.'s please. N.Y. residents please add
8¼% sales tax.

Mr/Mrs/Ms _____

Address _____

City _____ State/Zip _____

Please allow four to six weeks for delivery.